DEAD
RECKONING

DEAD RECKONING

MERCEDES LACKEY *AND* ROSEMARY EDGHILL

SCHOLASTIC INC.

ISBN 978-0-545-61455-9

12 11 10 9 8 7 6 5 4 3 2 1   13 14 15 16 17 18/0

Printed in the U.S.A.   40

First Scholastic printing, September 2013

Book design by Regina Roff

Dedicated to our tireless agents
Russell Galen and Ann Behar;
we couldn't do this without you

DEAD
RECKONING

AUTHORS' NOTE

Dead Reckoning takes place in 1867, when the world was a very different place. While we've done our best to strike a balance between the historical attitudes and language and modern (and far more enlightened) usage and attitudes, there are places in the story where we've had no choice but to use the words that would have been used during the period. While we know better, our characters (alas) do not.

CHAPTER ONE

West Texas, April 1867

Jett Gallatin expected trouble in Alsop, Texas—but not zombies.

As the evening breeze blew dust and tumbleweed across the town's main—and only—street, a gleaming black stallion picked his way along it. The stallion seemed to be the one choosing his own path; his rider sat motionless in the saddle, reins loose, hat pulled down too low for anyone to get a good look at whatever it concealed.

There wasn't much to the town yet, just a street with a livery stable at one end and a church at the other, but last year money on four hooves had come to Alsop. The railroad had reached Abilene, Kansas, and a beeve worth five dollars in Texas was worth forty if you could get him to the railhead in Abilene. Alsop had reaped the reward of being one of the towns near the head of Jesse Chisholm's trail; the town's new prosperity could be seen by the fact there were more horses in front of the saloon than there were places to hitch them.

Prosperity draws folks like flowers draw bees. Did it draw Philip? Mother Mary, please let it have, Jett Gallatin thought.

The stallion's rider would never be mistaken for an ordinary cowhand. Jett wore silver-studded black, from the silver-heeled boots and Spanish spurs to the silver-studded hatband on the wide-crowned black hat. This wasn't an outfit made for punching cows—nor was the well-worn custom gun belt with its matched pair of ivory-handled Colts. Everything about the meticulous arrangement of both revolvers told the tale of someone who lived and died by the gun—the holsters tied down, the gun belt tightened so it rode high, comfort sacrificed for the sake of a split-second's advantage in a gunfight. The sleek black stallion was no cow-pony, either, and his silver-studded, carved black leather saddle and tack weren't the sort of thing a working cowhand could afford. Everything about Jett Gallatin told the world the black-clad drifter was either a gambler or a shootist—or both—but no one in their wildest dreams would think Jett Gallatin was a girl. For her freedom, for her life—and for her brother—she played the kind of young gun a boy would want to be and a girl would yearn after.

And you all go on thinking I'm a boy, thanks, Jett said silently. *That's what you're supposed to do.*

For an instant she let herself remember those golden peaceful days when passing as a boy had been only a game she'd shared with her twin brother. *You can't just dress like me—you have to* be *me. Give a pretty girl the eye. Otherwise you'll never fool anybody*, he'd told her over and over. *Jasper* told her: Jasper and Jett Stuart, twin brothers who went places and did things Philip and Philippa Sheridan's parents would never have approved of. Now Jasper was gone, and Jett *Gallatin* searched for him . . . and Philippa Sheridan of Court Oaks Plantation in Orleans Parish was someone she used to be, a lifetime ago. She'd named herself "Gallatin" for Gallatin Street in New Orleans, where she and Mama had gone to hide the night Court Oaks burned. Even now, sometimes, she couldn't sleep at night, remembering her home burning, burning, *burning* . . .

Finally the stallion stopped next to the rail in front of the saloon. A rancher or a homesteader would have headed for the general store for the local news, but a cowhand would make for the saloon for beer and whiskey, a good meal, and better company. A gambler or a drifter would choose the same destination, and so—she hoped—that's what Philip would do. *If there's any trace of him here, this is where I'll find it.*

She swung her leg over the saddle pommel and dropped gracefully to the ground. *Oh, Philip, if you hadn't taught me to play the boy so well, I'd be dead now.*

She was just seventeen. She should have been getting ready for one of the many gala cotillions New Orleans boasted—*had* boasted—each spring. She thought with longing of the dress she would have worn—yards and yards of silk taffeta and lace and huge hoops, her waist laced small enough for a fellow to put both hands around. Philip would have been standing beside her, tall and strong and proud, ready to lead her out for the first dance.

But things hadn't been the way they should be for six years—not since February 1861, when Louisiana seceded from the Union, one of the first seven states to do so. Her brothers and their friends marched off to war, and most of them never came back. Her father and her four older brothers, dead in Mr. Lincoln's War. Her mother, dead in the occupation of New Orleans. Philip . . . the last news she had was five years old. Philip had written to tell them that Papa was wounded, a Union prisoner, and he was going with him to Rock Island to nurse him. A few months later, there'd been a letter from the prison commander's wife telling them Papa was dead—but they never learned what happened to Philip. He could have gone anywhere—even back to the Army if he'd managed to cross the lines. All Jett knew for sure was that he'd never come home. But she refused to believe he was dead. They were twins—if anything happened to the one, the other always knew it. He had to be here—in the West, where Tyrant Johnson's yoke lay lightly on the necks of exiled Southerners.

She had to believe that. It was all that kept her keeping on.

She didn't tie up Nightingale with the other horses. She looped his reins at the saddle horn as the stallion gazed scornfully down his aristocratic nose at the dusty cow-ponies. She patted his shoulder—bidding a temporary farewell to a good friend—and stepped up onto the weathered wood sidewalk in front of the saloon. A feeling of weary familiarity descended on her as she stepped through the batwing doors and paused, stripping off her gloves as she let her eyes adjust to the gloom. Sawdust covered the floor, kerosene lamps—the only source of light—hung from wall brackets, and a "chandelier" made from a wagon wheel was suspended from the exposed rafters. This was the sort of place Jett Gallatin was all too familiar with by now. *Four years ago I had no idea places like this even existed.*

There were almost a dozen men in the saloon—
eleven, to be precise—plus the barkeeper. At this time
of day, the locals would be at their supper tables, so
these were men without homes or steady employment.
A trail boss riding shorthanded might pick up one of
them to help out on a drive, but he knew he'd be taking his chances if he did. You had no way of knowing
if a man was any good until you'd tried him—and halfway between South Texas and Abilene was a bad place
to find out someone was an owlhoot.

As Jett walked slowly up to the bar, the only sound
in the saloon was the jingling of her silver spurs. The
silence persisted as she put one foot up on the gleaming brass rail and leaned over the bar. *I wonder if there's
going to be trouble this time*, she thought with resignation. She knew no one would guess she was a girl, but
no matter how good her disguise, nothing she tried to
make her look older stood up to close scrutiny. She
looked like a boy, not a man, so she relied for protection
on the flamboyant and menacing costume of a gunslinger. It was just lucky she was as good with a gun as
her costume proclaimed she was. She'd had to be.

"Where you from, stranger?" The bartender drew a
beer without her asking and pushed it in front of her.

"Up the trail," she replied. She fished out her money
pouch and laid a silver dime on the counter. *Union coin*

and Union tyranny, she thought with a reflexive sneer. "Looking to see what's down the way." She picked up the beer and sipped it thirstily. At least the bitter stuff cut through the trail dust.

"Been a few strangers through town lately," the bartender replied.

She nodded. "Cattle drives come through here?" she asked, half turning away. She already knew they did; she used the conversation to cover the fact she was watching for trouble. Her next questions would be about finding a bed for the night and the prospects of signing up with a drive. Harmless natural questions for a stranger to ask, and it wasn't impossible for a gambler to want to change his luck. If the bartender gave her the right answers, her next question would be . . .

Ah, never mind. Without bad luck, I wouldn't have any luck at all.

A stranger in town was always fair game for the local bully. There wasn't a lot of law out here, and, well, everything depended on how good you were with a gun—and with intimidation. *Good with a gun, yes. Intimidation . . . not hardly.*

She'd just spotted Trouble sitting by himself at a table. He had half a bottle of whiskey in front of him, and he'd been eyeing her furtively from the moment she came in. Her rig-out caused as many problems as it stopped, mostly with fools who forgot a boy could be as deadly with a gun as any man.

Now Mister Trouble tried to lock eyes with her. She pulled her hat down a little lower over her eyes—meaningfully—but he didn't take the hint.

The barkeep answered her question—though she'd already stopped listening—and when she didn't say anything more, he walked down to where he could keep an eye on his other customers and began to polish a glass with the hem of his dingy apron. As soon as the barkeep moved, Mister Trouble heaved himself to his feet and wove tipsily toward her. He was fat and unshaven, wearing clothing that hadn't seen a washboard in far too long. She kept her expression bland, though she wanted to snarl in exasperation. Barring a miracle, Mister Trouble was going to start something she'd have to finish, and then she'd have to light out ahead of whatever law this place had to offer. She really, *really* didn't want to have to draw down on him, or worse, shoot him. She'd been hoping to stay a few days and make some inquiries.

Wonder if throwing my beer in his face will cool him down peaceable-like?

She guessed she'd find out before she got much older.

It took the drunken ranahan a fair amount of time

to make his unsteady way up to the bar, but there was no doubt in Jett's mind he was aching for trouble. Any chance their encounter was going to end peaceably was becoming smaller by the minute. At least she didn't have to worry about sun glare; it was full dark outside by now.

So what's he going to say? she wondered, in the peace that always descended on her in the last moments before violence became inevitable. *"You ain't from around here, is ya?"* or, *"We don't cotton to strangers 'round here"?* or, *"Them's mighty big guns fer sech a little feller"?* She eyed the other customers of the bar to see how they were going to react to the unequal fight. Was Mister Trouble the town clown or a bully everyone feared? If he was a bully, she might be applauded for putting him down. If he wasn't—if he was someone everyone liked, even if they didn't respect him—she'd have to get out of this without seriously hurting him, or she'd have a posse on her heels. Her insides tightened up, and everything got a little sharper.

Most of the bar's customers didn't even seem to notice that misfortune—someone's misfortune, anyway—was brewing, and she couldn't read the faces of the rest. She glanced toward the barkeep, hoping for a better clue, but just as she took her eyes off Mister Trouble, she heard Nightingale whinny in warning. She took three long backward steps away from the bar, her hands going for her guns as her gaze turned toward the swinging doors.

And then every horse outside the saloon—even Nightingale—screamed in fear.

The batwing doors swung inward, and a wind as cold as the breeze from an icehouse—too cold for the season—poured into the bar. Even through the cold, Jett could smell a stink like a New Orleans cemetery at high summer. The bar's customers began to curse and complain, but before they could really get going, a horde of . . . unholy things . . . shambled in through the open doors. They were wearing everything from dirt-caked Sunday suits to the ragged tatters of denim overalls. They'd been people once. Now they were dead half-rotted bodies with white-filmed, sightless eyes. Some bore the marks of bullet holes or knife wounds. Some had the grotesque stretched and broken necks of hanged men. Some had been gnawed by varmints. They were all carrying weapons—pickaxes, spades, pitchforks, and even clubs.

Jett clutched her gun butts, though she wondered if the rosary she wore around her neck might be more use. There was a horrified silence in the saloon as its customers realized what had just come through the door, a thump as the barkeep dropped whatever he'd been holding, and then a boom as he whipped his shotgun up from under the bar and fired both barrels. It blew an arm off one of the creatures and knocked another to the ground. But the first didn't seem to notice the missing limb, and the second merely got up again with a fresh gaping crater in its chest.

As if that had been a signal, every living man was on his feet and shooting into the mob of the undead. The saloon filled with the thunder and lightning of gunplay and the smell of gunsmoke, but the barrage had no visible effect.

The zombies kept coming.

The stink of gunpowder mixed with the stench of rotting corpses. Some of the shooters reloaded to fire again, while some had flung aside their useless guns and were looking wildly for any other sort of weapon. The barkeep vanished behind the bar again, and came back up with a fire axe. One of the brighter rannies got the notion to pick up a chair and smash it into the face of one of the things, and then all hell was out for noon. Jett heard a sickening crunch as a living man went down beneath a corpse's club.

Jett still hadn't drawn her own weapons. Her retreat had placed her on the opposite side of the saloon from everyone else, but if she'd had any hopes the living could win this donnybrook, they were dashed within seconds. More and more shambling corpses were shoving their way into the saloon, and while the door on the back wall probably led to the street, it was at the far end of the room and she couldn't get to it. As she backed all the way down to the end of the bar, she saw one of the dead grab the axe from the barkeep's hands. His screams were mercifully brief.

The locals were surrounded, outnumbered, and out of bullets. The situation was hopeless. For the moment, the zombies were concentrating on the men attacking them, and if she didn't want to make this place her last stand, Jett had one chance and seconds in which to take it. She took a deep breath and jammed her Stetson on tight, then made a running dive for the saloon window, ducking her head into her shoulder to save her face from the glass. She hit the window with a splintering crash of wood and glass and turned her dive into a somersault over the plank walk.

She tumbled out into the street and rolled to her feet. The cow-ponies had all fled—the hitching rail was empty, except for a few trailing pieces of broken reins. She couldn't see Nightingale anywhere. She heard screaming, and as she looked frantically around, she saw movement in the street. The street was full of the things—a dozen she could see, maybe more she couldn't. They hadn't just attacked the saloon. They'd attacked the whole town at once and from the sound of things, nobody else was having better luck than the men in the saloon had.

Worse, the shattering window had drawn the zombies' attention.

She groaned in despair as she backed slowly away from the milling corpses. She would have made a run for the church, but they were between her and it. *Maybe I can outrun them*, she thought desperately. Cowboy boots weren't meant for walking, let alone running, but just now Jett was powerfully motivated.

A flicker of light behind her caught her attention. She risked a glance toward it, and saw one of the storefronts was on fire. *Broken lamp*, she thought inanely. In the firelight, she could see figures heading for the street. From their shuffling gait, she knew what they were.

She was surrounded now. Fear nailed her feet to the ground.

As the undead moved closer, she crossed herself quickly, breathed a prayer—and thrust two fingers into her mouth and whistled shrilly. If she hadn't removed her gloves as she'd walked into the saloon, she would have died here. But she and Nightingale were much more than horse and rider. They were partners. And because of that, he didn't flee when ordinary horses bolted in panic—and he came to her rescue when even a human partner would have thought twice.

Even so, he was almost too late.

In the distance, she heard a stallion's wild scream

of challenge. Nightingale was coming. All she had to do was stay alive until he got here. She gazed around herself wildly, searching for anything she could use as a weapon. She spotted a Winchester leaning against a wall—it would serve as a club if nothing else—but before she could dash across the street to get it, she saw more zombies coming out of the doorway beside it. There was nowhere she could run and nothing to fight with. They were going to kill her, and Nightingale would die trying to save her, and—who would search, for Philip once she was dead?

Fear gave way to fury, igniting a fire in her that burned away everything else. "Come on, you useless Bluebellies!" she shouted. "Come on, if you want a fight!" The nearest zombie was only a few feet away now. She ran toward it and punched it as hard as she could—then yelped in disgust and jumped back as dead, half-rotten flesh slid beneath her blow. Her punch had torn the corpse's face half off. It didn't stun the zombie, but it knocked it backward. It fell into the two directly behind it, and all three went down, but there were more than enough to take their places. One of them raised its arm and swung it at her as if the arm were a club. Its forearm caught her on the side of the head and knocked her sprawling.

The corpses closed in.

She struggled to her knees, only to be felled by

another blow. They weren't fast or nimble, but they were impossibly strong, and nothing she did could hurt them. If any of them had possessed a weapon—a club, a stick, a length of wood—she wouldn't have survived the next few minutes. But the ones in the street were obviously the ones who hadn't had weapons, and the ones who'd come to join them had dropped—or lost— theirs. She scrabbled backward on heels and elbows, dragging out one of her Colts as she did. When the nearest zombie reached for her, she held the pistol out at arm's length and pulled the trigger. Her arm flew up with the recoil; a Peacemaker had a kick like an angry mule. She'd seen what happened in the saloon: bullets hadn't stopped them, but the impact knocked down whatever it hit. Her attacker spun away into the advancing mob.

She tried to get to her feet—to keep moving—to run—but she was outnumbered. Dead flesh pummeled her, dead fingers clawed at her face, her neck, her clothes. Soon one of them would hit her hard enough to snap her neck or knock her out. Soon the ones with weapons would arrive.

Rescue arrived first.

She didn't see Nightingale until he burst through the zombie mob and stood over her protectively. The stallion was covered with foam, his eyes white-rimmed in terror. But he'd come for her. She reached up, dazed by the blows she'd taken, to claw at the stirrup-leather and use it to drag herself to her feet. She was almost knocked sprawling again when he reared to strike out at the nearest enemy, but she clung to him, clawing her way upward into the saddle, using her gun butt to pull herself up because she was clutching it too tightly to let go, even if she'd wanted to. The moment he felt her weight settle, Nightingale bounded forward. She felt cold dead hands grab her legs, her saddle, anything they could reach, and she battered at them with her gun butt until their hands were so ruined they could no longer grip.

Then Nightingale was through them. She finally got her feet into the stirrups as he galloped blindly into the night. It took her both hands to get her pistol back into its holster.

Only then did she let herself realize what had just happened.

Ten miles outside Alsop, a stream the locals called "Burnt Crick" cut across the Staked Plain. In summer it was no more than a dry streambed, but winter rains turned it into a broad torrent fast enough and deep enough to drown unwary cattle, and in spring it still filled most of its bed. Cottonwood trees lined both banks. Beneath their shelter sat a wagon.

On the far side of the stream a young man stood beside his brown-and-white paint mare gazing across the creek, just as he had for the last hour. The two of them were concealed from view by the trees and scrub. The young man wore fringed buckskin breeches and moccasins, a cavalry hat without hat-cords or creased crown, and a blue Army coat. He'd arrived at Burnt Creek in late afternoon only to find his favorite camping spot already occupied. He had business in Alsop, but by the time he got there it would be dark, and he didn't want to try to find a bed in the town. He should have ridden on, but something about the wagon held his attention. It was a Burton wagon, the same kind the traveling drummers sold their snake-oil tonics from, but instead of being brightly painted, it bore a sober coat of whitewash. That wasn't enough to draw his scrutiny, but the fact there was no wagon tongue to hitch the horses to *was*. In fact, there were no horses in sight to hitch to the wagon even if there'd been a way to do it.

The Burton's only occupant seemed to be a young blond female in an outlandish costume—loose blue serge trousers gathered at the ankle, a short dress of the same stuff, and a poke bonnet hanging down her back by its ribbons. If he needed any further proof beyond her costume to tell him the girl was from somewhere far away, the poke provided it. No woman in the Territory, from sodbuster to townie to rancher, would uncover her head while the sun was above the horizon.

If her team had run off before he got there, it didn't seem to worry her. He'd watched as she lit her fire, and she seemed to be perfectly comfortable out here all by herself. The tin coffeepot she set out was commonplace enough, as were the iron griddle and cookpot. The one held flatbread and the other held beans. Soon enough the aroma of coffee and beans drifted across the stream, and she was piecing out flatbread to bake on the griddle. But despite her obvious competence, his concern only grew. The only thing she had to defend herself with was a Remington coach gun, and even though it was within easy reach, there were plenty of dangers out here for a man, never mind a lone female.

The sun was already on the horizon. *You should ride on if you want to make camp while there's light left*, he told himself, but somehow he couldn't make himself mount up and head out. *You surely don't mean to leave her all alone out here*, he scolded himself. *Perhaps she doesn't know there's a town so near.*

He could go and tell her. He could bring her with him to Alsop—Deerfoot could carry double—and take his chances there. She could rent a buckboard from the livery stable, and tomorrow Sheriff Mitchell could ride back here with her and help her look for her missing horses.

It seemed like the best plan. He lifted himself onto Deerfoot's back and sent her toward the stream with a nudge of his knee.

Honoria Verity Providentia Gibbons looked up at the sound of splashing and reached for her firearm. A handsome pinto mare was crossing the stream. Gibbons wasn't a very good shot, but that was why she carried a coach gun. With a coach gun, you didn't have to be good—you only had to be willing to pull the trigger. At first Gibbons didn't think the mare wore either saddle or bridle, but then she realized she was tacked out Indian-style, with a blanket for a saddle and only a single braided leather cord for a bridle. Most observers would see the horse, the rider's darkly tanned skin, and think, *"Indian,"* but the rider was no Native—even from here Gibbons could see his hair was wavy, and a few shades lighter than his skin. *Well, that's interesting. I wonder if he's an Army Scout?* She watched the horse and rider approach with curiosity tempered with wariness.

"Hello, the camp," the man called when his mount reached the bank.

"Hello, stranger," she replied, setting down her gun and waving to him to approach. "Welcome. I have coffee—" She broke off to rescue the flatbread before it scorched, wrapping her hand in the end of her rather bedraggled shawl to pull the griddle away from the fire. "And bread and beans," she finished rather breathlessly. "You're welcome to share them."

"That's kind of you, ma'am," he replied. He signaled to his mare to halt and slid easily off her back. She followed him as a dog would as he walked toward the campfire.

No matter his appearance, he has lived some time among the Natives, Gibbons thought. *No one accustomed to wearing boots walks toe-heel instead of heel-toe, in boots or out of them.*

"Honoria Gibbons," she said, extending her hand. "But you must call me 'Gibbons,' as my friends do. Pleased to make your acquaintance, Mister . . ." She paused expectantly.

"Wapeshk Wakoshe," he replied, shaking her hand gingerly. "But I think it will be simpler if you call me White Fox."

She narrowed her eyes a bit in concentration. To her pleasure she recognized the language-group—Algonquin—and his pronunciation gave her the dialect. "Your accent is *Meshkwahkihaki*, I think?" she said. "But you are far from home for a Red Earth man, Mister Fox," she added, for the westernmost of the Sac and Fox tribes lived in the new state of Nebraska.

She smiled when she saw his pupils dilate a little. It was the only sign of his surprise. *Raised among them from childhood, I think, and not some frontiersman who has merely lived as their guest.* Most people would miss the subtle clues she'd noticed, but Honoria Gibbons took no small amount of pride in the fact she was not "most people."

White Fox was startled. The *wasichu* said there were no spirits, but either this girl spoke to spirits, or she saw as truly as one of the Red Earth People. But even if she was more than she seemed, she was still alone out here.

"Perhaps you do not know there is a town up the road," he said, politely averting his eyes from her face. "It is no more than ten miles from here. I was headed that way myself, and I would be glad to take you there. Tomorrow you can return to search for your horses. They will not wander far from water." She said nothing, and he hesitated, not wishing to frighten her. "Not everyone in the *Llano Estacado* is friendly," he finally said. "You'd be more comfortable in town. And safer."

Honoria Gibbons smiled as if he'd said something amusing. "Oh, I think anyone who attempted to interfere with me would discover it to be a very bad idea."

Her left foot moved a little as she spoke, and he froze as a slat dropped down on the side of the wagon. The muzzles of three deadly Gatling guns extended from the slot and pivoted to his position, though he was certain her wagon was unoccupied.

Perhaps she wasn't as helpless as she appeared, he decided.

There came the same scraping sound of wood on wood he'd heard a moment before. The muzzles retracted and the slat popped back up into place. "Yes," she said. "A very bad idea indeed."

"I reckon you know your own mind, ma'am," White Fox replied calmly. "Would you mind if I stayed tonight and shared your fire?"

"Not at all!" Gibbons replied cheerfully. "Coffee?"

He turned to Deerfoot, whisking the saddle-blanket free and slipping the loop of her bridle from her lower jaw so she could graze freely. The mare wandered off to the river, and he coiled the rein between his hands, the blanket tossed over one shoulder as he squatted down beside the fire and poured himself a cup of coffee.

"I should be quite glad of the company, actually," Gibbons continued. "You seem like a gentleman who can make intelligent conversation."

As she regarded him with utter fearlessness, White Fox realized this eccentric and possibly mad female might be the most beautiful girl he'd ever seen, from her flawless skin and golden hair, to the dark eyes—blue, he thought—alight with a fierce intelligence. And he sensed she was utterly unaware of her beauty.

"Beans, Mister Fox?" Gibbons asked brightly.

"If you were to go in search of my horses, Mister Fox, I am afraid you would search in vain," Gibbons said, handing him a plate of beans and flatbread. The night had fallen swiftly, and she'd lit the kerosene lanterns on the near side of the wagon before settling to her own meal. White Fox looked politely puzzled, but Gibbons knew enough about the Red Earth People to know he wouldn't do anything as rude as ask a near-stranger a direct question.

"This is an Auto-Tachypode," she said grandly, gesturing at the wagon. "Papa and I built it together. It does not require horses to provide its motive power."

"I do not see how that is possible," White Fox said doubtfully.

Gibbons laughed gaily. "I shall give you a demonstration in the morning, Mister Fox! Then you will see."

"Perhaps I shall," White Fox agreed.

Gibbons stifled a grin and applied herself to her

meal. She paid little attention to the taste—food, after all, was merely fuel for the brain, and unimportant except in that bad food was difficult to choke down— but White Fox devoured her cooking with relish, and even asked for seconds. When supper was over, he indicated his tobacco pouch and looked at her inquiringly. She nodded her permission, and he busied himself rolling a cigarette. She was grateful they were outdoors. While she wouldn't dream of dictating someone else's behavior, nicotine was a drug, and a pernicious one at that, and Honoria Gibbons did not ingest any mind-altering substances such as tobacco, alcohol, or opium. She prized clear thought far too much.

And besides, tobacco smoke *stank*.

By the time he'd gotten his cigarette made and lit and taken his first draw, he'd obviously decided their acquaintance had progressed enough that he might ask her some questions.

"You say you built this device with your father," he observed, nodding toward the Auto-Tachypode. "Will he be joining you soon?"

Gibbons shook her head, pouring herself another cup of coffee. Coffee, after all, stimulated mental alertness. "I travel alone, Mister Fox."

White Fox shook his head. "This seems unwise to me. You are certainly quite clever, but against wild beasts or outlaws, cleverness might not be enough."

Gibbons stifled a tiny sigh of exasperation at hearing the familiar sentiment. In her experience, there was no obstacle that did not fall before the power of the mind. Far be it from her to point out yet again that the majority of the lady pioneers here in the West spent the greater part of their lives either alone while their husbands were out hunting or trapping or tilling the soil—or performing those tasks themselves when one of the perils White Fox had listed carried that husband off. Both men and women had lectured Gibbons on the unsuitability of her chosen vocation, and when she marshaled her arguments, said, "But that's different!" (*How* it was different, no one was ever quite able to explain to her satisfaction.)

"I am afraid I cannot share your opinion, Mister Fox," Gibbons said tactfully, wiping her tin plate clean with the last of her bread and setting it aside. "And Papa needs . . . a certain amount of protection from himself," she added carefully. "America is full of charlatans, and he is forever hearing from people who want him to invest in all manner of idiotic schemes. That is why I am here."

This was oversimplifying things to the extreme, for to say Jacob Saltinstall Gibbons was a genius was rather like saying Leonardo da Vinci had been a passable painter, and with such genius came a certain amount of eccentricity. Those eccentricities had moved the wealthy Gibbons family to provide their youngest son with all the money he wanted so long as he stayed far, far away from Boston, but soon their remuneration had been overtaken by events. The gold fever of 1849 had drawn her then-widowed parent and his infant daughter westward—for Jacob Gibbons had eagerly sought the opportunity to test some theories he'd formed regarding mining equipment—and very much to his surprise, he'd gained a more-than-respectable fortune from his engineering patents.

But his newfound wealth brought problems of its own. In San Francisco his dear friend Doctor Rupert Arthur Gordon kept him from being taken by charlatans, but soon the con men began to cast their nets from afar.

"Idiotic schemes?" White Fox asked.

"As many as there are leaves on this cottonwood tree," Gibbons said, sighing. "Finding the Lost City of Atlantis, creating the Philosopher's Stone, building a mediumistic telegraph to communicate with the dead . . . I was just in Kansas City, exposing a gentleman who claimed to be able to summon twisters at will." She snorted inelegantly. "I assure you, such was not the case! I soon discovered he had confederates further west, who would telegraph to him when the right sorts of storms were on the way."

The charlatan's "spotters" had possessed clever rigs they could use to tap into telegraph lines wherever they could shinny up a pole. What had gotten him slapped into jail was not the fraud—for her father was to have been the first paying victim—but the purloining of the messaging service without paying for it.

"And before that, I was in the Arizona Territory, looking for some bizarre creature called a 'chupacabra.' Its would-be captor had sent photographs of it to Papa, wishing to be compensated for the expense of tracking the beast down and shipping it to San Francisco. The photographs were faked, of course, and though the Mexican farmers assured me the creature truly existed, their 'chupacabra' turned out to be merely a wild boar."

"I have heard of the chupacabra," White Fox said doubtfully. "I have never seen one, nor did the tracks shown to me belong to anything but beasts I already knew well."

"So you see." She shrugged. "It is my job, self-appointed though it may be, to track such villains down, uncover them as frauds, and send Papa the proof. At least sending me keeps Papa from sending money instead. And I confess, I do enjoy this far more than I would going to operas and plays and other such nonsense."

"And what are you pursuing now?" White Fox asked boldly. Apparently he'd forgotten she was a female, in his interest in her tales—momentarily at least.

"Mysterious disappearances," she told him. "Papa believes great phantom airships sail the skies, contraptions like aerial clipper ships. The crews of the phantom airships are said to have abducted individuals and even entire communities . . . and of course there is a man who swears he can put Papa into communication with the captain of one such airship—for a modest fee." She shrugged. "It is true there have been many unexplained disappearances here of late, but I have yet to see a sign of anything even remotely like a clipper ship in the sky."

"Nor have I," White Fox answered. He tried to keep his tone light, but Gibbons realized his interest had sharpened the moment she'd begun to speak of disappearances. "And you do not believe in these . . . airships?" he asked.

"I am keeping my mind open to the possibility," she admitted. "After all, Papa and I built this"—she patted the side of her wagon fondly—"so others might have built airships. But I am a Scientist and a Skeptic—all I know for certain is there have been enough unexplained disappearances of late to engender stories in the newspapers. Most of them came from this area."

Now White Fox looked genuinely startled. He opened his mouth as if to speak, and then closed it again. His cigarette had burned down nearly to his fingers; he flicked the end absently into the fire and continued to regard her closely.

"Do you have some intelligence touching on these disappearances, Mister Fox?" she asked bluntly, hoping he might be able to put her on the right track. He regarded her for a very long moment indeed, and Gibbons began to believe she might have misjudged his character. Finally—though grudgingly—he nodded.

"I, too, seek an answer to a disappearance," he admitted. "My investigation is the fulfillment of a pledge, in a manner of speaking."

"Was this disappearance recent?" she demanded eagerly. "Can you tell me more?"

"There was—until a few months ago—a town of freedmen in Kansas called Glory Rest," he said reluctantly. "I do not imagine you would think its disappearance important, or even worth investigation—"

She sat up indignantly. "Mister Fox! Pray give me some credit for human feelings! These missing—a *whole town*?—were as much human beings as you and I! Mothers, fathers, sisters, brothers, living in freedom for the first time! Tell me the details—everything you know is relevant!"

He blinked at her fervor. "If I am to do that, I must begin at the beginning. I am a scout for the Tenth Cavalry out of Fort Riley, Kansas."

"Ah!" she said in satisfaction at the confirmation of her earlier hunch, "Buffalo soldiers! Brave men, and true—I have read a very great deal about them!"

He blinked in surprise. "Then you already know of the 'Negro Soldier' units—"

She waved her hand dismissively. "Of course, of course. Pray go on."

"I am not myself a soldier, but a civilian contractor to the Army. One of the soldiers of the Tenth, Caleb Lincoln, asked me to go to Glory Rest to discover why his mother's letters had ceased to arrive, and his Captain gave me leave to do so. Glory Rest is perhaps a hundred miles from Fort Riley. It is a small town—its inhabitants strive—*strove*—to make their living by farming the land. When I reached it, the town was completely deserted."

Gibbons chewed her lower lip a moment as she mentally reviewed what she knew of that region. "Not an attack by the Apache or the Cheyenne?" she asked carefully. Both tribes raided, and destroyed settlements when they could. It was understandable—their land and their freedom were being destroyed by Anglo settlement—but it was also lamentable. Innocent people bore the punishment for the Federal policy that the first inhabitants of this land had no claim upon it.

White Fox shook his head. "The settlement was in great disarray, it is true, but I saw nothing I could not consider the work of storms or scavengers. There were a few small fires obviously caused by untended oil lamps, but I saw none of the signs that would tell me Glory Rest had been attacked by a raiding party. But every person who once lived there was gone."

"And of course, since it was a Freedman Settlement, no one had reported it. Nor would it be mentioned in a newspaper." She tried not to sound too disapproving, but—facts were facts, and it was better to stare them in the face.

He nodded. "Rather than return to the Fort with a greater mystery, I chose to seek answers. Roughly a week ago I was in San Antonio and heard that an entire cattle drive—riders and cattle both—had vanished. I am on the back-trail of that drive now."

Gibbons felt the little tingle of excitement that marked a moment when she had hit a true trail. Although a few moments ago she would have waved cheerfully to White Fox's departing back come morning, from this moment on he would have a difficult time shaking her loose from his heels. "And have you found anything yet?" she asked.

He shook his head again, clearly frustrated.

"Nothing. The drovers and the cattle simply vanished, as if—as if your 'phantom airship' truly exists, Gibbons. As if the earth swallowed them, or they walked into another world. I have only this—in the last letter Trooper Lincoln had from his mother—"

Suddenly he broke off, turning to stare intently into the darkness. A moment later, Gibbons heard what had summoned his attention; the sound of a horse galloping toward them, as no horse should gallop on so uncertain a road in the dark—unless the case was dire indeed.

They both jumped to their feet. White Fox laid a hand on his pistol, and Gibbons snatched up the coach-gun. Either the rider was an outlaw being hotly pursued or an innocent being pursued by outlaws.

And in either case, I want to get off the first shot, not the second, Gibbons thought.

CHAPTER TWO

In defiance of common sense, the further she got from immediate danger, the more frightened Jett became. She'd grown up with tales of the walking dead, for Mister Averell—Court Oak's overseer—had been a Free Black and turned a tolerant eye to the conjure ceremonies held on the plantation grounds. The Court Oak servants had been happy to recount marrow-chilling tales of duppies and *zuvembies* for their young charges—but she'd never seen one.

She'd never expected to, either. The *Llano Estacado* was about as far from the moss-draped oaks of Louisiana as she could imagine. *And Tante Mére swore the* zuvembie *only punishes the wicked, and I cannot believe everyone in Alsop was black with sin—*

Jett didn't know how long Nightingale had been running through the darkness when she saw lights ahead. The warm glow of a campfire, the paler light of kerosene lanterns. She must have made some movement Nightingale interpreted as a command, for he headed straight toward them. She barely had time to realize he might be running straight into a whole nest of zombies before he reached the edge of the circle of firelight. She recoiled in fear, and to her anguish, he took that as a signal to skid to a stop. She immediately realized why, for his head hung down and his breath whistled in his throat. His sides heaved as he struggled for air; foam dripped from his mouth and covered his withers. All she wanted was to spur him on, put more distance between herself and the zombies, but she knew Nightingale had given her his all, and to force him onward would kill him.

Standing before the fire were a—living—man and woman. The man took a step forward, obviously intending to grab Nightingale's rein. Had the zombies followed her out of Alsop? She had to warn them.

"Stay back!" she gasped. "Get your horses—get out of here—run! Now! There's"—her mouth spoke the word her mind still couldn't quite accept—"there's *zombies* behind me—a horde, an army of them—they're killing everything they see! Run, I tell you—*run!*"

She knew she had to keep going—there was no safety in the darkness. She would lead Nightingale onward. Surely, *surely* he could walk, at least—anything to take them far from Alsop! She tried to swing down from the saddle, but her body would not obey her. She clawed desperately at the saddle-horn, but she could not close her fingers around it. She felt herself swaying, slipping . . .

Strong arms caught her and eased her fall. She tried to stay on her feet but only managed to sink to her knees. "Run," she croaked. "Run."

"You aren't going anywhere, my good woman," the female said briskly. "You're in no condition to fight off a kitten, and as for your animal, I think he is in worse shape than you. He needs rest and water."

If there was anything that could have snapped Jett back to full consciousness, it was the stranger's words. Few had ever seen past Jett Gallatin to Philippa Sheridan, and none in a few moments by only the light of a fire.

"Miss Gibbons is right," the young man agreed. "If there is trouble behind you, it cannot arrive quickly. And I think we have the means here to answer it," he added with a glance toward his companion.

He held out a hand, which Jett used to lever herself

to her feet. It was the hardest work she'd ever done to walk the few steps to the fire and seat herself on the wooden box the woman had been using for a seat. "My horse—" she said. She needed to see to Nightingale.

"Mister Fox will see to your animal," Miss Gibbons said firmly.

"He can't—" Jett began, but Mister Fox was already lifting her saddlebags from the saddle—and Nightingale let him. *Has the world gone mad since sunset?* Jett thought, numbly accepting the cup Miss Gibbons pushed into her hands. The coffee was hot and strong, and she sipped it greedily.

With a few deft motions, Mister Fox unbuckled the cinch and pulled the saddle from Nightingale's back. To Jett's great relief—for it needed to be done and she knew she could not manage to do it herself—he did not stop there but picked up her saddle blanket, rubbed Nightingale briskly dry, and then began to walk him.

"Now. Tell us what happened to you. And without any supernatural fol-de-rol, if you please," Miss Gibbons said.

"If I had a dollar for every damnyankee know-it-all I've met in the Territories, I could buy them up at auction and get me a fancy box to put them in, too," Jett snapped. "You think I'm lying, you just head back up the road to Alsop. You'll see." She reached up to tip her

Stetson back and hissed in pain as her fingers brushed a bruise.

"You're injured!" Miss Gibbons exclaimed.

"Had worse," Jett answered gruffly, but Miss Gibbons was already leaping to her feet. As she hurried off toward the back of her wagon, Jett realized that what she'd first taken for a skirt was actually some kind of odd pantalets. "The world's gone mad," she repeated.

"Perhaps it has," White Fox said quietly, as he passed her. Nightingale walked behind him as tamely as a dog on a leash. "But whatever the cause, your injuries were not inflicted by what Miss Gibbons terms 'supernatural fol-de-rol.'"

"I told you to call me plain 'Gibbons,' Mister Fox," Miss Gibbons said crisply, returning with a carpetbag in her arms. To Jett's gratitude, not only was the first item she extracted from it a bottle of French Brandy, but she poured a generous measure of it into Jett's coffee cup. When she'd finished, she soaked down a pad of cotton wool with the brandy and began dabbing at Jett's forehead.

"I can tend my own hurts," Jett snapped reflexively.

"Oh, don't be unreasonable!" Miss Gibbons scolded. "I dare swear you didn't even realize you were hurt until a moment ago."

She made a grab for Jett's hat and Jett removed it in

self-defense. "She always like this?" she called toward Mister Fox.

"I cannot say," he answered gravely, leading Nightingale back in her direction once more. "My acquaintance with . . . Gibbons . . . is only a few hours old. So perhaps we should all introduce ourselves. I'm a scout for the Tenth Cavalry. They call me White Fox."

"And I'm Honoria Gibbons, and I will take it kindly if you call me 'Gibbons,' and not 'Miss' or 'Miss Gibbons.' And you are . . . ?"

"Jett Gallatin," Jett answered. "Folks who want a handle call me *Mister* Gallatin." She hissed again as Gibbons poked a sore spot. Her neck and shoulders were covered with deep scratches, and she suspected she'd be black and blue in the morning.

"Oh, don't be such a baby!" Gibbons said irritably. Jett endured further poking in silence until at last Gibbons sat back. "Nothing more I can do without better light. You're from Louisiana, are you not?" she added, as if the two ideas were somehow related.

"I was," Jett answered bleakly. She drained the last of her brandied coffee and, to her great relief, felt steady enough to get to her feet. She walked over to White Fox, who put the end of Nightingale's reins into Jett's hand—no matter how thirsty he might be, the stallion could not be allowed to drink until he'd cooled out. There was a paint mare browsing nearby, but no sign of a wagon team. She clutched the reins like a lifeline, then threw an arm across Nightingale's withers to steady herself and continued to walk him. If the other two continued their conversation, their voices were pitched too low for her to hear.

At last, when he was cooled out enough that he wouldn't instantly founder if left to himself, Jett walked Nightingale down to the creek for a drink. She knelt on the bank beside him and splashed water over her face and neck, then unbuckled Nightingale's bridle and slipped it off. As he wandered over to the mare, she walked back to her saddlebags and saddle. Her shirt was in ruins, and bloody besides. She located her other "everyday" shirt and tossed it over the saddle while she shrugged out of her frock-coat and leather vest. She turned her back to the campfire as she pulled off the remains of her shirt. Gibbons and White Fox would see the muslin bandage wound around her torso to bind her breasts flat, but there was no help for it. And they already knew her secret. She pulled the shirt on and stuffed the hem into her trousers, then picked up her coat and vest and walked back to the fire. When she sat down, White Fox handed her another full cup of coffee, and she smelled the brandy in it when she raised it to her lips.

"I'd be dead now if it weren't for Nightingale," Jett said in a low voice. "He fought them off. I don't know how many there were. I was in the saloon when they came, but they were all over the town."

"You called them 'zombies,'" White Fox prompted quietly.

"When the dead get up and walk again, that's what we call them," she answered tartly. "As you say, Miss— Gibbons, beg pardon, ma'am—I am, I *was*, from New Orleans, from Orleans Parish, and we understand hoodoo there. I'd always heard conjure could call a man up out of his grave and make him do his caller's bidding, but closest I ever came was coming on a place . . . after. And if you don't believe in it, you tell me what could take both barrels of a Winchester in the chest and keep coming. I saw that with my own eyes."

"I don't know, *Mister* Gallatin, but just because I don't know doesn't make those people you saw the reanimated dead," Gibbons said doggedly.

Despite herself, Jett smiled at the other woman's stubborn fierceness. "Reckon you might as well call me Jett so we don't get ourselves all tangled up here," she said. "But I'd take it kindly if you didn't tell all you know about me," she added.

"I would never betray a confidence," Gibbons said severely. "You have my word."

"'Preciate it," Jett said. "There's plenty of rannies who don't take kindly to this sort of thing," she said, waving a hand to indicate her outfit.

"Oh, men *always* object to being shown that a female is just as capable, just as competent, as they are," Gibbons announced. "But perhaps you would be so kind as to tell me everything you saw in Alsop tonight. And—I am afraid we've eaten all the biscuits, but there are some beans left over from our supper, and I can open another can of peaches."

"'Preciate it," Jett said again. "Bacon and hardtack gets a might tedious after a time."

By the time Jett finished her meal, Gibbons had extracted every detail of the attack on Alsop. Nothing Jett had told her seemed to have shaken her conviction that zombies did not exist. "Well, we'll see in the morning," was all she'd say.

"One way or another," Jett said grimly. *The devil we will. I'm not going back there, and you're not going there either, you crazy female.*

A short while later Gibbons announced it was time for bed, and White Fox went to check on Deerfoot and wash up. Gibbons offered Jett space inside her wagon, but Jett merely shook her head, saying she wanted to sit up for a while. Whoever had gathered the wood for the fire had collected enough for a week, and Jett had no worry she'd deprive Gibbons of a breakfast fire no matter how much she burned. Gibbons retreated to the wagon, dousing the lanterns as she did, and soon afterward White Fox returned. Without his hat, and with his hair slicked back and damp from washing, he looked much younger than she'd originally thought.

A Yankee's still a Yankee, she told herself stubbornly. *And I seem to have fallen into a nest of 'em.* She couldn't manage to work up her usual anger at the invaders who'd destroyed her home and her family, tonight, though. Bad as they might be, they weren't as bad as the unquiet dead.

White Fox unrolled his bedroll under the wagon with a quiet word of good night, and soon the little camp was utterly still. Jett tossed another chunk of wood onto the fire and poured the last of the coffee into her cup, tipping the pot upside down to let the grounds empty. When she finished drinking, she took pot and cup down to the creek to rinse them clean. She'd put her vest back on earlier, but now she shrugged into her frock coat, wincing a bit. She was stiff and aching, and every movement told her about some new place she was bruised, but she knew if she didn't move around, she'd just stiffen further. And she was alive. That was more than she'd expected earlier.

There was a full moon tonight, and the sky was bright with stars. In the distance a coyote gave tongue, soon joined by a chorus.

Durned critters always sound like their hearts're

breaking, she thought, grumbling under her breath. *Don't know what they got to cry about. I never heard tell of a coyote army nor a coyote war.*

When she came back to the campfire, she stacked the dishes neatly on one of the boxes, then went to collect the rest of her gear and put it in order. Her saddle blanket was still damp, so she hunted around until she found a branch sturdy enough to hang it from. When she took a seat by the fire once more, she shook out her ruined shirt and folded it carefully before tucking it into her saddlebags. Maybe she'd come across some town with a laundry where she could get it washed and mended—if it was worth repairing at all. If it wasn't, she could always use it for rags.

She was relieved her cigarette case hadn't been a casualty of her fight this evening. It was gold, with an ace picked out on the front in diamonds, and she'd won it in a card game. Someday she might need to sell it if she couldn't raise the wind any other way, but until then it added to her masquerade as a prosperous and indolent gambler. She opened it and extracted a thin black cheroot, and picked up a bit of wood to light it.

Mama'd have the vapors to see me using tobacco, Jett thought sadly. *And Papa'd whup me till I couldn't sit down.* Gentlemen smoked and ladies did not; before the war, she'd been too young to smoke when she'd been playing the boy. But it was one of the things that helped make her masquerade convincing.

She wondered sometimes if it was really a masquerade any more.

The fire popped loudly, and she jerked in alarm, heart racing. White Fox and Honoria Gibbons were both sound asleep—but they hadn't seen what Jett had seen. She didn't think she'd sleep at all, and she didn't want to, either. She'd keep watch, and kill two birds with one stone. She turned so she was sitting with her back to the fire and stretched her legs out in front of her.

It was where White Fox found her when dawn began to brighten the sky. He'd slept lightly, as he always did, and a part of him expected the young gunslinger to have crept away in the night. But when he rolled out from under the wagon, he found her feeding the fire back to life.

"Got some Arbuckle's in my kit," she said, seeing him. "Figure I could add some bacon to those beans, too."

White Fox nodded silently. After he'd washed, he made a wide circle around Gibbons's wagon, but he saw no sign that any creature who did not belong here had approached in the night. When he returned, Jett had sliced several chunks of bacon into the beans left over from last night's meal, and the coffeepot was already heating. He raided his own supplies for salt and meal, and by the time Gibbons appeared, breakfast was all but ready.

In the light of morning, Jett had a better view of Gibbons's outlandish costume. There was actually more than one, for last night's outfit had been royal blue, and today's was a vibrant scarlet. It consisted of voluminous pantalets that clearly revealed her legs, because they were gathered tightly at her ankles. Over it she wore a long tunic with soutache embroidery across the bosom and shoulders, and beneath that tunic a white muslin blouse. It was entirely obvious that Gibbons was not wearing a corset of any kind.

"I see you are admiring my Rational Dress," Gibbons said proudly. "It was invented by Miss Libby Miller—a noted female suffrage activist—to free women from the tyranny of corsets and petticoats. I confess I am disappointed it has not been more enthusiastically adopted," she added, looking momentarily crestfallen, "but you of all people will certainly see how much more convenient it is to have the freedom of one's limbs!"

"It's very . . . rational," Jett said awkwardly. Jett might dress as a man, but privately she longed for the pretty and fashionable dresses she'd left behind. She thought Gibbons's costume was the ugliest thing she'd ever seen in her life—but she could not bear to hurt Gibbons's feelings by saying so. "You can't sit a horse in that," she added, feeling something more was called for. "Can you?"

"Certainly not!" Gibbons agreed merrily. "My Auto-Tachypode is far more efficient. I have every faith that someday they will be as widespread as Rational Dress, and horses will be a thing of the past."

"Doubtless you know best about that," Jett said dryly. She drank coffee for a few moments in silence. "Tell me—have you thought better of this nonsensical idea of yours?"

"If by that you mean do I intend to give up my idea of seeing Alsop for myself, I certainly have not," Gibbons said. "It is Mister Fox's destination as well—not that I require his protection in the least."

"Oh, of course not," Jett muttered. "But you cannot mean to go to Alsop, White Fox," she added, turning to him. "I know Gibbons does not believe me—but you, at least, must know I am not lying." Perhaps if he changed his mind, Gibbons would change hers.

"I must," White Fox said. "My trail leads there, and I must find answers, no matter the cost. Many people— Negroes, whites, and Indians—have gone missing of late. Perhaps your zombies are the cause."

"P'raps you'll just end up missing, too," Jett grumbled.

"Really, you are the most fearful gunslinger I have ever met," Gibbons said sternly. "Why, you said yourself the creatures fear daylight! We shall be perfectly safe!"

"Well, if you're going to Alsop, I reckon I'm going with you," Jett said. Even if Gibbons was a crazy damn-yankee and White Fox worked for the Bluebellies, she couldn't let them ride into danger by themselves.

"Can't stop you!" Gibbons said cheerfully.

Jett was beginning to think Honoria Gibbons did everything cheerfully.

"I'm about to start the Auto-Tachypode! You'll want to move well away! Your horses will not appreciate the commotion!" Gibbons called, stepping up into the back of the wagon. She didn't wait to see whether White Fox and Jett took her advice. If they didn't this time, they certainly would in the future. Horses simply didn't seem to like the Auto-Tachypode.

Wagons such as this one normally provided a tidy and weatherproof traveling home for their owners, but while Gibbons thought of this as more her home than her suite of rooms in her papa's Russian Hill townhouse, even she had to admit it was cramped. Most of the interior was taken up with the Gatling guns and their firing mechanism and with the Auto-Tachypode's motive mechanism, a collection of cogwheels, pulleys, and pistons as elaborate as the interior of a Swiss watch. But while one might wind a watch to permit it to function, the Auto-Tachypode's motive power came from steam. A steam boiler—a marvel of miniaturization, and her own invention—allowed the Auto-Tachypode to function. She had filled the reservoir last night as soon as it had cooled, and had begun stoking it even before she had dressed to greet the day.

She consulted the pressure gauges with a critical eye. The boiler had built up a good head of steam. Everything was in readiness. She exited the back of the wagon again, being careful to latch the doors firmly behind her. She had no interest in chasing her boxes of supplies over half the desert—and even less in being laughed at by her two companions.

She was pleased to see Jett and White Fox had taken her warning seriously. They were on the far side of the creek, watching the proceedings with curiosity. She walked around to the front of the wagon and took her place on the wooden bench. While the bench itself had been part of the wagon's original structure, that was the last thing about it that was conventional. She pulled the gleaming wooden tiller toward her and ran her hand over the small forest of brass levers installed at the right-hand side of the seat. *It is not that I am nervous*, she told herself. *I simply wish this to be a true exhibition of the mechanism's capabilites.*

"Here goes nothing," she muttered under her breath. She grasped the largest of the brass levers and pulled back on it strongly. The moment she released the clutch there was an earsplitting shriek of released steam followed by the clattering banging racket of churning pistons. The entire wagon began to shake violently.

"Are you all right?" Jett shouted anxiously to her.

"Never better!" Gibbons shouted back.

She released the brake. The shaking stopped, replaced with a low mechanical vibration, and to her secret glee, the Auto-Tachypode began to move forward with majestic grace. She pulled the tiller toward her gently, and it turned toward the stream. At that point, both horses thought better of remaining where they were. They didn't bolt, but their riders were forced to wheel them about and trot them further away. As the Auto-Tachypode bumped gently down into the streambed, Gibbons congratulated herself once again at having had the forethought to augment the wagon's wooden wheels with tires of vulcanized rubber. Not only did their textured surfaces provide additional traction, the rubber acted as a sort of shock absorber and provided a smoother ride. The wagon climbed the far bank as easily as it had descended the near one, and began chugging its way toward Alsop at a stately two miles per hour.

At first the horses would have nothing to do with the strange contraption, but after half an hour or so they were willing to walk alongside it, apparently having decided it was some odd new variety of locomotive. Gibbons happily answered her companions' questions about her invention, though she privately doubted she'd won any converts to this new method of transport. Jett thought it was too slow, and White Fox thought it was too noisy, though both of them agreed a steam engine that did not have to have tracks laid for it was of a certain amount of use.

"It is only a prototype, after all!" Gibbons said. "Once it has been thoroughly tested I shall build one capable of sustaining a higher operating speed, and even of pulling a number of wagons behind it!" She did not think it was worth mentioning just now that the Auto-Tachypode was capable of attaining a speed in excess of fifteen miles an hour—though it was a risky business, as it required the engine to build up such a head of steam that it was in constant danger of exploding. It was true that the main body of the boiler had been cast in one piece to avoid precisely that, but Gibbons had a healthy respect for the dangerous power of live steam. She had seen far too many deadly accidents at the locomotive yards where she'd researched her invention.

It was midmorning by the time they reached Alsop, and Jett would have thought she'd dreamed the previous night's attack . . . except for the fact that not so much as a barking dog greeted their extremely noisy arrival. In a way, she was grateful for the noise that contraption of Gibbons produced. It kept things from being so quiet she'd turn tail and run for it.

"I'm going to check the livery stable!" Jett shouted over the racket of the Auto-Tachypode. White Fox raised a hand to indicate he'd heard, and she spurred ahead toward the stables.

This isn't right, she thought as she dismounted. The corrals outside the building were deserted, though the horses should have already been turned out for the day. The stable doors were open, and she entered warily, one hand on her gun-butt. The interior was dark—no one left a lantern unattended in a barn full of hay—but enough sun shone through the doorway to show her rows of stalls, some with saddles hung on the partitions.

But there were no horses here anywhere. No horses—and no people.

She made a quick and careful circuit of the stable's

interior. The bunk in the cubby where the hostlers slept was cold, and so was the potbellied stove. She picked up the enamelware coffee pot on top of it and looked inside. The coffee had cooked down to sludge before the stove went out. *Would've been a full pot around sundown*, she mused. *Looks like there wasn't anybody left around to drink it, though.* She checked the tiny house built out behind the stable—most shopkeepers lived over their stores, but the owner of a livery stable couldn't do that. The bed was made, and there was no pot on the stove, but that was the only difference between the house and the hostler's cubby. She shivered despite herself, and hurried back to where Nightingale stood waiting patiently.

"Not even a stable cat," she said to him as she swung back into the saddle. "That isn't right."

As she headed back to the others, there was a sound Jett and Nightingale were both familiar with: the ear-splitting whistle of escaping steam that meant a boiler being vented. It was clear Gibbons meant to stop here a while. *Just as long as we clear out by sunset*, Jett thought worriedly. She didn't know the zombies would return with sunset—but she didn't know they *wouldn't*, either.

By the time Jett rejoined them, Gibbons had done whatever she needed to do to prepare the Auto-Tachypode for an extended period of inactivity. Deerfoot was drinking thirstily from the half-empty water trough outside the saloon, and White Fox leaned against the hitching rail glancing watchfully around himself. Jett swung down from Nightingale's back and flipped his reins up over his saddle-horn. He shook himself all over like an enormous dog, nosed at her shoulder companionably, and ambled over to the water trough.

"This is where you were when you were attacked?" White Fox asked quietly.

Jett favored him with a sardonic smile. "Reckon that smashed window tells the tale," she said, tipping back her Stetson.

"Then come along!" Gibbons said, jumping down from the wagon's bench. "It is time to begin investigating your story!"

Jett opened her mouth to say it wasn't a story, it was the unvarnished Gospel truth, and closed it again. Gibbons would find out soon enough. But when she followed Gibbons in through the saloon's bat-wing doors, for a moment Jett doubted herself as much as Gibbons obviously did. There'd been a fight here for certain—tables and chairs were broken and overturned—but the saloon was utterly empty of both the living and the dead.

"This can't be . . . ," she said slowly.

"Oh, don't distress yourself, my good—*Jett*," Gibbons

said airily. "Unless one is trained in the principles of scientific observation, it's very easy to—"

"Someone died here," White Fox said quietly. "More than one, I think."

He knelt in the sawdust that covered the floor. On an ordinary evening, it would have been swept out onto the street at the end of the night and fresh would have scattered before the saloon opened in the morning, but last night's sawdust still covered the floor. It was scuffed and scattered, but in several places it had been darkened with blood—so much blood that the blood-soaked sawdust had stuck to the floor as it dried. He brushed the floor clear around the darkened places to reveal the wood was blood-soaked as well.

"Nobody bleeds that much and gets up to go dancing," Jett said sharply.

"Still doesn't mean they were killed by zombies!" Gibbons answered cheerfully.

"*Then where in tarnation is everybody in this durned town?*" Jett shouted, rounding on her. You couldn't punch a lady, but oh, how she wanted to! "Answer me that, if you're so smart!"

"Just because I don't know doesn't mean you're right!" Gibbons shouted back, a matching fire in her own eyes.

"You want some damnyankee notion of evidence?"

Jett strode across the floor to a charred crater in the plaster wall. "Here's where the barkeep put both barrels into one'a those things!" She spied something on the floor and pounced on it. "And here's the axe he tried next!" The blade was still clean.

"*Post hoc ergo propter hoc*—all that proves is that there was a saloon brawl," Gibbons answered, her eyes flashing dangerously.

After this, therefore because of this. Jett wondered if it would improve Gibbons's opinion of her to know Jett was probably as fluent in Latin as she was. It hadn't been considered 'feminine' for a girl to have much book-learning, but as the lone girl on an isolated plantation, Jett had shared everything with her brothers, including their school-days.

"*If* you say so," Jett answered, throwing up her hands. She turned to step out onto the street again— zombies or no zombies, the deserted saloon gave her the willies—but she suddenly noticed something. "Hey. Where'd White Fox get to?"

The indignantly baffled look on Gibbons's face did much to restore Jett's good humor, even if it did nothing to answer her question. She was about to suggest they go looking for him—she had no intention of leaving Gibbons alone, even if Alsop seemed deserted— when White Fox walked in through the doorway that led to the saloon's back room.

"There's no one upstairs," he said. "All the rooms are empty."

"Then the whole place is empty," Gibbons said briskly. "Let's keep looking."

The main street of Alsop contained a general store, a dining parlor and boarding house, a feed and grain, a bank, a telegraph and post office, a newspaper office, and a jail. The church was about a mile outside of town, and a few houses—probably owned by the few citizens of Alsop who did not live above or behind their businesses or workplaces—formed a ragged line between the church and the town. Jett had already checked the livery stable, and the church was far enough away that the three of them were in unspoken agreement to save it for last. By the time they'd checked the first few establishments, it was clear there was no one at all in Alsop.

The three of them split up to search more quickly. Jett frowned as she gazed around the general store. When the sun set, Jett intended to be far away from Alsop. What she found almost more unsettling than the complete absence of living things was the fact that nothing else seemed to have been disturbed. *Just walked off and locked everything up behind them when they did.* She'd had to smash the glass pane in the door to get in.

No. Wait, she thought. *I saw those things come walking out this door last night plain as day.*

Maybe the people of Alsop were still here. Hiding. They might not have come out for the noise of Gibbons's steam-driven whirligig, but . . .

She drew her pistol and ran out into the street. Pointing its barrel skyward, she pulled the trigger over and over again. Gibbons and White Fox came running at the sound of gunfire, staring at her incredulously.

"Wait," Jett said urgently, before either of them could speak. The three of them stood in silence for several seconds. And then—faint and distant—they heard the sound of shouting.

The shouting continued, indistinct but vigorous, and they finally traced it to its source—the jail. Jett stepped in front of Gibbons and opened the door, gun drawn.

"Well it's about time!" the man in the cell said irritably. "Where's Sheriff Mitchell? He was supposed to give me my breakfast—not to mention my supper!—and let me out of here *hours* ago!"

The cell's occupant was unshaven and disheveled, his long silver hair curling down over his shoulders. He wore a frock coat and a brocade vest, though the string tie and starched collar that should have completed the outfit were missing—but even though he looked disreputable, he was clean.

"First things first," Gibbons said crisply, stepping around Jett and walking up to the door. "Who are you?"

"Finlay Maxwell," the man answered, drawing himself up proudly. "I have the honor and privilege to be the Town Drunk of this fine metropolis, a position I have held for the last four years. It is a sign of civilization for a society to be able to support truly useless individuals such as I."

"Don't seem like there'd be much money in being a drunk," Jett said quickly. If Gibbons decided to lecture Maxwell on the evils of drink, they'd never get anything out of him.

"Dear sir, I am an *actor* by profession," Maxwell said haughtily. "A—dare I say it—a celebrated thespian who has performed before the crowned heads of Europe! It was the most trifling misunderstanding about the disposition of the receipts from our highly successful western engagement that caused my theatrical troupe to decamp without me."

"A trifling misunderstanding, I'm certain," Gibbons said dryly. "But certainly they didn't lock you up here when they left."

"Certainly not, my good woman. I do not scruple to admit that—every now and then—I am forced to rely on Sheriff Mitchell's kind hospitality. And yesterday was one such occasion. I had barely arisen from my healing slumber in the embrace of the grape when the night was made clangorous with the sound of guns. Naturally, Sheriff Mitchell and his minion, the worthy Deputy

Aldine, sallied forth to deal with the fuss, never to return. And what I saw thereafter I can barely credit." He paused dramatically.

"Well?" Jett demanded.

"My dear young man, you can hardly expect me to summon the angels of memory in my parched and famished state," Maxwell said.

Gibbons gave a sharp huff of annoyance and thrust her hand into the pocket of her voluminous panta-loons. She extracted a small silver flask and thrust it toward the bars. Maxwell plucked it from her grasp, deftly unscrewed the cap, and drained it at a single gulp. He sighed with deep satisfaction as he handed it back.

"As I said, there was a good deal of gunfire," Max-well continued. "And more shouting than I cared for. I kept a lookout through my window"—he gestured behind him toward the barred window in the back wall of his cell—"and after about a quarter of an hour, the town was silent. But the revelations of the evening were not complete, for there, passing outside my coign of vantage, came a vast and silent army."

"What sort of army, Mister Maxwell?" White Fox asked.

"As to that, my dear lad, I cannot fairly say. They all appeared to be sick. Or drunk, and I assure you, ma'am and sirs, the celebrated Finlay Maxwell, Esquire, is a connoisseur of the inebriated state. Regardless of their condition, I was about to bestir myself to beseech them to relieve my unjust confinement when I saw that a number of them were carrying bodies. And so I decided that '*tacere*,' as the Greeks would say, was the better part of virtue. I kept my vigil in silence—and it was just as well I did, for there was one last mystery to unfold." He paused again.

"You might as well tell us everything now, Mister Maxwell, because I'm out of brandy," Gibbons said.

"Ah, yes, but you still hold within your gift that pearl beyond price—freedom!" Maxwell said, gesturing toward the wall.

White Fox took down the ring of keys Maxwell had indicated. He moved toward the cell, but Gibbons plucked the keys from his hand before he could open the cell door. "Your 'mystery,' if you please, Mister Maxwell," she said, holding the keys up meaningfully.

"Oh very well," Maxwell grumbled ungraciously. "I watched the nightmare army depart Alsop, and the stench of the grave was in my nostrils. I knew then that I was in the presence of the Legions of Hell, my own life spared by Divine Providence. And yet, that ghastly army of the dead possessed a living General, for I saw him with my own eyes urging them onward. I know no more."

"I was right," Jett said smugly.

"That still doesn't make them reanimated dead," Gibbons said stubbornly. "Plague, autohypnosis, drugs—or outright fakery—there's a perfectly reasonable scientific explanation. I just need to find it."

"Whatever it is Mister Maxwell saw," White Fox said with calm certainty, "it has left a trail I can read." He took the keys back from Gibbons and unlocked the cell. When he swung the door wide, Finlay Maxwell strode through it, glaring at all three of them reproachfully.

"Hectoring a starving man—withholding not mere sustenance, but the very waters of life—I hope you're properly ashamed of yourselves, the lot of you!" Still grumbling, he made his way to the door of the jail and disappeared up the street.

"Where do you suppose he's going?" White Fox asked curiously.

"Probably straight to the saloon to drink himself blind," Jett answered. "Can you really track them?"

"Living or dead, by your own testimony they are corporeal beings," he answered. "They will leave some trace of their passage that I can follow. It . . . the trail will be easiest to follow if I start at once. I will return as quickly as I may."

"You mean 'we,' Mister Fox—anyone who's lo[ ] for trouble had best have company doing it[ ] be all right here by yourself?" Jett asked, (since Alsop was currently zombie-free) she knew Gibbons should be perfectly safe.

She knew she ought to mount up and ride away right now. But White Fox had already made it clear he was staying—or at least coming back. She just couldn't leave him to deal with this by himself. And she'd be lying if she didn't admit, at least to herself, that he was mighty easy on the eyes. But the same things that made it possible for Jett to masquerade as a boy were the same things that guaranteed someone like White Fox wouldn't look twice at her, even if he did know her true sex. She was too tall, too skinny, and dark like her Creole great-grandmother. While Gibbons . . .

Gibbons was small and plump and blond, and those big blue eyes of hers could stop any beau dead in his tracks as quickly as a bullet from one of Jett's pistols. Quicker.

"I've been fending for myself since you cut your milk-teeth, Jett Gallatin," Gibbons said derisively (and inaccurately). "Just be sure to bring me back one of your zombies . . . if you actually find one."

Jett had been about to sigh for "can't be" and "never happen" when Gibbons's remark made her exchange a disbelieving glance with White Fox. When she turned to give Gibbons the full force of her incredulous stare, she realized Gibbons hadn't noticed White Fox's considerable charms. White Fox might have been Finlay

Maxwell for all the consciousness of him Gibbons displayed.

"Surely—" White Fox began disbelievingly.

"*Surely* I need one of them to find out how they tick, Mister Fox!" She regarded both of them stubbornly. "Do you or do you not want this mystery solved? Well? I am the only person here with the scientific training to discover how these so-called 'zombies' came to be. If they exist at all!" she added with a snort.

"They do. You just wait and see," Jett said, more cheerfully than the subject probably called for.

CHAPTER THREE

The trail the marauders had left was easy for White Fox to follow. He was not willing to say, even within his own thoughts, whether they were living or dead—but without Jett as a witness to the attack, Alsop would have been just one more deserted settlement like Glory Rest. He would have arrived this morning to find an uninhabited town, and there would be one more mystery to add to . . . far too many others.

He'd intended to backtrail Alsop's destroyers alone, but he was forced to admit having Jett accompany him only made sense. If they found what they were seeking—living enemy or dead—she could return to Alsop and telegraph for help while he kept an eye on them, following them further if needful. And her company was not as onerous as he'd feared. She didn't talk when there was nothing to talk about, and though she was far from an expert tracker, she knew enough to stay out of his way and let him work without interference.

If I had not had her account and Mister Maxwell's to go by, I would not have thought to follow this trail, he thought. *And by evening, wind and dust would have wiped away all trace of those who passed this way.* Even now, he was not entirely certain whether the wagon whose passage he could detect had traveled with the marauders or had simply passed by some hours before them. Whichever it was, he could find no trace of the animals that should have drawn it, and that was more puzzling still. Until he'd made Gibbons's acquaintance, he could not have imagined a wagon that could move without horses. Surely there could not be *two* of them . . . ?

"Smoke," Jett said, speaking for the first time in several hours.

White Fox glanced up from where he knelt in the dust. She pointed. There was nothing to see but heat-haze and sagebrush, but the wind was blowing toward them, and once he withdrew his attention from the ground, he realized he smelled it as well. The scent was so faint most would have missed it entirely.

"You came from this direction, did you not?" he asked.

"Sure did. But I was making for Alsop, hoping to get there before dark. Wind was blowing the other direction, too," Jett answered.

"Perhaps whoever lit that fire will have information about the attack," White Fox said, swinging up onto Deerfoot's back again.

"P'raps. And perhaps they know more'n they should," Jett said distrustfully.

White Fox dismounted several times to check the trail, but whoever—*whatever*—they were following had taken a path as straight as a crow's flight once they'd left Alsop. It was not long before the trail crossed a well-used pathway and vanished. The pathway was rutted with wagon wheels and scarred with hoofprints, but it was too hard-packed to hold any lighter impression, and he could find no trace of the trail on the far side.

"I think they turned down this trail," he said quietly.

"Ranch road," Jett said, thinking aloud. "Don't know as I credit Mister Maxwell's tale of some ranahan giving them orders, but this is the closest spread to Alsop . . ."

"If they merely came to kill, why carry off the bodies of the townspeople?" White Fox asked.

Jett nodded. "And if the fella givin' 'em their marching orders is from around here, here is where he'd be from. And if not, then no reason this place wasn't attacked, too. I'm thinking it wouldn't be a bad idea to get a look around before we go riding in."

They crossed the road, looking for someplace where they could see without being seen. Less than half an hour later they found a stand of scrub pines. They didn't give much cover, but it was the best they could find.

The ranch in the distance looked utterly ordinary at first glance. Main house, bunkhouse, corrals, storage sheds, a windmill to bring water up from the grudging earth. But even a few minutes of observation showed White Fox that this ranch wasn't entirely ordinary. In addition to the buildings any ranch would possess— both of adobe and of timber weathered to gray by the elements—there were several whose tin roofs gleamed as bright as silver in the sun, and their walls were of new timber.

"Never saw a bunkhouse that big in my life," Jett whispered, pointing toward one of the new buildings. "Don't see any people, either." Despite that, she seemed content to remain where she was, watching for signs of life. A few minutes later her patience was rewarded. A woman in a calico dress and poke bonnet stepped from the doorway of the main house and walked toward the windmill, a tin bucket in each hand. She set them down at the foot of the pitcher pump and began working the arm. The creak and thump carried clearly in the quiet. When both buckets were full, the woman called back to the house, and a younger female came running across the yard to join her. Each of them picked up one bucket, and they began to walk carefully back the way they'd come.

White Fox heard Jett sigh.

"Well, they aren't zombies," she said grudgingly. "And after what I saw last night, I don't think the zombies would leave anyone alive wherever they went. But they came here," she finished, a faint questioning note in her voice.

"Whatever attacked Alsop came here," White Fox agreed. "It would have taken them perhaps six hours to cover the distance."

"Meaning they got here around midnight," Jett said. "And they *could* have just walked straight across and out the other side. But they'd need to be under cover by daylight." She sighed again. "So somebody needs to go down and have a look around. And that means me."

White Fox regarded her quizzically. He'd seen her terror last night, and knew she still believed she'd narrowly escaped being slain by the undead. And one or two *living* people—or even a dozen—was no surety that more of the creatures she feared did not await her.

"I know you aren't a hostile, White Fox, but some folks wouldn't see that. And they might just take you for a blue—for a soldier, and that'd be just as like to spook them. So I'll go and scout around while you see if those critters really did just sashay right on through."

"Will you be all right going by yourself?" he asked.

In answer she drew one of her pistols and spun it before dropping it fluidly back into its holster again. "Been alone for a while and haven't had any trouble yet."

Jett backtracked to the ranch road and then set Nightingale ambling along it. She'd been about to take offense at White Fox's question when she realized he'd have asked the same question of a man. The thought warmed her. He was the first man in the last two years to know her secret, and he hadn't lectured her about wearing trousers once.

A few hundred yards along, she passed under the archway that was a common feature of ranches. Usually there was a clapboard sign with the name of the spread and a copy of its brand hanging from the crossbar, but there wasn't one here. As she neared the house, she saw something she hadn't been able to see from the trees. There was a cross cut out of sheet brass covering most of the door. It was polished so bright it was nearly painful to look at.

The door opened as she approached, and the same woman she'd seen earlier stepped out, regarding Jett curiously.

"Afternoon, ma'am," Jett said, touching her hat brim in greeting. "Don't mean to startle you. Name's Gallatin. I'm looking for an outfit that might need a few extra hands."

The woman smiled up at her. "I'm sorry, Mister Gallatin, but I'm afraid this isn't a ranch anymore. It's Jerusalem's Wall. My name is Sister Agatha, and we are The Fellowship of the Divine Resurrection."

"Pleased to make your acquaintance, ma'am. Reckon I'll keep looking. Mind if I water my horse before I push on?"

"Oh, but you must at least stay for dinner, Mister Gallatin. Charity is the first duty of our Fellowship."

"Much obliged, Miss Agatha," Jett said, swinging down from the saddle.

"It is Sister Agatha, Mister Gallatin. We leave worldly names behind us when we join the Fellowship. Come inside when you've seen to your animal."

Jett nodded and led Nightingale over to the watering trough that stood beside the pump. Being invited to stay was a good excuse to find out about this

Fellowship. She wasn't particularly surprised to find a place out in the middle of nowhere calling itself "The Fellowship of the Divine Resurrection." This wouldn't be the first such she'd come across, and she doubted it would be the last. Most of them were harmless enough, and few of them insisted their guests abide by their ways. The West was a place where you could come to shed your past, and plenty of folks took the opportunity to shed a lot more than that. Places like the Fellowship were usually heavy on the idea of everyone holding their worldly goods in common and light on Bible preaching, though most of them could claim someone, man or woman, who'd had a "Divine Revelation" or two. Those "Revelations" could be about something as innocent as not eating meat or as outlandish as not wearing clothes and nobody getting married. She'd actually found some of them to be a comfort, since one of their prayer meetings was as close as she was likely to get to the inside of a church for the foreseeable future. She knew God would forgive what she had to do to find her brother, but that didn't mean His priests would.

She gave Nightingale a good long drink and then led him back to the hitching rail beside the door. She flipped his reins up over the saddle-horn just as she always did. "Behave," she told him, patting his shoulder. He turned his head and blew a fine spray of water against her cheek.

Sister Agatha opened the door as Jett approached and beckoned her inside. Jett removed her hat—one of the many things a man would do and a woman wouldn't; there'd been so many things she'd had to learn—and followed Sister Agatha. This close to the border, there was as much "rancho" as "ranch" in the buildings. Her boot-heels made sharp clicking sounds on the red tile floor.

"Come into the parlor and rest. It's nice and cool there. Isn't the sun dreadful?" Sister Agatha said.

"Sun gets pretty hot," Jett agreed neutrally. She was willing to bet hard cash on Sister Agatha having come from somewhere back east—and not too long ago, either.

"Now, you just make yourself comfortable and I'll bring you something nice and cool to drink."

Before Jett could protest that Sister Agatha wasn't to go to all that trouble, the woman had scurried off. At least it gave her a chance to look around. The house was built in a typical Mexican style: the main part of it balanced by two wings, giving the whole the shape of a squared-off C. There was a deep porch running across the back of the house between the wings, and a roof built out over to the edge of it, ensuring that the main part of the house would be in shade for most of the day. Whoever'd been the original owner of Jerusalem's Wall had done well for themselves—there were French doors opening out onto the porch, and every pane of glass in them would have had to come by freight wagon and flatboat from the East.

But the French doors were the only sign of gracious living left here. The parlor furniture was sparse, stark, and all bare wood. The half-dozen chairs, benches, and small low table did little to fill a space that had probably once contained velvet-upholstered mahogany furniture, a Regulator clock, and even a pianoforte. She could see faint shadows on the lime-washed walls where paintings and trophies might once have hung, but now there wasn't even a mirror over the fireplace.

Just as well you don't go getting too comfortable here. Those zombies might not have come from here in the first place, but Jerusalem's Wall was sure where they headed after they left Alsop.

Her musings were cut short by Sister Agatha's return. She carried a clay pitcher in one hand and a tin mug in the other. She filled the mug and handed it to Jett, then set the pitcher down on the bare wood of the room's only table. Jett managed to keep from wincing, although it was clear there wasn't any need to protect the wood. If the Fellowship got tired of water-marks, they could just sand the surface down and it would be as good as new.

"Drink up!" Sister Agatha urged.

Jett sipped cautiously. The liquid was cool, but it

was also bitter and almost foul-tasting. After a moment she identified it—tentatively—as the worst herb tea she'd ever drunk in her life.

"It is one of Brother Shepherd's own recipes," Sister Agatha said. "It came from a *Revelation*."

"I imagine it'd have to," Jett muttered under her breath. "You aren't alone here, are you, Sister Agatha? I imagine it'd get pretty lonely."

"Oh, not at all! We are seventy souls here at Jerusalem's Wall. Most of the menfolk are tending to the cattle and horses, but some are at work in the forge, and you will meet them when we gather for supper. I am so grateful I am not a man—it would be a great burden to me if I was not able to hear Brother Shepherd's preaching every day."

That's odd. I never heard of a forge that didn't make more noise than a tinker's cart falling off a cliff. And sound carries out here.

"So, most of the menfolks don't come back to the house every day?" No matter what Sister Agatha said, Jett was pretty sure she was lonely and looking for someone to talk to . . . and that would make her an excellent source of information.

"Oh, no! They—"

"Sister Agatha, it grieves me to find you here in idleness," a new—male—voice said. "Has not our own Blessed Founder said it is the woman's place to labor, for her labors are as sweet devotion and honest prayer?"

Sister Agatha gave a startled gasp. "Oh forgive me, Brother Raymond! I was only—we have a guest—" She didn't wait for Brother Raymond to reply but scurried out of the room with a good deal more speed than she'd shown entering it. Jett clenched her teeth and pasted on a cheerful—and utterly false—smile. It was amazing how much Divine Revelation always seemed to involve women doing all the work and keeping their mouths shut.

"Jett Gallatin," she said, holding out her hand (and taking the opportunity to set the tin mug aside). "Hope I didn't get the lady into any trouble."

"She will scourge her soul with prayer and hope to hear the Revelation more clearly," Brother Raymond said darkly. He was a stocky man about a decade younger than Finlay Maxwell. His face and neck were burnt red by the sun, and he wore a collarless muslin shirt, baggy homespun pants, suspenders, and work boots. *Good thing this isn't still a ranch*, Jett thought to herself. *Brother Raymond looks like a sodbuster born and bred. And I can make a durned good guess where he was born, too.*

"What brings you to Jerusalem's Wall, Mister Gallatin?" Brother Raymond asked, ignoring Jett's outstretched hand.

"Looking for work," Jett said blandly. "Sister Agatha invited me to stay for supper, but if I'd be any trouble . . ."

"Charity is the first duty of our Fellowship," Brother Raymond said, echoing Sister Agatha's words. Innocent enough. Charity was one of the virtues, and most Churchly folks Jett had met on her travels practiced it, whether they were Methodists or Mormons, Quakers or Catholics.

"Well, that's real neighborly of you," Jett said. " 'Preciate it. Wouldn't mind the chance to ask a few questions."

"Questions?" Brother Raymond's voice was suddenly hard with suspicion.

"Looking to catch up with my brother. He, ah, he lit out for the Territories when we lost the war, and last I heard from him was a while back. Wondering if you folks might've seen him." She knew she wouldn't need to make it any plainer. If Brother Raymond hadn't been wearing a gray uniform three years ago, she'd eat her hat.

Brother Raymond relaxed immediately. "You will find we of The Fellowship of the Divine Resurrection have renounced all Earthly quarrels and allegiances, Mister Gallatin. It is God's Law that will rule over God's Kingdom, and the time of that Kingdom is fast approaching. I must ask you to set aside your hatred while you abide among us."

"Just looking for my brother," Jett said mildly. "Only kin I've got left." She'd learned a long time ago that if people thought they knew all about you, they stopped wondering. And her story was a plausible one. After all, it was the truth.

"When God's Kingdom comes, *all* the Saved will be as brothers," Brother Raymond said. "Our Blessed Founder has told us so, and should you doubt my words, I must tell you that once Brother Shepherd was a man like you, a man consumed by hatred and the love of violence. Then one day seven years ago he was vouchsafed God's Seal of Divine Grace—but he found to his sorrow his words fell upon ears not ready to hear them. And so he came West, into the wilderness which God in His Infinite Providence appointed to our use. Here he has gathered about himself pure souls who will become the cornerstone of the Great Temple that God will raise up from our humble faith."

There ain't one blessed thing humble about you, "Brother" *Raymond,* Jett thought to herself. *And I guess if I was a yellow-bellied coward, I'd've had a Revelation that meant I had to light out before the War, too.*

But she'd never have been a successful gambler if the men across the card table could tell what she was thinking. She made herself look interested and impressed, and Brother Raymond seemed to take this as an invitation to do some preaching of his own. Except for those few facts about Brother Shepherd, his speechifying was long on vague promises and short on hard information. She didn't bother to try to work the conversation around to the walking dead. She suspected it would hurt his feelings.

There didn't seem to be any place for her to jump into the conversation anyway, and she began to think Brother Raymond had enough words stored up to be able to go right on preaching at her until sunset, mostly about her violent and unChristian ways. She was finally rescued by the familiar clatter of an iron triangle signaling dinnertime.

"Come, Mister Gallatin," Brother Raymond said grandly.

Jett picked up her hat and followed him.

They walked through a second room—this one completely empty of furniture—and then into what was obviously the dining room. It held benches and long trestle tables, but the tables weren't set, and the room was empty. It was clearly not their destination.

"Prayer before food, Mister Gallatin. I trust you agree it is far more important to feed the spirit than the body?" Out of the corner of her eye Jett caught Brother Raymond smirking, and wondered how many "guests" at Jerusalem's Wall had beat a hasty retreat when they realized they'd been offered a meal and were getting a sermon instead.

"Ain't ever had trouble feeding both," she answered mildly, and was rewarded by seeing Brother Raymond's mouth settle into a thin line of discontent.

The chapel doors stood open and the hallway was filled with people moving toward them. The ranch chapel had probably been part of the original building, and not something The Fellowship of the Divine Resurrection had gotten up itself. A lot of spreads were so isolated that if they wanted to do any God-bothering, they needed to make local arrangements. There were circuit preachers who rode among places without a minister in residence, staying a few days to marry and bury (or at least say a funeral), baptize any new young'uns, and offer up a good serving of hellfire. In between, a rancho's chapel would be used for prayers and Bible readings.

The place looked more like a lecture hall than a chapel, with benches of the same rough construction as she'd seen in the parlor and the dining room and an unadorned lectern at the back. The only thing that didn't fit in was the pipe organ in one corner. It was the finest thing she'd seen here at Jerusalem's Wall, all gleaming brass and polished mahogany.

All the men Jett saw were dressed much the same

as Brother Raymond, and the women like Sister Agatha. Jett drew more than a few curious looks as she followed Brother Raymond inside. The light in the chapel came entirely from kerosene lamps attached to the walls. There were four on each side of the room and two at the back, and a fan of lampblack on the wall above each one, indicating the room saw a lot of use. Jett wondered if she'd been wrong about this originally being the chapel. Not only was there nothing here resembling an altar, there weren't any windows.

No, wait. There used to be. She looked carefully to be sure. *I can still see where they filled them in.* That was more than strange, but plenty of these so-called "holiness churches" had odd ways about them. It might not mean anything.

Brother Raymond led her up to one of the benches in front of the lectern. He was still—obviously—trying to make her uncomfortable, but better men than he had tried and failed. She didn't like having people at her back, but she still had her guns and her knife and she hadn't seen a single firearm here anywhere, not even so much as a shotgun. She pretended to fidget on the bench, using the movement to let her look around the room. There were maybe three dozen people here, most of them women. Sister Agatha had said there were seventy people living here; she wondered how many beeves Jerusalem's Wall had if they needed forty or so hands to wrangle them. That was twice as many as it took to drive a herd to Abilene—and some of those drives numbered a thousand head of cattle. Of course, spring *was* branding season too . . .

There was an expectant rustle behind her. Brother Shepherd must have arrived.

The man who walked up the center aisle was short for a man—about Jett's height—with thinning gray hair cut short. His skin was pale and smooth, and he had much the look of a law clerk: stoop-shouldered and soft. Jett was willing to bet he didn't lift anything heavier than a pencil from one end of the year to the next.

The room settled into expectant silence as Brother Shepherd took his place behind the lectern. Brother Raymond had spent a good deal of time on the subject of Brother Shepherd's humility and how all the Fellowship were equal, but it was obvious to Jett they all kowtowed to this Blessed Founder of theirs. She settled her hat on her knee and prepared to be bored.

"My dear brothers and sisters in the Divine Resurrection, I bring you greetings once more from the angels Cassiel, Dumah, Jehoel, and The Heavenly Throne of Revelation. Truly we are fortunate to live in an age where the Highest prepares to close the great book upon this earthy Jerusalem in preparation for the building of a Jerusalem of Fire. It is by your hands and by your unstinting labors that an army of Holy Angels is being forged to go forth upon this sacred task—a sinless, stainless army whose bodies are of the substance of the Almighty's first children, recalled to life without the stain of Eve or the mark of Cain to lead them astray—"

Jett revised her opinion from "law clerk" to "preacher." Brother Shepherd had the knack of hooking an audience, and the same ability Maxwell Finlay had to fill a whole room with his voice and still make you think he was talking just to you. He didn't just stare at the back wall, either, but glanced around his congregation. When he locked eyes with her, Jett saw his were such a pale gray as to be almost colorless. The uncanny effect gave her chills.

It hadn't taken her long to decide "Brother" Shepherd was crazier than a cage full of bats. It didn't mean he had anything to do with the zombies—she was prepared to believe that if he saw a zombie, he'd just start preaching at it. The fact he was still alive was a pretty good indication he hadn't seen any. Maybe they *had* just crossed Jerusalem's Wall on their way to parts unknown. She knew they'd come this way. White Fox hadn't lost the trail or followed the wrong one.

But the longer Brother Shepherd preached, the more worrisome his preaching got. *The last time I heard this much about fire, the preacher was talking about the Other*

Place, Jett thought sardonically. Brother Shepherd moved on from praising the congregation and describing the "Jerusalem of Fire" that was to come, to praising the army that would make it happen.

"It is the Blessed Resurrected who will go forth to work the Almighty's will! They will build the Jerusalem of Fire to which our Blessed Savior will return! You will say it is a great labor beyond the strength of mortal man—and I say to you, you are right! But the Blessed Resurrected draw their strength not from the things of this world, but from their baptism in the Divine Fire of the Jerusalem to come! The Blessed Resurrected are possessed of an angelic nature forged in Heaven's own fires, a fire that burns away all earthly taint—"

As Brother Shepherd continued describing the holy army of the blessed resurrected, something occurred to her that made Brother Shepherd's speechifying a lot less entertaining. If you stripped off all the 'holiness' jabberjaw and Bible-talk, what Brother Shepherd was describing . . .

"—by their angelic nature, the Blessed Resurrected need no Earthly substance! Those anointed by the fires of the Jerusalem to come neither eat nor drink—nor shall the Blessed Resurrected sleep while their work is unfinished, for their every hour is dedicated to the will of the Heavenly Throne of Revelation!"

. . . was *zombies.*

His "Blessed Resurrected" didn't eat, drink, or sleep. They were "silent before the walls of the fiery Jerusalem," which meant they didn't talk. They were "impervious to the pains of death," and the only thing Jett knew of that didn't have to worry about dying was something already dead. They were "perfectly obedient to the Will of the Lord and to the will of The Lord's Appointed Captains"—and Maxwell had said the zombies in Alsop had followed a living general. But there were too many breathing people here for this to be a haunt of zombies.

Could be coincidence, she insisted to herself. *Could be.* She'd almost convinced herself it was when Brother Shepherd headed into the homestretch.

"My truth is a truth revealed of the mind of the holy angels of the Almighty God! Alsop has long stood as a rebuke to the pure and stainless Throne of Praise, a cankerous woodworm within the walls of the Jerusalem to come, a Temple of Ba'al and of Mammon, filled with harlotry, with drink, with wagering, and with money-lending! But no longer! This very day Alsop stands cleansed by the hand of the Blessed Resurrected, by an angelic army obedient to the highest law! But rejoice! The angels of the Lord have revealed unto me, the most humble servant of Righteousness, that Death has been vanquished, nor will Almighty Heaven cast even the blackest malefactor into Hell! Those whom the angelic army cleanse die not, but rise up redeemed and sanctified to join the army of the Blessed Resurrected! Alsop is only the first such to join in the army of the Blessed Resurrected! It will not be the last!"

Jett concentrated on sitting very still. The only way for Brother Shepherd to know what had happened in Alsop was if he'd been there. And if he said Alsop was only the first to be "cleansed" that way . . .

It meant the zombie army was going on a recruiting drive.

Gibbons felt a certain amount of relief at White Fox and Jett's departure. They were good people, both of them, but they were not scientists, and they were inclined to believe in irrational things without ever bothering to examine their beliefs. She was used to solitude as she conducted her investigations. Having to explain every step as she took it—and probably argue about it—would be tedious in the extreme.

First things first, she told herself briskly. She intended to spend some time here in Alsop—she could hardly search an entire town for clues in just a few hours—and that meant it would only be sensible to move her Auto-Tachypode into shelter. The three of them might be the only people here *now*, but that could change at any time.

She walked up the street to where her conveyance waited. Swinging herself up onto the driving bench, she adjusted several levers, waited a few moments for the pressure to build in the boiler, then released the brake. But instead of being rewarded with the familiar rhythm of the pistons and a smooth forward motion, the Auto-Tachypode began bouncing up and down in place.

Well . . . drat, Gibbons thought.

Before it could explode, she grabbed the emergency levers and yanked hard. The double-walled iron floor of the firebox swung free, dropping its load of coals and ash onto the ground. From the roof of the wagon, a brass nozzle extended and a long arc of boiling water jetted out above and behind the wagon, to fall harm-lessly to the street. Last of all, she opened the regulator in order to let the remaining steam pressure escape.

Science is a process of trial and error, she told herself consolingly. The Auto-Tachypode was a great leap for-ward in mechanical transportation, but it was still a prototype, and as such, it failed to start properly at least one time in three. *I was certain I'd compensated for the steam loss in the low-pressure cylinder. Perhaps I need to rebalance the flywheel once more*, she thought brood-ingly. She jumped down from the bench again. Her machine wasn't going anywhere for several hours at least: she'd need to allow enough time for the cylinders to drain and the boiler and firebox to cool completely before an attempt to restart it, or else uneven expansion in the cylinders would lead to a larger explosion than the one she'd just averted. Meanwhile, she could take advantage of a luxury she'd never expected to find in a town like Alsop to further her investigations.

The telegraph and post office building was across from the jail at the far end of the main (and only) street. Both it and the jail were brick, the only non-wooden structures in the town. In the case of the jail, it was undoubtedly for the sake of constraining the inmates from escape or untimely liberation. In the case of the telegraph office, it was probably to reassure the townspeople that this new technology wouldn't destroy everything for miles around with its strange electromagnetic waves. She wrinkled her nose in amusement. *As if there have not been telegraph lines strung from one end of the continent to the other for six years already!*

Samuel B. Morse, Joseph Henry, and Alfred Vail had invented the telegraph in 1844, several years before she'd been born. The invention had made it possible to converse with someone a hundred miles away almost as easily as with someone in the same room. Telegraph lines were usually run along railroad right of ways, for in addition to providing the wires with an unobstructed path, they could also be easily inspected for accidental breaks or deliberate vandalism. For a town such as Alsop to have a telegraph was unusual, but as a waystation along the Chisholm Trail, it was not entirely unexpected. Trail bosses might have to let ranchers know of unexpected good or bad fortune.

She opened the door and stepped inside. The silence and sunlight gave the place much the feel of a cathedral, and so it was—a cathedral of Science. The outer office held a wide counter with bars like a bank teller's cage, a desk with pigeonholes for message forms, and a plaque on the wall with the rates charged for messages. (A piece of paper pinned up below it said that no incoming telegraphic messages would be available before four p.m. or after six p.m. and concluded with *"No Exceptions!!!"*) The expense of sending and receiving messages meant telegraphy was still beyond the budget of most people. *But that will change!* Gibbons thought joyfully. *Someday there will be a telegraphy office on every street and an Auto-Tachypode in every barn!*

She opened the gate beside the Postmaster's cage and walked inside. There was a set of wooden cubbyholes on the wall, a few of them containing letters their recipients would never open. A canvas mailbag hung on the wall, waiting to be entrusted to the next stagecoach that passed through. The schedule would be written down somewhere here; she made a mental note to search for it later. She conducted a cursory inspection of the Postmaster's station before heading back to the inner office. There was a cashbox with some small change, a collection of stamps and ink pads, two bottles of ink—one red, one black—and several pens. Nothing particularly informative. She moved on. The desk containing the telegraph mechanism faced one probably used by the Postmaster. That desk was neat to the point of meaninglessness, and when she tried the drawers, all of them were locked. She was excellent at picking locks, but that, too, could wait. She turned to the other desk, which was obviously used not merely to send telegraphic messages, but to transcribe incoming ones. There were neat coils of yellow tape held together with latex rubber bands stacked in the "Out" tray, and the "In" tray was empty. She turned her attention to the mechanism itself. The paper tape was motionless and unmarred beneath its waiting stylus, and when she placed her hand against the side of the cabinet she felt no vibration. The clockwork armature that moved the tape past the stylus must have run down. She hunted around in the operator's desk until she found the winding key. At least she knew no messages had come down the wire in the last day or so, for if they had, the paper would be torn and frayed by multiple punctures of the recording stylus.

She gave the machine a good winding, but did not release the gear that would cause the tape to move. Time enough to do that when she'd finished sending her own message. She sat down at the operator's desk, removed the cover from the transmission key, and checked to see that everything was in order. As she placed her hand over the key, Gibbons felt a thrill of wonder that she knew would never dim, for the electromagnetic telegraph was nothing less than the power of human genius harnessed for the betterment of all Mankind. *Neither false doctrines nor degenerate kings shall rule us any longer, only Science, and the pure and glorious search for knowledge!*

She began to tap quickly and expertly, using Mister Alfred Vail's code. Jacob Gibbons, like many wealthy (and eccentric) men, had a private telegraphic line that ran into his own home, and Doctor Gordon checked it frequently for messages, for Jacob Gibbons had many correspondents. Telegraphy operators could decode their message tapes by sight and would discard or ignore tapes not sent to their offices, so the first characters she sent were simply her father's name and city, over and over. It was also a common practice for operators to wait until the stylus began moving to release the gear of the recording mechanism, in order to save paper, which necessitated multiple repetitions of the message's "address."

ARE YOU RECEIVING ACKNOWLEDGE PLEASE, she sent at last, then lifted her hand from the key to release the gear on the tape machine. Fully five minutes passed before the needle began to move. When it stopped, she tore the tape free and inspected it.

YES RECEIVING HONORIA IS THAT YOU THIS IS GORDON PRAY CONTINUE.

She placed her hand over the key again and began to send, transmitting nearly as quickly as she might write a letter. Telegraphic code lacked the ability to convey punctuation—everything, including numbers, must be spelled out—but she inserted "stop" and "question" almost without thought. In a very few minutes, she had transmitted what she knew—she had found the town of Alsop, Texas, utterly deserted—and a request for every scrap of information in Jacob Gibbons's library regarding the reanimated dead. It was not an unreasonable request on her part: the library of the mansion on Russian Hill filled an entire floor and contained every book or paper ever written about the inexplicable.

After a slightly longer pause, the needle began to move again.

DAUGHTER THIS IS JACOB HOW I WISH I COULD BE WITH YOU TO SOLVE THE MYSTERIES OF DEATH ITSELF IS A GREAT ACCOMPLISHMENT BUT ONLY WORTHY OF YOUR GIFTS I SHALL BEGIN MY

RESEARCHES AT ONCE AND LET YOU KNOW MY PROG-
RESS FOUR HOURS FROM NOW YOUR PROUD FATHER
STOP.

Gibbons decoded the slightly garbled message easily
and with a certain amount of resignation. If she did not
solve this mystery quickly, the next thing that would
happen was that someone would attempt to sell Jacob
Gibbons a zombie—or some mechanism for making
one! At least she could use the telegraph to convey the
solution to the puzzle to her father as quickly as she
found it. She sent a last short message: THANK YOU I
SHALL AWAIT YOUR REPLY STOP LOVE YOUR DAUGH-
TER GIBBONS STOP.

That task completed, she stopped the tape again
and got to her feet. *Now to see what Jett and White Fox
missed!* The three of them had only been looking for
survivors during their previous exploration, and had
undoubtedly missed vital clues to the true nature of
Alsop's attackers.

She decided to begin with the church, for it was
the only building none of them had yet searched. She
hoped to find some survivors gathered there, even
though she knew that was a faint hope indeed, since
anyone possessing the use of their limbs—or their
hearing—should have declared themselves upon hearing the sound of the Auto-Tachypode's arrival, or Jett's
gunshots.

The church itself was entirely ordinary, its arched windows empty (as yet) of glass but secured by wooden shutters. The doors were closed, but of course not locked, and the first thing she did upon entering was to unlatch the shutters and throw them wide. The sunlight revealed precisely what she had expected to see: rows of polished wooden pews, a gleaming wooden floor, choir stalls and a piano, a pulpit beside the altar rail, a white-draped altar behind them, and a plain wooden cross affixed to the wall above it.

"Hello?" she called. Nothing but silence answered.

Her shoulders slumped just a little. Gibbons realized she'd been hoping more than she'd been aware of to find someone here. Not just because people would mean more witnesses who could provide precious data, but because the disappearance of all the townsfolk was more depressing than she wanted to admit, even to herself. This was the first of the "disappeared settlements" she'd seen with her own eyes, and Alsop had stood vacant for less than twenty-four hours. But Honoria Verity Providentia Gibbons was neither to be daunted by adversity nor sidetracked by tragedy. She squared her shoulders, set her jaw, and did a quick investigation. Nothing was out of place, and that told her the attack had run its course so quickly no one had been able to flee to the church for safety. While she still didn't credit Jett's story of *zombies*, she did believe

Jett had been here at the beginning of an attack by . . . someone. That fact was irrefutable, the empty town and Jett's bruises both bearing mute testimony.

Her next stop was the belfry. The church bell was rung from the vestry, but she could gain access to the bell tower from there as well. She had spent enough time in the "wild" West not to think it strange that a congregation that could not afford glass for its church windows should have a fine bronze bell in its belfry: the bell would not merely be used to summon the congregation to Sunday services, but to give warning to the town in case of trouble. The ladder looked well-made and sturdy, so without qualms she grasped its sides and began to climb. The belfry was at least thirty feet above the ground, making it the highest point in the landscape for several miles around. She would be able to gain a good overview of her surroundings from here.

At the end of her ascent she climbed out onto the narrow platform surrounding the bell and looked around. From this vantage point she could see faint pale scars across the desert entering and leaving the town, marks left by stagecoaches and freight wagons, for their routes were blazoned and they followed the same path each trip. To the south, she could see a small graveyard, one of the "Boot Hills" so beloved of dime

novelists. A disease which rendered its victims fever-
ish and delusional might account for what Jett had
seen, but there were no fresh graves in the graveyard,
and if a sudden plague were the source of the problem,
at least a few individuals would have succumbed to it
before it reached epidemic proportions. The only other
feature of the landscape was a sturdy wooden house
that undoubtedly belonged to the minister. *And his
wife*, she emended mentally, for there were several
clotheslines strung on wooden trees behind the house.
Aside from the house and its accompanying outbuildings, all she saw was desert, scrub bush, and the distant glitter of Burnt Creek amid its stand of sheltering
cottonwoods. East and west were similarly featureless,
and to the north, the town of Alsop was much as her
earlier reconnaissance of it had indicated it to be: a
single street with buildings along both sides. There
were a few backhouses, another set of clotheslines
behind the boarding house, and a small building—
probably a pump-house—behind the general store. All
the water for the town would come from that pump or
from the few water barrels she saw, though it was hard
to believe it ever rained here enough to fill them. But
aside from the tracks across the desert, where Alsop
stopped, the marks of Civilization ended as abruptly
as if severed with a knife.

She placed her hand on the side of the bell and shoved gently. It rocked slightly in its carriage and gave a faint mellow gong. She frowned. *Anyone seeing or hearing trouble would immediately give the alarm, yet no one rang this bell last night. Jett may be unbecomingly credulous, but she is a keen observer, if an untrained one. If the bell had rung, she would have mentioned it.* Why hadn't it been rung? *A good scientist does not theorize in advance of the data*, she reminded herself, and began her descent. There was one more place to search before returning to the town itself.

She pushed open the door of the minister's house, wondering if she would encounter attackers in hiding, or victims too injured to have hailed the three of them earlier. But it, too, was deserted, and from all the evidence she saw, the family—John and Rebecca Southey and their three children, John Junior, Michael, and Katie—had been elsewhere at the time of the assault. The dining room table wasn't set, and there was no indication the kitchen had been in use. Most telling of all, all the lamps were still full of oil. If any of them had been lit before the attack, they'd either still be burning now, or they'd have used up all their fuel.

One small mystery was solved when she found—among the papers in Reverend Southey's desk—a note from his wife saying she would return from visiting her cousin in a month and sternly enjoining him to take regular meals in town. It was dated a week ago. *So he would have been in town when the attack came, and there would have been no one here to ring the church bell.*

She found no particularly useful information in her investigations, unless she were to count the text of Reverend Southey's most recent sermons. He'd given one two weeks ago which took Hebrews 13:2 as its text: *"Be not forgetful to entertain strangers: for thereby some have entertained angels unawares."*

Well, it's always good advice I suppose, but was Mister Southey warning his congregation to be kind to newcomers—or warning them that such newcomers might be more than they seemed?

There really wasn't any way to be sure.

She walked slowly back into town. The Sheriff's Office was her first stop, for she hadn't stayed to search it after Jett and White Fox's departure, and if there was anything odd going on within a hundred miles, Sheriff Mitchell would probably have known about it. She could only hope he'd left some record. The battered rolltop desk was locked, and none of the keys on the jail keyring opened it, so Gibbons removed her bonnet and extracted two short wooden pins from her hair. A quick twist revealed them to be lock picks. She'd often found it useful to be able to get into—or out of—locked rooms, jail cells, and even handcuffs in the course of her investigations, and even the most dyed-in-the-wool villain would rarely disarrange a female's hair in search of weapons or tools. For all that the popular press regarded lock picking as some sort of arcane and criminal art, it was actually little more than dexterity, good hearing, and the application of sound scientific principles. Easy enough for one such as Gibbons to master.

It was less than a minute's work to gain access to the desk, but the results were disappointing. Not only did the mysteries of an alphabetical filing system seem to be beyond both Sherriff Mitchell and the worthy Deputy Aldine, apparently Matthew Mitchell was a thoroughgoing packrat. The drawers were crammed full of ancient Wanted Posters, mysterious odds and ends—a length of twine, one spur, a candle—and a collection of chewed pencils, a broken penknife, a box of Lucifer matches. In the bottom drawer she found the probably–inevitable tin cup and half-full bottle of whiskey. She'd nearly despaired of finding anything helpful when she reached those items, but that drawer also contained Sheriff Mitchell's Charge Book. No matter how disorganized he was in other respects, Sheriff Mitchell was a meticulous record keeper. She made a pleased sound of satisfaction and sat down to read.

The Charge Book contained such information as who was jailed for what and what the disposition of the case was—and of more interest, it also contained a daily report, where Sheriff Mitchell wrote down things that weren't official business (things that didn't involve anyone being charged, fined, held over for trial, jugged for thirty days, or tried by a jury of their peers) but might become so. There she discovered that in the fortnight before . . . the incident . . . Sheriff Mitchell had been under increasing pressure from the local ranchers to find out why (and how) a whole cattle drive had vanished. He'd been wavering between calling in the Texas Rangers and forming a posse on his own, though what they could have done was unclear.

I do not think even the Texas Rangers could have solved this riddle, Gibbons mused as she read. *They are very handy if you are quelling a riot or hunting an outlaw, but detection is not their forte . . . though I think not even Mr. Allan Pinkerton and his National Detective Agency could have gotten to the bottom of this puzzle.* She'd often found that even those dedicated to solving crimes and bringing the guilty to justice were at a loss if a mystery was truly outlandish. Their success came from a broad understanding of human nature, not from an application of scientific principles. Sheriff Mitchell's reports were one more datum, but she was far from having enough information to begin building her own theory.

From the Sheriff's office she returned to the saloon, for enough time had passed that she could attempt to start the Auto-Tachypode again. As she approached her vehicle, her ears were assaulted by the sounds of raucous off-key singing and a piano very badly in need of tuning. She looked in through the doors of the saloon to discover Finlay Maxwell in residence. Lacking any other place to sit, he'd appropriated the piano bench, and had obviously found the lure of the keyboard irresistible. A half-full beer mug—and a half-empty whiskey bottle—provided Gibbons with all the information she needed about what he'd been doing since he'd left the jail.

Clicking her tongue in exasperation, she returned to her original intention. This time the Auto-Tachypode started smoothly and without difficulty, and she drove it to the livery stable and parked it inside. From there, she resumed her search.

Over the course of the next few hours, she discovered that every establishment that would have been closed at the time Jett gave for the initial attack—just after dark—was completely untouched. That was interesting, for outlaws would certainly have made the bank, and possibly even the general store, targets of their predations. Even the storefront that served as the dentist's, barber's, and doctor's office was in pristine condition. Dentists kept gold on hand, and doctors kept an inventory of drugs. It was becoming clear that whatever the motive for the attack, monetary gain was not its purpose.

The majority of her time was spent at the office of the *Alsop Yell and Cry* ("Bringing Truth and Vital Intelligence to Menard, Concho, and McCulloch Counties!"). She'd been gratified to discover Ahasuerus P. Harrison—the paper's editor and publisher—kept an extensive "morgue." He'd pasted each issue of the paper carefully into large scrapbooks. As the *Yell and Cry* was a weekly four-page paper, each of the scrapbooks covered a year of its publication. There were fifteen of them; the paper had been founded shortly after the Compromise of 1850.

Quickly skimming the last several years of the paper, Gibbons discovered that what had happened to Alsop, far from being an isolated incident, was merely the latest in a long series of puzzling incidents. Entire homesteads had been going missing in the surrounding area for at least two years. The first occurrence had involved a hermit whose name (according to the paper) was "Spanish Pete." Reverend Southey had discovered his absence as he went to make a monthly delivery of supplies. After that, a new disappearance was recorded every fortnight or so, though none of them had been extensive enough to attract out-of-state attention. In every case, Mister Harrison reported the event not as an unexplained disappearance, but as a "leaving for greener pastures." That wasn't surprising: every single episode following that of Spanish Pete had involved a homesteader, a sodbuster, or a sheep-farmer—all people the ranchers would be happy to see gone.

Then the cattle drive vanished—cattle, cowhands, chuck wagon, and all. The *Yell and Cry* had published two editions since then. The first devoted a page and a half to the disappearance. Mister Harrison's editorial called for the return of law and justice to Menard County—and the return of the cattle to their owners. The following week, the *Yell and Cry* ran a full-page editorial excoriating Sheriff Mitchell and calling for his removal from office if something wasn't done. It said Sheriff Mitchell put the blame on Indians "to conceal his incompetence in bringing this matter to a swift and favorable resolution."

If he did, he didn't record any such notion in his Charge Book, Gibbons observed thoughtfully. And while Ahasuerus P. Harrison might think the homesteaders had just moved somewhere else for the convenience of the ranchers, Gibbons did not. There were simply too many of them—every small homestead in an area covering almost three thousand square miles. *Even at the most conservative estimate of the numbers per homestead, that's at least a hundred people. It seems to me that whoever attacked Alsop last night started small, with those the people in power—the ranchers—would be glad to see gone. But whoever is behind this must have seen that Sheriff Mitchell would investigate soon, and struck first.*

Jett's description of "zombies" didn't quite jibe with that motive. But Gibbons knew perfectly well there was a long history of whites dressing as Indians to commit crimes and place the blame elsewhere. It was possible the "zombies" were simply an ingenious variation on that tactic. Certainly terrifying one's victims would be a good way to discourage resistance.

She checked her watch. It was time to keep her appointment at the telegraph office. Perhaps her father had information that would help her unravel this mystery.

Chapter Four

The "prayer meeting" finally drew to a close, though Jett didn't think it fairly deserved the name. There hadn't been any prayers—despite what Brother Raymond had said—or even hymn-singing (despite the presence of the pipe organ in the corner). The entire event had been nothing more than a long unnerving harangue from Brother Shepherd. She supposed you could call it a sermon if you were feeling charitable, but she'd been to more than a few services offered by "holiness movement" settlements. There was usually singing. And more than one person preaching.

Maybe this was just an everyday holiness meeting. Maybe they have more churchly services on Sundays. She wanted to believe that, but the combination of Brother Shepherd's description of "the army of the Blessed Resurrected" and his knowledge of Alsop's destruction wouldn't let her. He *could* have ridden to Alsop and back before she and White Fox had reached Jerusalem's Wall today. But why would he? And White Fox would have seen the fresh tracks. *I'll be just as glad to give this place the air*, she thought. She'd slip out after dinner. There was no way she could bolt just now without raising suspicion.

When she followed Brother Raymond back to the dining room, the men sat down while the women headed for the kitchen. Jett hung back in order to sit as far from Brother Shepherd as she could. Some of the women returned immediately with plates and cutlery and began setting the tables. A place wasn't set for Brother Shepherd at all. Once the tables were set, the women sat down at one of the other tables. Apparently men and women didn't eat together at Jerusalem's Wall.

Supper consisted of beef and bean stew, tortillas, and pitchers containing "Revelation" herb tea and water. The table settings were the cheapest kind of tinware, and the pitchers were clay, but when the food was brought out, a silver pitcher and a crystal glass were set at Brother Shepherd's place. Jett expected a prayer to start the meal, but all that happened was that Brother

Shepherd filled his glass with some kind of pale amber liquid and everyone fell to.

The portions were generous—whatever else was going on at Jerusalem's Wall, they didn't stint on the victuals—and Jett expected at least to find the meal palatable, if not enjoyable. But one spoonful of stew was all she needed to discover it was as awful as the herb tea had been. *No salt. There's no seasoning in anything here. That's why they're serving tortillas. Bread needs salt to rise . . .*

Which was when she remembered something else from Tante Mère's ghost stories. Salt would kill a zombie. It was one of the few things that could. Well, not kill it, precisely, since they were already dead, but Tante Mère said the taste of salt reminded the creatures of who and what they had been when alive, and they would either turn on their creator or lie down and die again.

Or both.

Every hair on her body stood straight up, or tried to. She began to calculate, urgently, just how fast she could get herself out of here.

"So, Mister Gallatin, what brings you to Jerusalem's Wall?" Brother Shepherd set down his tumbler and regarded her inquisitively.

"Just passing through," Jett answered. She felt a surge of panic, since for a moment she couldn't remember what she'd told Brother Raymond, and she knew he and Brother Shepherd would have compared notes. "Looking for work, I guess, but mostly looking for news of my brother."

"Perhaps we've seen him," Brother Shepherd said smoothly. "What's his name?"

"Um . . . Horace," Jett answered. "Horace Gallatin." She didn't know why she lied. It couldn't matter if she gave either "Philip" or "Jasper" as her brother's name. But somehow she didn't want to tell more truth to Brother Shepherd than she absolutely had to. "He's got my look to him," she added reluctantly.

"No, he hasn't stopped here," Brother Shepherd said, shaking his head. "You're more than welcome to join our Fellowship, though."

"But you will have to renounce your ways of violence if you do so," Brother Raymond announced. "They have no place here at Jerusalem's Wall."

"I'm a man of peace," Jett protested mildly.

"Who carries a gun," Brother Raymond said harshly.

"Any feller goin' as a sheep among wolves in these parts is going to find himself skinned," Jett answered inarguably. "I'm not especially fond of the idea of dyin' so some varmint can—can lead himself further into sin."

She couldn't tell whether Brother Shepherd believed her or not, but her act of desperation turned out to be an inspired one. Brother Raymond wasn't the trusting sort, and she couldn't get any kind of a read on Brother Shepherd, but now some of the other brethren joined the conversation. In response to their comments, she spun a story that contained a little truth and a lot of what she'd just heard Brother Shepherd preach. Part of it was Philip's story. She knew she looked far too young to have fought in the War of Northern Aggression, but her twin brother hadn't been too young to go with the regiment as its drummer boy. Jett claimed to have been sickened by what she'd seen, and to have returned home after the war to find her family scattered. She said she'd known "Horace" had gone to Texas—as so many soldiers of the Confederacy had— and so she'd followed him, only to be shocked at the sin and lawlessness she encountered here.

"I'm right glad to hear about Alsop," she added. "Once Sister Agatha told me you folks weren't looking to take on a new hand, I figured to push on into town. But it sounds like the kind of place I'd rather steer clear of. Guess I'll head on up north instead."

"A wise plan," Brother Shepherd said. "You're welcome to stop here overnight," he added.

"Brother Shepherd will be Witnessing again before supper. We might even be privileged to receive a Revelation!" Brother Reuben added enthusiastically. He was the youngest man at the table, and Jett was willing to believe that whatever was going on among the Fellowship of the not-so-Divine Resurrection, Brother Reuben was wholly innocent of it.

To her relief, the meal was quickly over. Jett hadn't been able to force herself to eat more than a few bites, though the others had emptied their bowls. When Brother Shepherd rose to his feet, it seemed to be a signal. Everyone else stood as well, and the women began to clear the tables.

"Figure I'll unsaddle my horse and turn him out if I'm staying," Jett said, picking up her hat and moving toward the doorway. She didn't add—as she would have otherwise—that she could just go ahead and put her gear wherever she'd be sleeping. Somebody might follow her to show her the way, and that was the last thing she wanted.

She settled her hat on her head as she stepped outside. The sight of Nightingale waiting patiently for her was the sweetest thing she'd seen in a long time. With a few quick strides she reached his side and tucked a toe into the stirrup. A second later she'd vaulted into the saddle and was heading up the ranch road at a brisk gallop. She didn't care what the Fellowship thought about her abrupt departure: she never meant to come back here if she could help it.

Once she was well away from the compound, she headed for the stand of pines she and White Fox had used earlier to spy on Jerusalem's Wall. She'd told White Fox she'd wait for him back in the pines, but what she'd do if he didn't show up by dusk, she didn't know. The sound of hoofbeats behind her made her put a nervous hand on her pistol, but to her relief, it was only White Fox and Deerfoot. She brought Nightingale to a halt and waited for Deerfoot to catch up.

"I got some bad stew and worse news back there," she said when he joined her. "Looks like this place is some kind of commune calling itself The Fellowship of the Divine Resurrection. Their Brother Shepherd says it was *angels* in Alsop last night."

White Fox looked worried. "My discoveries were equally troubling. Perhaps between us we can make sense of our findings."

Jett nodded and quickly told him what she knew, from Jerusalem's Wall having enough livestock that it needed forty men to wrangle them, to the bizarre "service" she'd attended, to being served a meal prepared entirely without salt.

"And Br'er Shepherd wasn't shy about saying Alsop had been 'cleansed' by an army of the 'Blessed Resurrected,' and he said it was just the first town on their list, so I guess he's playing things close to the vest, iff'n your troubles are connected to Alsop's," she finished grimly. "And I don't know about you, but where I come from, a man bragging on something like that is responsible for it."

"You may be right," White Fox said. "Though I know not how a living man could have done all that you describe—or I have seen—nor do I believe the *wasichu* can summon spirits of vengeance that will act in such a fashion."

"If prayin' could wipe a town off the map, there'd be a lot fewer folks in a lot of places," Jett agreed, and White Fox nodded briefly before he began his own story.

White Fox had waited in the trees until he'd seen Jett enter the house, then circled around until he was concealed by the bunkhouses before riding down to investigate. He left Deerfoot behind one of the new buildings and moved cautiously on foot until he reached a place in a direct line from the gate. A working ranch was a busy place, but this one was both silent and nearly deserted.

Whatever he'd been tracking had always moved in a straight line: it had turned down the road heading into the ranch, so his first thought was that it had continued on the same path. But to his frustration, the ground here was just as hard as that of the ranch road had been, and whether his quarry had come this way or not, he could find no sign of tracks. He could continue southward and try again to pick up the trail there, but before he did there were some things he wanted to investigate here.

"When I approached the dormitory buildings, I could see what had been invisible at a distance. The buildings have shutters, but they cover only wood."

"No windows?" Jett asked. "The chapel's windows were bricked up too. Why?"

"I have no explanation," White Fox admitted. "But when I went to see if all the buildings followed the pattern of the first, I saw the original bunkhouse's windows had been boarded up as well. And further, the door was barred—from the outside."

He'd listened carefully at the door for some minutes, and when he was certain the interior was empty, he'd removed the bar. Just as he'd been about to open it, he'd heard the bell ring for dinner, and ducked hastily inside.

"It was empty of furniture," he said. "Even the stove had been removed. And in the center of the floor there was a second set of doors—chained shut."

"Sounds like you had more fun than I did," Jett

observed. "But why bar the door from the *outside*? And if you did, why chain the inside doors shut? Where do they go, anyway? No bunkhouse I've ever heard tell of came with a storm cellar."

"Once more I have no answers, Jett, only questions. Yet I can tell you this much: the trail we followed from Alsop stops at Jerusalem's Wall. Once I saw all the members of the 'Fellowship' had entered the ranch house and were likely to remain there, I spent more than an hour casting about to see if I could find the trail once more. I could not."

"Well, if you couldn't find it, odds are it wasn't there to find," Jett said. She inspected the sky. "I suppose we could wait around until night," she said reluctantly. "Do some more poking around when everybody's asleep in their beds."

"I do not think that would be prudent," White Fox said. "Without the key, the doors in the bunkhouse floor will remain locked. It is true that you might shoot the lock off," he added with a faint smile, "but that would be certain to attract just the attention we both hope to avoid."

"True enough," Jett said. "Back to town, then. If that fool Yankee hasn't either blown it up or burned it to the ground by accident."

"I believe you're wrong, Gibbons," White Fox said

mildly. "If she has done any such thing, it will be with all deliberate intent."

The telegraph machine began chattering precisely at the appointed hour. But even though Jacob Gibbons's communication filled several dozen yards of recording tape, it didn't provide much enlightenment to his daughter. It seemed there was blessed little in the way of useful information to be had. It was said a hoodoo doctor or hoodoo queen could cause a newly dead corpse to rise up and do his or her will. Some said the body had to belong to a suicide, others that it had to be someone who'd died of a curse. Some said a zombie could be killed by feeding it something containing salt. Other means of zombie destruction included feeding them holy water, or blessed wafers, or bringing them within the sound of church bells on a Sunday morning. But Jacob could tell his daughter little more than that.

All useless, Gibbons thought in exasperation. *I am willing to believe without a scrap of further investigation that there is not one hoodoo sorcerer within a thousand miles of where I'm standing. And I am not dealing with a story of* one *zombie, but of an entire zombie army!*

She wondered if there was any practical hope of getting a reliable count of the Alsop "zombies" out of either Jett or Mister Maxwell. The *Llano Estacado* wasn't particularly well-settled. It would be hard to hide an army of any size here—let alone a *zombie* army, which (logic insisted) would need to be replenished at frequent intervals as decay and putrefaction rendered its members useless.

Oh, what nonsense! Dead is dead, and the dead don't just get up and walk around!

Papa hadn't stopped with zombies, of course. He'd gone on to acquaint her with every type of fantastic creature that had a claim to the name "undead." But vampires were also solitary creatures, nor had there been an unexplained rash of anemia or disease in the area. Ghouls would disturb fresh graves. Liches were skeletal. Ghosts were often invisible and always incorporeal.

Jacob had concluded by saying he'd recently received unimpeachable scientific proof from one of his European correspondents that the Earth was hollow and urging her to seek out any deep caves or open wells in the area, for: "should the race of sub-Terrans be disturbed by human encroachment I feel certain they would react forcefully." And of course by urging her to seek out any phantom airships in the vicinity, for: "interrogating their captain or crew is likely to be a fruitful source of information."

Oh, that's all I need! Gibbons thought in frustration. *Now Father will wish to go on an expedition to the center of the Earth to meet these "sub-Terrans," and I am certain he can find someone willing to guide him there—for a fat fee! At least Doctor Gordon has a certain amount of sense. He will know better than to let Father go off on such a—a wild goose chase! At least until I have gone first . . .*

Fortunately, telegraphic communication lent itself to mendacious tactfulness. Gibbons was able to thank her Papa for the great help he had given her without letting him suspect how very irritated she was with him. She promised to let him know how her investigations proceeded—*"if the telegraph lines do not go down,"* she added carefully, for she had every reason to think that a possibility. Bad weather, high winds, and sabotage could all interrupt communication, and if Alsop had been attacked to conceal some dastardly plot by a person or persons unknown, their next move would be to cut the telegraph wires before some outsider arrived. *I am fortunate they have not been cut already,* she told herself. *Perhaps when Jett and White Fox return, they will have answers for me.*

But until they arrived, she had another task to occupy her.

Gibbons pushed open the door to the jail with a stack of blankets in her arms. She dropped the blankets on the nearest bunk and regarded her preparations with satisfaction. The general store had contained nearly everything she needed. A fine Winchester lever-action repeating rifle. The .44 ammunition both Jett and White Fox's pistols used. Cartridges for her own coach gun. Kerosene lanterns and a tin of paraffin oil. Tin pails to hold drinking water. Last of all, she entered the rooming house. In the kitchen she found tinned butter, loaves of bread only a little stale, a roast of beef that was still good, and most of an apple pie. She made a dozen sandwiches and wrapped them in oilcloth for safe keeping, and put the sandwiches, the pie, and plates and utensils into a hamper she'd also liberated from the general store. She doubted any of this would be necessary, but she also knew if Alsop's attackers hadn't been able to enter the jail last night, they'd be equally confounded tonight—if they returned at all. If they didn't, well, the jail was comfortable enough to spend the night in. And because she didn't care to trust that the drunken actor wouldn't stumble upon her vehicle by accident and break something, she had locked it. It would take a cannon to break into it.

On her way back from the rooming house Gibbons stopped at the saloon. It took her several minutes of hunting behind and beneath the bar to unearth a dusty and still-sealed bottle of "French" brandy (though she doubted it had been any closer to Paris than Chicago). While she didn't approve of spirits for intoxicating purposes, Gibbons had a great respect for their powers of revivification, and it was only prudent to prepare for every possibility. Finlay Maxwell was still in residence, although he'd apparently been defeated at last by the "water of life": he was asleep in a corner, a bottle clutched protectively to his chest.

Gibbons was heading in the direction of the jail to add the basket to the rest of her supplies when she saw Jett and White Fox heading up the street at a brisk trot.

"Come on!" Jett shouted, as soon as she saw her. "Get your buggy and fire it up! They're coming this way!"

It was later than Jett liked when she and White Fox started back to Alsop. She comforted herself with the reminder that it was still daylight. She knew zombies were helpless during the day. But as they rode, the shadows began to lengthen. The edge of town was a couple of miles distant when the wind shifted.

The wind was cold.

Nightingale raised his head, his nostrils flaring as he tasted the air. A moment later, Jett smelled what he had.

Rotting flesh.

"They're coming back!" she cried to White Fox.

Neither of them had to urge their animals to gallop. The horses obviously wanted to get far away from whatever they smelled.

As they approached Alsop, Jett saw Gibbons walking up the empty street lugging a large basket. She shouted out her warning, but instead of running toward wherever she'd tucked her steam-wagon, Gibbons stopped dead.

"If by 'they' you mean your *zombies*, I certainly hope so! You obviously haven't brought one back for me to study!"

"You— You— You—" Jett sputtered in disbelief.

"You must heed Jett's warning," White Fox said. "Unless this unknown enemy intends to assault Fort San Antonio instead, Alsop is their destination."

"Then my preparations can be put to good use," Gibbons said briskly. "I've equipped the jail with everything we'll need, and I am pleased to tell you I locked my vehicle against tampering. I suggest you take your animals to the livery stable, and then join me there. And bring Mister Maxwell with you—he's unconscious on the floor of the saloon!" she shouted over her shoulder as she walked on.

"She's crazy," Jett said flatly.

"Perhaps," White Fox said. "But she's also right. A jailhouse is designed to withstand attack from within and without." He swung down off his mare's back and tossed her rein to Jett. "I will see to Mister Maxwell. Take Deerfoot with you. If she must flee to protect herself she will come when I whistle for her."

"Any varmint living or dead that tries to make off with Nightingale will think better of the notion before he's much older," Jett answered grimly.

At the livery stable Jett saw Gibbons's wagon parked in the back. *Reckon that contraption wouldn't get far in the dark*, she told herself reluctantly. She'd still have preferred to make a run for it, but she had to admit there were more than a few hitches in that rope. What if the creatures decided to encircle the town this time? She might ride right into them . . .

It was the work of only a few moments to untack both horses. She led them into stalls at the front of the barn and left them loose. She left the stable door open, too. White Fox was right. Their ability to run was the best protection the animals could have. With their saddlebags slung over one shoulder—and Nightingale's tack, for there was enough silver on saddle and bridle to make it an attractive target—she headed for the jail at a quick jog. On the way she caught up to White Fox. He had Finlay Maxwell slung over one shoulder.

"Is he dead?" she asked.

"Dead *drunk*," White Fox answered succinctly.

As they entered the jailhouse, Gibbons dropped the

bar across the door to seal them in. Two of the cells were filled with her store of provisions. White Fox carried Finlay Maxwell to the third. It was one of the end ones. He laid Maxwell on the bunk and covered him with a blanket. Jett dropped her saddle with a grunt of relief and carried bridle and saddlebags to the cell at the opposite end from Maxwell.

"Well, here we are," Gibbons said brightly, lighting two of the lamps. Their warm, incongruously cheery glow filled all three cells. The two on the ends had a solid back wall and one side wall. The one in the center had bars on both sides and a tiny window above head height. The window was barred and too small for anyone to climb through even if it hadn't been.

"Caught like rats in a trap," Jett grumbled, dropping her saddlebags to the floor.

"You may make yourself useful, Mister Fox," Gibbons added, ignoring Jett. She picked up two of the blankets and handed them to him. "Your room is next door."

White Fox smiled faintly and carried the blankets into the adjoining cell. He returned for one of the unlit lanterns and set it on the floor of the cell he was to occupy.

Jett sat down on the cot by the wall, pulling off her

hat and setting it aside. She stared toward the back wall of the cell as if it were a window, and in the soft glow of the lamplight Gibbons could see Jett was some years younger than she'd originally thought her to be. She wondered how Jett Gallatin had come to live as a man. *I'll probably get these walls to talk before she does!* she told herself with a mental snort.

"While we're waiting to be overrun by your zombies," Gibbons said, "why don't we have something to eat? A cold supper is better than no supper. And you can tell me where that trail of yours led."

"Nowhere that made a darned bit of sense," Jett grumbled. "And I don't figure I want to listen to you tell me about how nothing I saw was so."

Gibbons blinked in surprise at the hostility she heard in Jett's voice. Certainly she didn't believe Jett had seen zombies here in Alsop last night. But neither did she think Jett had made up some story. "It's true I find the possibility of zombies unlikely in the extreme," she said slowly, "but it is not your *account* I dispute, merely your interpretation of it. It is very easy to be mistaken. If we discover you are right and I am wrong, I will assuredly tell you so. But meanwhile, I am investigating similar disappearances. I need all the data I can collect to make sense of them, and your report is vitally important."

Jett stared at her for a moment. "That is the

long-windedest 'sorry' I've ever heard. But I guess I wouldn't mind some of your cold supper while I tell you my part of the tale."

The three of them gathered in the cell Gibbons had turned into her temporary home, and over sandwiches and pie White Fox and Jett told Gibbons about tracing the trail back to Jerusalem's Gate, and what each of them had found there. Gibbons frowned as she considered the new information. It didn't fit into what she'd learned this afternoon, but she was too good a scientist to concern herself with that. In turn, she told them all she'd found in Sherriff Mitchell's Charge Book and the newspaper archives.

"That doesn't make sense," Jett protested. "If the cattlemen wanted everybody else to clear off their range, why leave Jerusalem's Wall alone? Or"—she frowned, thinking hard—"if the ranchers *weren't* running the settlers off, why didn't the paper complain about Jerusalem's Wall as much as about the rest of the settlements?"

"I really don't know what to tell you," Gibbons said with a shrug. "I have a number of facts, but so far they don't suggest a theory—and there's absolutely no point in coming up with a theory and looking for facts to support it. Some of the things about this Fellowship could be just oddities or coincidence, but I *would* like to know how this Brother Shepherd knew something had happened to Alsop. And what's in that double-locked bunkhouse, too."

Jett snorted. "White Fox wouldn't let me shoot the padlock off. But . . . *what* other disappearances? You said none of the stories in the *Yell and Cry* made any of the Eastern papers."

"No," Gibbons agreed. "Nor the Pacific ones. But there've been more inexplicable vanishings than just those few the *Yell and Cry* mentions. I investigate such outlandish happenings." Just as she'd done for White Fox, Gibbons told her story to Jett. "—so I came east on the trail of Father's 'phantom airships'—though I doubt their existence very much—and I met Mr. Fox, here. And he's on the trail of the same thing."

Jett glanced at White Fox. "So he said. First time I ever heard of the Bluebellies investigating much of anything."

White Fox could see the fear Jett tried to conceal with bad-tempered words. He'd seen her terror the previous evening and knew how intolerable she must find it to be trapped and waiting for the return of the enemy she had fled from.

"My investigation is in the nature of a favor to one of the soldiers at Fort Riley," he said. "I am a civilian scout attached to the Tenth."

"The Buffalo Soldiers," Jett said, nodding. "They're good folks to have at your back in a scrap."

He saw Gibbons was surprised at Jett's comment, but he was not. The Buffalo Soldiers were comprised of former soldiers, and there had been Negro soldiers fighting on both sides of the recent war. Nor was everyone in the South the monsters of cruelty Miss Stowe had portrayed in her novel.

"How'd you end up with them?" Jett asked. "If you don't mind me asking," she added politely.

"It is a story I am more than willing to tell," he answered. "Though I fear it is not particularly interesting nor unique. Some thirteen years ago, a mixed hunting party of Sac and Fox came across the wreckage of a wagon train. They rescued the young boy—a child of four—who was its only survivor, and raised him as their own."

"But wasn't anyone looking for you?" Jett asked, understanding without more explanation who that boy must have been. "I've never heard of the Agency leaving a white child in the hands of Indians."

"My tribe had little to do with the Bureau of Indian Affairs," White Fox answered. "The remains of the Meshkwahkihaki moved west of their own volition after Black Hawk's War and owned—under Anglo law— the land on which they lived. I was ten years old before I saw my first white man, a good and learned soul.

Doctor Singer was both minister and physician, offering both skills freely to anyone who would accept them. Through the years, he urged me to rejoin those whom he spoke of as being my own people, but he never strove to compel me to do so. I knew I would never find my place among them, but I also came to realize I was not truly Meshkwahkihaki either. Working as an Army scout gives me a place in both worlds."

There was more to his story than he'd told, but he did not feel it was yet time to share it. He had not become a scout out of free choice. Two years ago he'd been away from his village on a trading expedition. He'd returned to find his village destroyed, his tribe and their livestock slaughtered. He'd ridden to the nearest fort, bent on vengeance, only to find his people had not been the victims of yet another white massacre. Upon hearing his story, the fort's commander sent a troop to investigate, and—much against his will—White Fox had come to believe the soldiers and the nearby Anglo settlers were truly innocent of the outrage. He'd been offered a job with the Army after that and had taken it in hopes of finding some way to bring justice to his murdered people. He'd never discovered who had been responsible, but in his searching he'd found there'd been a similar massacre twelve years before, one identical in nearly every detail.

A wagon train.

In the spring of 1853, a party left Independence, Missouri, to begin the six-month journey that would take some of its members to California, some to Oregon, and some to Utah. There'd been nearly a hundred wagons in the train, for all three routes lay together until Omaha, Nebraska. From there, fifty wagons had continued toward Oregon.

The regiment that later came across the wreckage of that wagon train described it as a slaughterhouse. Every living thing had been dismembered as if with axes, and the wagons themselves had been broken into kindling. The time and place matched the wagon train from which he'd been rescued, and what the Mesh-kwahkihaki hunting party had seen had matched the army's description. He'd never thought to see a scene of such violence with his own eyes until the day he had discovered himself cruelly orphaned yet a second time.

He brought his tale to a close by recounting the mystery of Glory Rest in more detail than he had provided to Gibbons on the previous evening. "Caleb Lincoln, on whose behalf I went to Glory Rest, had good cause to be alarmed. And what I found there—and afterward—makes me—"

He broke off mid-sentence as the air within the jail suddenly turned chill and foul. Gibbons instantly leaped to her feet to douse both lamps. For long moments the three of them sat in the dark, straining their ears for some sound from the outside. The spoiled-meat reek was stronger with each passing moment, and White Fox thought of herds of buffalo killed by white buffalo hunters and left to rot where they fell. Then the silence was broken by a weighty thud—Finlay Maxwell had fallen from the bunk to the floor.

"Mister Maxwell, pray be quiet!" Gibbons said in a loud stage whisper, but her admonition had no effect. They heard thumping and banging as Maxwell staggered to his feet and lurched about his cell. More thumps told the listeners he was careening off the walls. Then the door of the cell rattled as he fell against it.

"If you don't shut your noise the zombies are going to get all four of us!" Jett whispered loudly. In the distance, the sound of a window breaking could be heard. There was another loud thump from the far cell, then silence.

White Fox rose to his feet as Gibbons struck a Lucifer match against one of the bars of their cell. In the light he could see Maxwell lying immobile on the floor. The match burned down quickly. Gibbons dropped it with a hiss and struck another. Then—before either White Fox or Jett could stop her—she flung open the door of their cell and dashed into Maxwell's.

"You bring those things down on us and I'll kill you myself!" Jett whispered furiously.

There was another scraping sound as Gibbons

struck another match. In its glow, White Fox could see she was now kneeling beside Maxwell's body.

"He's dead," Gibbons said in bewildered tones.

"And we're gonna be if you don't stop striking lights!" Jett hissed.

White Fox got to his feet and moved silently through the darkness toward the center cell.

"Whoof!" Gibbons gasped as she collided with him.

"I wish to see—" he began, just as Jett ran into him from behind.

"Will you both get out of my way?" she demanded.

The window looked out on the back of the buildings, and Jett had to stand on the bunk, then lean out as far as possible to see through it. For a moment she didn't think there'd be anything to see from back here. Then she saw movement.

Half a dozen zombies shuffled past the window. Every one of them was carrying something, and the smell of them was enough to make her regret the meal she'd eaten. *So much for "men resurrected into the nature of angels" who don't need food or any worldly goods!* She didn't care how much proof Gibbons insisted on. Jett knew Brother Shepherd was behind this—somehow.

Another zombie shuffled by, closer than the first ones. Its head rocked and lolled on its shoulder with every step it took. Its neck was obviously broken. Even dead she recognized him—it was Mister Trouble, the bully who'd been about to challenge her last night just before the zombies attacked. Not only had he died in the bar fight—he'd come back. *He smells just as bad dead as alive*, she thought, on the edge of hysteria.

She dropped down before Gibbon started bellowing about getting a chance to look out the window. Jett felt around in the darkness until she found her, then put her mouth by Gibbons's ear to breathe a description of what she'd seen.

"I need to see!" Gibbons answered in an urgent whisper. Jett led her over to the window and knelt down as she guided Gibbons's foot into the stirrup she formed with her hands. Gibbons quickly stepped up onto Jett's back to peer through the window.

At first Gibbons thought it must be some trick to befool the credulous. None of the manifestations she'd seen so far would be easy to create under these frontier conditions, but since she'd been a child of twelve she'd been uncovering the tricks used by con-artists of every description. "Card ice" or "dry ice" was easy enough to manufacture if one had a few simple chemicals, and a wagonload of it would account for the cold. The stench of putrefaction wouldn't even need to be artificially manufactured: all one would need was rotting meat and a strong stomach. Add to that an artful costume and some greasepaint to counterfeit the pallor of the grave, and—presto!—zombies.

But the parade of the dead passing by in front of her began to shake her conviction, loathe though she was to admit it. A missing limb could be faked easily. A broken neck or crushed skull . . . could not.

For a single moment, terror overwhelmed her. She fought it down with the best weapon in her arsenal against emotion: logic. She did not have the leisure to be afraid. She had to find the method behind this. Once she had the method, these horrors could be wiped from the face of the earth. Science first. Then vapors.

"I must have a specimen to study!" she whispered in near-hysterical excitement as she jumped down from Jett's back.

"You're crazy," Jett answered flatly, getting to her feet.

"How am I to determine how they are created without studying one?" Gibbons demanded in exasperation— grateful to feel exasperation instead of fear. Jett ought to be *glad* she was trying to find proof that zombies were real instead of calling her unfounded names.

"It would be far too dangerous," White Fox whispered.

"It will save hundreds of lives—perhaps thousands!" If Jerusalem's Wall was behind the zombies, well . . . Brother Shepherd had already said he was sending his "blessed resurrected" on a rampage.

"It will get us *dead*!" Jett insisted. "If—" She was undoubtedly about to go on, when the door of the jailhouse began to rattle. All three of them froze.

The rattling continued for a few seconds, then it was replaced by loud thumping. Something far stronger than any man was trying to break down the door. It was a heavy door and a heavy bolt, but as the thumping continued, Gibbons began to fear the door wouldn't hold. The terror returned, and this time logic wouldn't keep it at bay. Logic said: *That door can't hold forever.* She heard a faint, distinctive click as Jett slowly eased the hammer back on her Colt.

Then all of a sudden there was silence once more. Before Gibbons could demand help to get to the window again, Jett had leaped to the bunk and was peering out.

"What is it? What do you see?" Gibbons demanded urgently.

"It's the preacher-man," Jett answered. "It's Brother Shepherd."

Brother Shepherd looked to be in fine fettle this evening. He was wearing a long frock-coat and a low-crowned hat, and he looked like a doctor—or the preacher his people claimed he was. What he certainly didn't look was *reanimated*. He was standing at the back of a freight wagon, wholly unconcerned by the zombies lurching past him to deposit their plunder in it. She was about to tell Gibbons and White Fox more, when suddenly Brother Shepherd threw back his head and began caterwauling.

The sound was half Rebel yell, half lamentation. It made the hair stand up on the back of her neck. There seemed to be words mixed into it somehow, but she couldn't make them out. "Sounds like somebody stepped on a cat," she muttered under her breath.

"It's no language I know," she heard Gibbons whisper.

Jett jumped down from the bunk. Brother Shepherd kept right on yowling. "Maybe if you—" she began.

She broke off with a hiccup of indrawn breath. There was an unmistakable sound of *movement* from the other cell.

The one that contained Finlay Maxwell's body.

"He isn't dead," White Fox said, sounding baffled.

"But I checked," Gibbons protested.

"He *was*," Jett said.

"It isn't locked," White Fox said.

"Who locks up a *corpse*?" Gibbons demanded.

Just like before, they could hear the sound of Maxwell thrashing around his cell. Only it wasn't Maxwell now. It was a creature that meant to do Brother Shepherd's bidding. Once it got out of its cell, it would open the jailhouse door . . .

"I need light!" Jett said urgently. She was already moving before either Gibbons or White Fox responded. She shoved open the cell door and launched herself into the darkness, navigating by memory. A moment later she had the jailhouse key-ring in her hands.

Someone lit one of the lamps, turning the wick down as far as possible. The faint glow was enough to let Jett see where she needed to go. The thing that had been Finlay Maxwell was in front of the door to its cell pawing blindly at the bars. The door rattled in its frame. Jett launched herself forward, shoving the key into the lock.

It didn't turn.

The wrong one! Jett thought frantically. She fumbled for the next key on the ring. The thing in the cell reached through the bars, patting clumsily at her as if it didn't know what she was and moaning faintly. The key-ring fell from her fingers, hitting the floor with a jangle. She bit her lip hard and snatched it up again. Which key had she already tried? She couldn't tell. She chose one at random and jammed it into the lock.

The tumblers clicked as Jett turned it.

At the sound, the zombie's movements quickened. It clawed at her arm, her shoulder, its mouth open in a horrible silent scream. She jerked the key from the lock and threw the key-ring as far behind her as she could. The thing in the cell clutched at her with impossible strength. Soon its hands would find her throat . . .

Strong arms—*living* arms—encircled Jett's waist from behind. White Fox dragged her free of the zombie's grasp. The moment they reached the far cell, Gibbons blew out the lamp in the center cell. Jett blinked back tears, grateful for the concealing darkness. She wouldn't let them see her cry. She wouldn't let anyone see her cry. She sat down on the bunk and tried to stop shaking.

Somewhere in those frantic minutes spent trying to lock the zombie's cell before it could get out, Brother Maxwell's squalling had grown fainter. Now the loudest sound was the thumping and rattling of the former Finlay Maxwell as it tried to free itself.

"You have the heart and spirit of a great warrior, Jett Gallatin," White Fox said quietly.

"You'd've done the same," she said gruffly. She knew it shouldn't matter, but she felt strangely warmed by his praise.

"You got there first," Gibbons said, sitting down beside her. She took Jett's hand and pressed something small and cool into it. "Here. Brandy."

Jett managed to unscrew the cap. She tilted the tiny flask to her lips and drained it. The liquor burned down her throat. "Thanks," she said. She took a deep breath. "Looks like you've got your zombie after all."

She heard Gibbons make a small sound of annoyance, but when she spoke, her voice shook a little. "I know he was dead. What I want to know is—how did he come back to life?"

Jett saw a flicker of shadow. White Fox had returned to the center cell, taking care to stay out of Maxwell's reach, and was looking out the window once more. "They're leaving," he said when he returned to their cell. "Brother Shepherd and his . . . zombies."

"Oh, good," Jett said shakily. "I can't stand crowds."

Gibbons sat on the floor of her cell while the other two took turns at the window. She had seen all she could stand. And right this moment, it was all she could do to sit in one place and shake, with her knees pressed up into her chest and her arms wrapped around them.

The bottom had dropped out of her universe. In her world, the dead did not walk. There was no magic, there were no supernatural explanations. Science had a name and a cause for everything—or if it didn't now, it would soon. Things like this did not happen.

But they had. And that meant everything she had faith in was wrong.

She wanted to cry. She wanted to run home to San

Francisco and hide in her rooms forever. She wanted to drive her Auto-Tachypode to the nearest railhead, abandon it, board a train, and never, ever, leave a place that was safe again.

She put her head down on her knees and let herself cry silently. She didn't frighten easily; she would have said she didn't frighten at all until today. But how could anyone have looked on the faces of those . . . things . . . and not been afraid?

She couldn't let the others know how afraid she was. If they knew, they wouldn't trust her judgment. She had to get to the bottom of this, and find the cause—more importantly, the "cure."

But right now . . .

Right now, Gibbons wished, very badly, for her Papa.

CHAPTER FIVE

By unspoken agreement all three of them stayed awake the rest of the night, even though Maxwell was safely imprisoned and Brother Shepherd and his zombie army were gone. It would have been impossible to sleep in any event: the caged zombie battered tirelessly at the door to its prison. At first, Gibbons had wanted to go straight to the reanimated corpse and examine him. But after Fox and Jett objected forcefully—and Jett threatened to knock her in the head if she tried—she finally agreed to let the zombie be. Not because she thought Jett would knock her unconscious. But because after about half an hour of watching the crea-ture, she realized that if she got anywhere near it, it would have a very good chance of killing her. It wasn't fast, and it was clumsy, but death seemed to have granted Finlay Maxwell an unholy strength.

So they settled as far away from the thing as possible, and mostly to try and keep Jett's mind (and, truth to tell, her own) off the horror trying to claw its way out of the cell, she asked about the one thing she was pretty sure Jett truly cared about.

"Your stallion, he's—well, remarkable is an understatement. Did you train him? I've never seen anything like him outside of Liberty Horses in a circus."

"My brother and I had him and his sister from the time they were suckling foals," Jett said slowly. "Nightingale and Lark. They were bred from a fancy stud out of Arabia as our birthday presents. I was to have the filly, of course, and my brother the colt. We'd been reading about knights—not the King Arthur sort, but the Crusader kinds, and how they'd trained their horses to fight with them, and we thought that was a champion idea. We saw the Liberty Horse acts with traveling circuses too, and our head stableman agreed to let us train 'em as we wanted, so we pretty much started training them before they were even weaned."

"Aha," Gibbons said, enlightened. "Yes, the old knights, particularly the Germanic ones, made their horses into weapons. I can see now what you did. But how is it you have the stallion now?"

"When my brothers went off to fight, nobody thought we'd lose," Jett said bleakly. "You don't send the horse you intend to be your foundation stallion off to war. If Lark was killed, we'd lose maybe eight, ten foals at most. But if Nightingale died or was taken, we could, potentially, lose hundreds. So my brother took Lark, and I got Nightingale. He—" Jett paused, and the silence continued long enough for Gibbons to be sure there was something painful about it. "The Yankees didn't get him. It's about all we had they didn't get."

Quickly, Gibbons spoke up to turn Jett's thoughts back to something happier. "So tell me more about how you trained them. I know very little of horses."

As she had hoped, horses, or at least Nightingale and Lark, were Jett's passion, and she was more than willing to wax eloquent about how she and her brother had turned their mounts into something so remarkable that foolish people might start pointing fingers and whispering about witchcraft. It was more than interesting enough to keep Gibbons from thinking too closely about the horror on the other side of the jail. Even White Fox found it interesting enough to add some tidbits about how Indians trained their horses. But at last the sky turned from black to gray to blue, and in the first moment of true daylight, Finlay Maxwell's body dropped to the floor, lifeless once more.

"I want to take a look at him," Gibbons said

decisively. She'd managed to bottle her feelings back up and put them where they belonged—out of the way. There was no place for feelings in Science.

Jett shook her head, but made no other protest. She got to her feet and picked up Gibbons's coach gun. "Here," she said to White Fox as she handed it to him. "This'll be a darned sight more use than your pistol."

Despite that, Gibbons noticed Jett kept a hand on the butt of one of her Colts. For that matter, Gibbons wasn't nearly as sanguine as she wished to appear as she picked up the ring of keys and advanced on Maxwell's cell. He certainly *looked* dead. More dead (in fact) than he had the night before. Of course, by now he'd been dead *longer*, and while he didn't have any bruises from the hours he—*it!*—had spent trying to batter its way out of its cell, the struggle had left the body looking a bit more . . . beat up.

Gibbons unlocked the door and stepped inside, then knelt down beside the body and placed the back of her hand against its cheek. It was cold. She felt for a pulse in both neck and wrist, because no matter what she'd seen outside the jail last night, Maxwell's condition might stem from some natural cause. Datura—among other things—could cause both the frenzy she'd witnessed and the near-coma that had followed it, and Jimsonweed—or *loco* weed—was a common local plant.

But if the former Finlay Maxwell still possessed a pulse, it was far too weak for her to find. Gibbons thought he probably *was* as dead as he looked, but Science was not a venue in which to entertain guesses and suppositions. First she'd identify his condition beyond doubt. Then—if he was dead—she'd start searching for what had reanimated his corpse.

Because if corpses *were* being reanimated, she wanted to know how.

Jett watched approvingly as Gibbons relocked Maxwell's cell (there was no point in taking chances). She'd been as scared as she could ever remember being last night, but with the return of daylight, Jett had other things to worry about.

"I'm going down to the livery to see if the horses are still there," she said, picking up her Stetson. She glanced back at the provision-laden cell as she moved toward the jailhouse door.

"I suspect it will be for the best if we continue to sleep here," White Fox said, seeing the direction of her glance.

"Didn't do much sleeping last night," Jett commented sourly. She lifted down the bar securing the outside door. As she swung it open there was a faint sound and a piece of metal fell free. The creatures bat-tering at the door last night had torn the facing plate of the lockset from the doorframe. "But I don't think they'll be coming back, somehow," she added, and stepped out onto the wooden sidewalk.

When Gibbons and White Fox joined her, they could see what she'd meant. Overnight, Alsop had been trans-formed from a deserted town into a devastated one. Most of the street-level windows were broken. Doors stood open, and some of them had been wrenched completely from their frames. There'd obviously been substantial and systematic looting.

"My Auto-Tachypode!" Gibbons gasped.

She took off at a dead run for the livery stable. Jett and White Fox were only a few paces behind her. When they got there, it was empty—both of zombies and of horses—but the Auto-Tachypode didn't seem to have been touched. While Gibbons examined her machine for signs of damage, White Fox and Jett examined the stables.

"They carried off most of the oats," White Fox said, gesturing toward the back of the barn. "But they left the hay, the blankets, the carriage, Gibbons's con-veyance."

"Hay would take up too much space, I think," Gib-bons said, emerging from the inside of her wagon. She frowned in puzzlement. "And the Auto-Tachypode does not look particularly valuable—if one is not aware of the treasure of Science its form conceals! But there are no signs they even tried to break down its doors. Certainly I would have expected them to at least *try* to get into it."

"Are you bragging or complaining?" Jett asked. "Just as well. Your buggy may be our only way out of here now."

"Our horses weren't taken," White Fox said. "They fled. We may hope they will find their way back to us soon."

Jett nodded without speaking. If Nightingale could, he'd come back to her. *I should have stayed here with him. Or brought him into the jailhouse*, she thought, even though she knew either course would have ended in disaster. The zombies had been all over Alsop last night. She couldn't have escaped them again—and even if she had, Brother Shepherd had been here too, and probably armed. She might outrun a zombie, but she couldn't outrun a bullet. And Nightingale would have given them away for sure if he'd been in the jailhouse when Finlay Maxwell came back from the dead. All she could do now was hope the miraculous luck that had kept the two of them alive for so long hadn't run out.

Gibbons disappeared inside her wagon again,

emerging with a bulging carpetbag. "We must make a detailed search of the town," she announced. "But that can wait until after breakfast!"

Any drinking establishment worth its salt served food. Beans and eggs, or plates of stew—both accompanied by sourdough biscuits—were common fare. Most saloons served as tavern, restaurant, and hotel—and sometimes even as courtroom and hospital—but in Alsop there was a restaurant and rooming house next door to the saloon. A well-beaten path between their back doors proved that food went one way and beer went the other. Despite the depredations wreaked in most of the town, the rooming house's kitchen had escaped essentially untouched; White Fox speculated that the looters were interested mainly in bulk provisions. As Gibbons stoked up the huge cast-iron stove, Jett went to inspect the general store for additional supplies. It had been looted, and much of what remained had been smashed or ruined, but she found an unbroken bag of Arbuckle's and some cans of Eagle Brand in the wreckage. At least there'd be coffee, and milk to go in it.

Good thing Gibbons stocked up on bullets when she did. There sure aren't any here now. Or firearms, either.

She no longer wondered what zombies would want

with things like iron frying pans and bolts of cloth. The question was: what did *Brother Shepherd* want with them?

Over flapjacks, beans, and coffee, Jett got the chance to ask that question. White Fox had carried one of the tables into the kitchen area. The smoke from the chimney might be seen at a distance—or more likely *smelled*—but anyone riding into Alsop wouldn't see anything but the broken window of the dining room.

"So Br'er Shepherd can make zombies—somehow," Jett said.

Gibbons nodded reluctantly. "You were right after all, Jett. And what I need to do is—"

Jett held up her hand so she could finish. "And he took over Alsop, killed everyone here, turned them into zombies, then came back to loot the place. Why? What's he get out of it besides the chance to lord it over less than a hundred people?"

"Perhaps that is sufficient," White Fox said in doubtful tones.

"No. It can't be," Gibbons said urgently. "*Think*, both of you! He has discovered some method by which he can cause the dead to rise up and follow his orders. That secret could make him a rich and powerful man."

"Except for the fact he's crazier than a daystruck owl," Jett said. "I don't think the bank was touched last night, but even if it was, there can't be more than a few hundred dollars there—and that's figuring in the paper money, too. If Br'er Shepherd was to use his army to hold up a stagecoach, there wouldn't be a lawman in the Territories who could stop him. Or he could hit the assay office in Denver—there isn't a desperado alive who doesn't dream of lifting that cashbox."

Gibbons looked thoughtful. "A herd of cattle is worth a great deal of money—but only if one can get it to the railhead in Abilene. I don't think zombies, from what I've seen, make very good cowhands. If we assume Shepherd is behind the disappearance of the trail drive, he must have taken them for a reason beyond personal enrichment."

"To keep Sheriff Mitchell from looking into all those people who went missing, like you said," Jett said, and Gibbons nodded.

"But surely he could have found a simpler way to discredit the Sheriff," Gibbons pointed out. "White Fox, you spoke of disappearances north of here—and far beyond anything the *Yell and Cry* has reported. We know people have been vanishing for at least two years, and that's only within a few hundred miles of Alsop. You mentioned disappearances on Tribal lands even farther away. And—according to you, Jett—Shepherd is telling his congregation his "blessed resurrected" will soon be sweeping across Texas and the Territories, doing much what they did here in Alsop. He'll need numbers for that. So, I think . . . I think he's been *experimenting* up until now."

The prospect of an army of reanimated corpses sweeping through the West, killing everything in its path was enough to cause all three of them to fall silent. White Fox was the first to speak. Throughout the meal and the discussion that had accompanied it, he'd been looking more and more troubled. At last he reached into his shirt and pulled out a beaded buckskin pouch. Most people called them "medicine pouches" but Jett had one herself: plain or fancy, they were used as often to hold tobacco and small valuables as for any kind of Indian magic.

White Fox extracted an oilcloth bundle little larger than a deck of cards from the pouch. "I promised Caleb Lincoln I wouldn't show this to anyone, as its disclosure could get him and his family into trouble," White Fox said. He unwrapped the bundle, revealing a small handmade book. Its leather covers were stained and worn. "His mother sent this to him in her last letter. It was why he was so anxious to see how matters stood at Glory Rest. He told me it was a treasured family heirloom and said I was to return it to his mother if I found her and his family safe and well. And to rely upon it for help if they were not."

"A prayer book?" Jett asked in disbelief. It was the size and thickness of the breviary her mama had conducted the Sheridan family's evening prayers from.

Gibbons plucked the book from White Fox's hands and riffled through it. Its pages were covered edge to edge in cramped time-faded writing. "No," she said. "A spell book."

Someone who knew of Gibbons's love of logic and her devotion to Science would find it odd that she was as familiar with the principles of sorcery as she was with the principles of physics. But such was the case. While many disciplines were freighted with such a weight of past ignorance and historical irrationality that rendered new research difficult if not impossible, others could be considered as useful records of phenomena observed but imperfectly understood. As such, these "parasciences" were able to illuminate many aspects of the physical world.

"I see now why Trooper Lincoln warned you," Gibbons said as she skimmed the small volume. "This could be quite inflammatory in the wrong hands."

"I can't see how a spelling book could be trouble," Jett said, grabbing for the book.

Gibbons twisted sideways, holding the book out of

Jett's reach. "Not a spelling book. A *spell book*. It's a *grimoire*," she said. "A manual of *Conjure*."

Jett recoiled as if she'd been told the little book was made of red-hot iron.

"Conjure is folk magic," Gibbons began pedantically. "One part Dahomeyan Vodun, one part Catholicism, one part Indian practices, and one part folklore."

"You don't have to tell *me* what it is!" Jett snapped. "You think we never knew about the dances they held down at—"

"Then don't behave as if I'm suggesting you take up *Satanism*!" Gibbons said irritably.

Jett sat back with an aggrieved sigh. "What does it say about zombies?" she asked after a pause.

"I have no idea—yet," Gibbons said, brandishing the book in emphasis. "It took only a quick glance to tell what the book is, but it will be another matter entirely to extract actual information. Everything has been written down in bits and pieces. I'll need to comb through the entire text to see if there's anything about zombies. And if it's of any use."

"I suppose I might be some help with that," Jett said reluctantly. "I can help you match it up with what I know, anyhow."

Gibbons smiled at her radiantly. "Thank you! That will be very useful! But first," she said, getting to her feet and tucking the little book into the pocket of her pantaloons, "we must search the town for clues."

Jett sat on the corral fence down at the livery stable, her boot-heels hooked over the center board. The sun was high, and heat-haze danced and shimmered, blurring the horizon. There wasn't much to see, anyway—just desert, desert, and more desert, from here to the Rio Grande.

Two days without sleep had begun to take their toll, and Gibbons had ordered her to take herself off to rest. Jett had been too weary and heartsick to rip up at Gibbons about her high-handed dictates, but she didn't rest, either. She went back to the livery.

This morning the three of them had spent hours searching every building in the town, and all they'd found were new mysteries. Jett was more than familiar with the look of a place that had been looted by an invading army. Alsop didn't look like that. Even if you assumed zombies couldn't climb stairs, they'd had plenty of time to cart off everything at ground level Br'er Shepherd could possibly want—and smash what could make trouble for him. Gibbons expected to find the telegraph lines down. Jett expected the bank to have been robbed. Gibbons was right—the lines were down, and the machinery had been smashed—but the bank was untouched, much to Jett's surprise. Most of what had been taken was food. Food for livestock, food for people—anything available in bulk that could be easily carried away. Maybe a few other items, but while it was obvious the General Store and the livery had both been hit hard, the destruction made it less obvious what was missing, particularly in the case of the former. And the destruction looked to have been caused by accident rather than intentionally.

Jett'd thought she'd be able to get White Fox to track the missing horses after that, but Gibbons had a long list of errands she wanted him to run. Gibbons had decided to make the saloon into her base of operations, and Jett had helped carry all the broken furniture into the street, then swept the saloon floor clear of sawdust and scrubbed it down with lye and water. It wasn't much cleaner than it'd been when she started, but at least the bloodstains had been bleached away. But there was plenty more fetching and carrying that Gibbons had in mind, and Jett didn't really have the heart to drag White Fox away from that task. She was afraid of what he might find. If Nightingale had been panicked enough to gallop until he was winded, he might have broken his leg—or his neck. He might have run into a Comanche scouting party—Alsop was on the southern border of the *Comancheria*, but since the whites didn't honor the border, the Comanche saw no reason to, either.

He might have been killed by the zombies after all. Or shot.

Or he could be down by Burnt Creek this very minute wondering where the devil I've gotten to! she told herself irritably. She'd go and check, only Burnt Creek was a day's walk from Alsop. It was only a few hours away by horse, but she was fresh out of equines. And Gibbons didn't seem inclined to take her steam buggy out for a spin. Right now she and White Fox were busily converting the saloon into something Gibbons called her "laboratorium." Whatever that might be.

She'd promised to help Gibbons with her research later, but Jett wasn't convinced Gibbons needed help— not hers at least. The thought of stepping back into the jailhouse with the zombie gave her a cold grue, let alone the thought of facing a whole army of the things. *This isn't my fight. It's nothing to do with me. I'm looking for my brother. Phillip needs me. If I don't look for him, who will?*

Jett tilted her Stetson further down over her eyes and sighed, wishing she were anyplace else. *Only you can't run out on White Fox and that fool Yankee and you know it. If she's right about what Br'er Shepherd is planning, he won't leave anyone aboveground from the Mississippi to California—and that includes Philip. If I couldn't convince Gibbons until she saw for herself, I sure can't convince the United States Army. So—*

Suddenly a dark splotch appeared in the heat-shimmer of the horizon. Jett stuck two fingers in her mouth and whistled shrilly, hoping her eyes—and her heart—weren't playing tricks on her. But a moment later Nightingale came trotting toward her, Deerfoot behind him. She jumped down from the rail and a moment later she was running her hands all over him—neck and chest and legs—looking for injuries as Nightingale tried to grab her hat. He finally succeeded, gripping the brim in his teeth and pulling it off her head as she laughed and grabbed for it.

"You fool nag! Don't you know I was worried sick about you? Where have you been?" She rose to her feet and swung an arm across his withers.

As Deerfoot trotted past her, Jett turned to look up the street. White Fox was standing outside the saloon. He'd obviously heard her whistle. She blushed hotly. He'd heard her slopping Nightingale all over with sugar like a—like a *girl*. To the world, she was *Mister* Jett Gallatin: gunslinger, cardsharp, drifter. She had to remember that. It didn't matter if she slipped up here and now—but she wouldn't always be surrounded by folks who knew the truth.

Maybe someday, she thought wistfully. *When I've got Philip back, when we settle down somewhere.*

White Fox led Deerfoot back in Jett's direction. She stepped away from Nightingale to retrieve her hat and the stallion followed her, nudging at her hopefully.

"You think I carry sugar around with me all the time on the chance you'll turn up?" she demanded gruffly. She dug around in her pockets until she turned up a piece. Having received his treat, the stallion turned away and walked sedately into the barn, obviously expecting breakfast.

"Fool," Jett repeated, and followed him.

She'd tossed some hay into the stall Nightingale had chosen and was looking around for a water pail when White Fox entered the barn. "They seem to have taken no hurt," he said. "Once we have tended to their needs, Gibbons requests your assistance."

Jett restrained herself from snorting in derision. It didn't seem to her that Honoria Gibbons needed anybody's assistance with anything.

But less than an hour later Jett was standing in the saloon gazing at a makeshift map tacked to the wall of the saloon. It had been assembled from pages removed from an atlas, and showed Texas and a good bit of the Territories: all of Kansas and part of Nebraska, west into Utah and Arizona. There was a bright red wax-pencil "X" to mark Alsop, and a number of smaller

"Xs" in pencil both clustered around Alsop and dotted across the rest of the map. Crossing the map from east to west were three meandering pencil lines. Jett wasn't sure what they were. Wagon-train routes? Cattle-drive trails?

"This is why I wanted your help," Gibbons said. She crossed the room holding an open atlas in her arms, obviously the one that had been sacrificed to create the map. "I hoped if I charted all the disappearances, the pattern would tell me something. Anything you can add will help."

"I can tell you plenty about disappearances east of here," Jett said. "Don't need to wonder why they went missing, though."

"Show me." Gibbons walked over to the bar and set down the atlas. "Don't assume you know why someone disappeared. I'm looking for a pattern."

Jett stepped closer to the map and peered at the penciled marks. Now she could see there was a date written faintly beside many of them. "Each of these is where somebody went missing," she said, puzzling it out. She frowned. "Isn't that one going to Mexico?" she asked, pointing at the southernmost of the three jagged lines. "What are they, anyway?"

"Railroads," Gibbons said succinctly. "And that isn't Mexico."

"Sure looks like it to me," Jett said. She pointed at a

word at the bottom of the map. "Mexico. Says it right here."

Gibbons gave an annoyed huff. "It might *say* Mexico, but it isn't Mexico. These pages are from an old atlas. That area's been part of the U.S. for four years."

"Says who?" Jett scoffed.

"*Says* Mister James Gadsen, the United States Ambassador to Mexico, that's who," Gibbons said. "He bought it from Mexico."

"Must've cost him a pretty penny," Jett said. She inspected the map for a few more seconds. "Those aren't railroads. There aren't any lines west of Kansas."

"Not yet," Gibbons said, sounding even more annoyed. "But there will be! There are already telegraph lines. The railroads will follow. And the first *transcontinental* railroad will take one of these three routes." She gestured at the map.

"Which one?" Jett asked with interest.

"This one," Gibbons said, pointing at the center line. "The Union Pacific's laid track almost all the way across the Sierra Nevadas, and they won't stop there. The Central Pacific is coming west. They're going to meet the Union Pacific halfway."

"Well, if they've already made up their minds, why put in all three of them?" Jett asked.

"Because you don't need just *one* railway line!" Gibbons said. "And . . . the Central Pacific still might go

159

south. Everybody's worried about snow on the central route."

"No snow in Texas," Jett agreed. "Don't know what railroads have to do with zombies, though."

"Probably nothing," Gibbons admitted. "But the more information we can collect in one place, the more likely we'll see some connection. And of course there are more settlements along the path of the railroad."

"Whether it's there or not," Jett pointed out.

"It's *going* to be there," Gibbons insisted. "And that's why towns are being built along the route. Being on the railroad line means faster growth, better transport— if you order something from New York or even Chicago, it can take three months—or longer—for it to get here by wagon."

"Or for something from here to get there," White Fox pointed out. "Now that the railroad has reached Abilene, the ranchers drive their cattle there to sell. They, too, are becoming wealthy from the railroad."

Jett turned to him, looking puzzled. "Too?" she asked.

"The railroad companies must purchase the rights of way before they can lay their track," White Fox said. "Those who own land along those rights of way stand to enrich themselves greatly."

"Or be left holding the bag if they guess wrong, but that isn't pertinent to our current problem!" Gibbons said briskly. She advanced on Jett, flourishing a pencil. "Everything you can remember, please."

By the time Jett had charted every disappearance she'd ever heard of, the shadows were beginning to lengthen. She'd added twenty or so possible locations to the map, and White Fox had promised to send a message to Fort Riley to see what he could add as well. Gibbons had suggested they spend the night in the jail once again, since it was the safest place to be if the zombies returned, but Jett had flatly refused. The moment Gibbons had opened the jailhouse door, the zombie had flung itself at the door to its cell, reaching through the bars in a vain attempt to reach *them*.

The three of them spent the night in the livery stable. Gibbons's contraption seemed like a good place to hide if the zombies returned.

The next day was devoted to something Gibbons apparently considered even more vital than making a record of the missing and figuring out just *why* Brother Shepherd felt the need to create a zombie army to slaughter the "wicked" (something much at odds with Br'er Raymond's insistence that The Fellowship of the Divine Resurrected was completely opposed to violence just to begin with). Jett and Gibbons spent the morning combing through Trooper Lincoln's little spell book for useful information. To Gibbons's indignation, there wasn't much in the grimoire about zombies.

Jett already knew what *didn't* kill a zombie—which was what Gibbons seemed to want to know most—so she'd cudgeled her memory for everything she remembered from the ghost stories Tante Mère had loved to tell her and Phillip. The only specifically zombie-related information she'd been able to come up with was that you could kill one by feeding it salted porridge with a silver spoon—and certainly that seemed as if it ought to work, considering the salt-free meal she'd "enjoyed" at Jerusalem's Wall. Despite her vigorous ridicule of Jett's "silly superstitions," Gibbons had sacrificed one of her own silver spoons to experimentation, and at high noon—when the creature lay as if dead—they'd put a bowl of salty porridge into its cell.

The two of them returned a little after dusk to see whether it had worked.

"It's as dark as the inside of a goat's stomach in here," Jett muttered, breaking the silence.

Gibbons snickered as she walked over to the lantern. "I suppose you—"

Suddenly there was a sharp thud, and the cell door rattled. Gibbons jumped in surprise and dropped her tin of matches. The rattling continued as she retrieved the matches and lit the lamp. In its soft glow, Jett could see that the zombie was on its feet again. The porridge was untouched, and from the creature's behavior, the only thing it was interested in devouring . . . was them.

"You're wearing a cross, are you not?" Gibbons asked as they regarded the zombie straining to get at them.

"Yes . . . ," Jett answered slowly. "Rosary, anyway. It's got a cross on it," she added, since she knew Gibbons wasn't Catholic.

"Is it, um, blessed?" Gibbons asked, awkwardly.

Jett nodded. Gibbons held out her hand, and Jett slipped it over her head and handed it to Gibbons reluctantly. "What are you . . . ?" she began. "Hey!" she yelped as—to her horror—Gibbons strode purposefully toward the cell.

"Hold it still!" Gibbons demanded as the zombie flailed wildly at her.

"*How?*" Jett demanded. But she gritted her teeth and seized the zombie's outstretched arm. It didn't feel *alive*, despite the fact its owner was flailing around like a gigged frog, and Jett groaned in revulsion.

Fortunately she didn't have to hold on for long.

"Let go!" Gibbons cried a moment later. She jumped back, with Jett's rosary swinging from her fist.

The touch of a blessed object will break a curse.

Apparently Gibbons meant to try all the things Jett had told her until she found something that worked.

Jett let go of the zombie's arm and staggered back clumsily. Its fingertips grazed the front of her shirt in the instant before Gibbons yanked her out of the way. She grabbed at Gibbons to keep from falling and was surprised to discover Gibbons was shaking.

Why, she's just as scared as I am! Jett thought. Watching Gibbons charge right up to the cell, it hadn't occurred to Jett she was seeing bravery and not idiocy. *She may be a damnyankee, but she's got grit when it counts.*

"Are you all right?" she asked hoarsely.

"It didn't work!" Gibbons said in frustration. She took a deep breath. "Never mind! I'll find something that will."

By now they were standing in the open doorway once more. Jett stepped out onto the sidewalk. "I still don't see why you're worrying so much about figuring out how to kill 'em, anyway," she grumbled. "White Fox and me can ride back to Jerusalem's Wall and drag Br'er Shepherd out by the ears. Or just ride out to any of the big spreads around here and tell the boss who's got their cattle."

"And what if stringing him up—since I doubt the cattle barons will turn him over to the law—just sends his zombies on an uncontrolled rampage?" Gibbons demanded.

"What if it doesn't?" Jett answered crossly.

"Even though that makes just as much sense, since I am currently without facts on which to base a theory, that only means Brother Shepherd's discovery—whatever it is—remains at Jerusalem's Wall for anyone to use. It isn't enough to discover he's behind this if we have no way of destroying his zombie army."

Jett sighed. "Guess you might be right." Gibbons had the uncanny ability to make raving lunacy sound like absolute common sense. "What do we do after we kill off all his zombies?" The more times she said the word "zombie" aloud, the more peculiar it sounded.

"Why, we search his laboratorium of course! It is impossible to imagine he doesn't have one!" Gibbons said optimistically.

The zombie rattled the bars of its prison, and her smile dimmed just a bit. She pulled the door closed behind her and followed Jett onto the sidewalk. "Here," she said, holding out Jett's rosary. "Thank you for loaning it to me." Jett took it with a twinge of reluctance (even though she knew Gibbons had only touched the zombie with it briefly) and tucked it into her pocket.

"I shall think of something," Gibbons said firmly. "I know it."

Gibbons stared morosely at the makeshift map pinned to the wall of the saloon. White Fox was out hunting, in hopes of adding some fresh meat to their diet, and Jett had gone up to the graveyard to acquire some "graveyard dust," another of her folk remedies. Gibbons didn't think it would be any more successful than the others, but she had to try it anyway. She was glad she was alone right now. She hated to fail, and she was currently out of new ideas.

If the graveyard dust doesn't work, the only thing left is to pray *over the creature, though I don't have any idea what prayers to say over a zombie! We don't have either garlic or roses—and anyway, Father said they were for use against vampires—so I can't try those. And all of these things are sheer hoodoo, besides—I know they are!*

She chewed on her lower lip, glancing from the notebook in her hand to the map on the wall, then made another careful "X" on her map. It was too old to show most of the recent towns—and individual home-steads wouldn't have been indicated anyway—but White Fox had drawn careful maps of his information, and she was following them now. If she couldn't solve the most important problem, at least she could collect more data.

Brother Shepherd has *to have used modern methods to create his legion of undead*, she thought, glaring at the map in frustration. *He certainly isn't a hoodoo doctor. I even have a sample of his work. I should be able to deduce his methods and counteract them!*

She added the last marks to the map and then blinked at it in surprise. *There* is *a pattern!* she realized excitedly, and the spark of discovery was enough to make her temporarily forget her other problem.

"It's obvious," she said, waving her fork toward the map on the wall.

White Fox had returned with a brace of rabbits, and while they'd been cooking, Jett had taken her pouch of graveyard dust down to the jail and sprinkled it over the unmoving body in the cell. Gibbons had spent that time rechecking every site on the map. She didn't want to share her discovery until she was sure it was true.

"Well, Jerusalem's Wall is here. Makes sense—most of the disappearances are here, too," Jett said.

"They're not just *here*," Gibbons said. "They're *there*!" She gestured toward the wall again.

"Clear as mud," Jett muttered.

"No," White Fox said. "Gibbons is correct. The disappearances aren't centered around Jerusalem's Wall as one might expect. They follow two routes. The cattle trail north—and the southern railroad route."

"There isn't a southern railroad. You said so," Jett pointed out.

"But if the railroads did use the southern route—now—they wouldn't have to pay to secure right of way," Gibbons said triumphantly. "He hasn't cleared all of it yet, but I suspect he intends to. And if there's no one there, no one can claim ownership of the land."

"No," White Fox said, sounding sad and troubled. "Before I left Fort Riley, General Custer said the Comanche have resumed their raids north of the Comancheria. They would not do that without reason."

"They're being shoved north by other hostiles," Jett guessed. "The Apache, Wichitas, and Mescalero are clearing out."

"Now we know why," Gibbons said in satisfaction. "This isn't about preparing for some 'Jerusalem of Fire' and it isn't killing for killing's sake. It's about luring the railroads to build on the southern route because they can do it for free. And I'll bet you anything that when they do, this Brother Shepherd is going to file claim to as much land on both sides of it as he can grab."

"And once he owns the land, he can ask any price he wishes for it," White Fox said. "He'll make a fortune."

"I bet he's got"—Jett snapped her fingers as she tried to think of the word—"undated Deeds of Claim on file in Austin. Once the railroad goes through, he gets someone to backdate his claims. If the land's empty, who's going to argue?"

"And so he's chosen to kill—or terrorize—everyone in its path," White Fox said. "With an army of undead."

"So which came first?" Jett asked. "The zombies? Or the Fellowship of the Blessed Resurrection?"

"That," Gibbons said thoughtfully, "is a very good question."

White Fox couldn't decide how a task that had seemed simple (if dangerous) had become so large and complicated in less than a week. The more they uncovered of the cause and reason for the destruction of Glory Rest and so many other settlements, the less they seemed to know. And so much of it was guesswork. They knew the settlements were being attacked by undead creatures. They knew the man calling himself "Brother" Shepherd was involved. Beyond that, what they truly knew was less substantial than a handful of wind.

And if I hadn't had the luck to meet both Jett Gallatin and Honoria Gibbons, I wouldn't have known even that much. I would have been among those who died here four days ago.

So many chance events had combined to save him. His decision to stop at Burnt Creek to watch over Gibbons. Jett's arrival with the warning about Alsop. Gibbons's preparation of the shelter that had saved all of them. He knew the *wasichu* placed little credence in omens or guardian spirits, but White Fox had to believe they had guided him to this place to do their work. And more than that, had given him allies any warrior would be proud to fight beside. Gibbons's unflagging bravery as she searched for the truth. Jett's courage in facing her fear and allying herself with them for a cause she had no stake in.

He stepped out of the telegraph office, a salvaged basket full of neatly rolled tapes under one arm. Gibbons wanted to go through the messages sent to Alsop to see if any of them might contain another scrap of information. Alsop hadn't had a telegraph office for long enough for the received messages to become a nuisance; the basket was only half full.

He was about to return to the saloon when the sound of a gunshot shattered the quiet. He turned toward the sound, and saw a tin cup balanced atop the fencepost of the livery stable corral spin into the dirt. As he walked in that direction, five more shots followed in quick succession, and five more targets disappeared. Before the last one hit the ground, Jett dropped the empty pistol into its holder and tossed her second Colt from her left hand to her right. Her long black frock-coat swirled as she moved, and six more targets followed the first.

"What are you doing?" White Fox asked when he reached her.

"Practicing," Jett answered. "Nothing else to do while Gibbons is making up her mind about what to do about Br'er Shepherd." She gestured toward the jail. "And trying to kill our houseguest." She holstered the second gun and went to gather up the plates and dishes and set up her targets again.

"And how long do you intend to continue . . . practicing?" White Fox asked.

"Making too much noise for you?" Jett asked, pausing in the middle of setting a cup on the top of the fence. "I could go out by the church and practice there."

"No," White Fox said. "I only wonder . . . why."

Jett tossed the cup to the ground and leaned back against the fencepost. She folded her arms across her chest, regarding him steadily beneath the brim of her black Stetson. The impersonation was a good one. They might have ridden the trail together for some time before he suspected the truth.

"This rig-out saves me a lot of problems," she said, gesturing at her clothes. "But if I can't back up the tale I'm telling, well . . ."

"A hard life, spent always at war," White Fox said.

"I didn't start the war!" Jett said sharply. Her words turned his into something he hadn't intended.

"The war is over," White Fox said. "Don't you think—"

"Jett! White Fox! I think I've figured out where I went wrong!" Gibbons said, running up to them.

"Do tell," Jett said, digging into her pocket for bullets and beginning to reload her guns.

"I thought I was on the wrong trail when we tried the porridge," Gibbons said excitedly. "But now I don't."

"It didn't work," Jett said, spinning her gun's cylinder before dropping it into its holster. Her hand was still full of bullets.

"It didn't *eat* it," Gibbons said.

Jett began to load the other gun. "So, you're going to walk in there when it gets up tonight and hand-feed it?" she asked neutrally.

"Don't be silly!" Gibbons scoffed. "That would be unduly reckless. But the three likeliest methods of destroying a zombie all involve salt. Porridge has salt, and so does graveyard earth."

"Sure," Jett answered. "Depending on the graveyard, I guess, but the river's plenty brack around New Orleans. I guess that means the stuff I dug up today won't work."

"We must wait for tonight in order to rule it out, I think," Gibbons said kindly. "The third method involves having the zombie ingest blood from an (obviously still living) close relative, but that will be impractical as we don't know any of Finlay Maxwell's family. But my point is that all three folk-remedies involve salt—blood is quite saline, as I'm sure you know—so once you eliminate the obfuscatory trappings of rank superstition, it's clear that it's the salt that's the important part, not any of the rest of the mumbo jumbo!"

White Fox carefully suppressed a smile. Jett and Gibbons engaged in a constant war of words, bickering much as sisters might. He wondered if either of them even suspected their growing friendship.

"'Obfuscatory trappings of . . . ,'" Jett said slowly. She spun the second Colt around her finger and dropped it into place.

"'Superstition,'" Gibbons supplied helpfully. "I know you grew up with zombies, Jett—"

Jett choked and began to cough. Gibbons moved forward to pound her on the back, but Jett waved her off. "No, no, no, you just go on, I'm fine," she said in a strangled voice.

"—but these creatures don't seem to be anything like *your* zombies."

"You can stop going on as if I grew up with a hope chest stuffed full of the things!" Jett protested.

"I don't think Mister Shepherd is practicing hoo-doo at all," Gibbons continued, ignoring her. "I think he's some sort of scientific necromancer."

Jett groaned faintly.

"And if you are right, and salt will kill one, what do you propose?" White Fox asked.

"*I* want to see her hand-feed the varmint," Jett muttered.

"You will!" Gibbons promised. "But only if this doesn't work!"

"Perhaps it would simply be best to burn it when morning comes," White Fox said quietly. The building now reeked of decay; the cloying scent of rotting meat underlain with a sharper, more poisonous scent. In the light of the lantern, all three of them could see the thing in the cell hadn't been destroyed by the graveyard dust. If anything, it seemed even more energetic.

"And lose the chance to find out what actually kills one?" Gibbons demanded. "No!"

"At least we know something else that *doesn't*," Jett said in disgust. She nodded toward the cell. "Pretty darned lively for something that hasn't had food or drink in five days."

"That's why I think it may not be—exactly—dead," Gibbons said seriously. "I know what you saw—I saw it too! But if the process puts the creatures into some sort of animate coma—which might well explain the drop in temperature in their presence, for should this process lower their temperature to unnatural levels, proximity to one would be akin to proximity to a hundredweight of ice. . . . But I digress! If Brother Shepherd's scientific necromancy does not create true death, but a deep coma, it would explain the chanting we heard that night as perhaps some form of control. Individuals in a state of coma later recount entire conversations that took place at their bedsides, you know."

"That's because they're in bed to hear them—not marauding across the *Llano Estacado*, killing everyone in sight," Jett pointed out. "And it sure as anything *smells* dead."

"Obviously the two cases aren't entirely identical," Gibbons said hastily. "But let us see what tomorrow brings."

CHAPTER SIX

According to the records kept by the *Yell and Cry*, the two closest ranches to Alsop were Flatfield and the Lazy J (now Jerusalem's Wall). White Fox had ridden out before breakfast that morning for Flatfield. He said he wanted to find out what Mister Sutcliffe knew about the local disappearances—and warn him not to send any more drives by way of Alsop. And if Mister Sutcliff could spare a rider, White Fox hoped to send word to Fort Riley as well.

Jett had wanted to be the one to go—this ghost town was making her stir-crazy—but White Fox pointed out that an army scout was likely to get a warmer reception than a suspected outlaw. *I suppose he's right*, Jett thought glumly, *but it's been almost a week I've been cooling my heels here now, and I am fresh out of patience.*

It didn't help matters at all that Honoria Gibbons of San Francisco had the heart and soul of a schoolmarm—and a tongue hinged in the middle and oiled at both ends, as the saying went around here. She seemed to think that just because Jett didn't shoot her, Jett was actually interested in hearing every single theory Gibbons had about Br'er Shepherd, The Fellowship of the Divine Resurrection, and zombies.

"First things first," Gibbons said, bounding to her feet. "We've got a lot to do today."

"We've got *what* to do today?" Jett demanded. "Dishes?" Gibbons hadn't even stopped to clear away their breakfast dishes, and Jett had a suspicion that left to herself, Gibbons would simply throw the dirty dishes out after each meal. Even granting that there were plenty of clean dishes and cups in Alsop, it just didn't seem respectful somehow.

"You do them if you care so much!" Gibbons called over her shoulder. Jett was taller than Gibbons by a good few inches, but she had to hurry to keep up with her.

"Where are you going?" she demanded, even though she knew the answer to that. The only things down at this end of the street were the Post and Telegraph Office and the jail, and she was pretty sure Gibbons wasn't expecting a letter.

Of course Gibbons didn't answer. Jett caught up with her just as she opened the door of the jailhouse.

"Phew!" Jett said in revulsion. "We should throw some eau de cologne around in here!" She made a mental note to look for some around Alsop before she came back here again—she could at least soak a neckerchief in it and tie it over her nose.

"Certainly we should not!" Gibbons answered (though she was making an equally disgusted face). "An unknown variable would interfere with my experiment!"

"Exp—? Would you say something that makes sense?" Jett demanded.

"Certainly!" Gibbons said crisply. "Finlay Maxwell didn't become a zombie by any of the so-called traditional means. He was in perfect health, and yet he dropped dead for no particular reason and rose as a zombie!"

"He was *drunk*!" Jett said.

"If that was all it took to make a zombie, there'd be thousands of them in every city on Earth," Gibbons replied inarguably. She walked into the jail and plucked the ring of keys off their nail. Jett hung back by the door. The sun was up, so to all intents and purposes it was a corpse in the cell—but Jett had seen that corpse get up and walk enough times that she didn't trust it to lie dead when it ought to. Since she already knew no amount of argument could stop Gibbons once she'd taken a notion, she held her peace, her hand hovering nervously over the butt of her Colt, as Gibbons unlocked the door of the dead man's cell and stepped inside.

Gibbons knelt down beside the corpse and dug something Jett couldn't see out of a pocket. Then she pried its mouth open. (Jett made a small unhappy sound of protest. Gibbons ignored her.) She tipped the bag over "Maxwell's" mouth and poured.

"Salt is salt," she said matter-of-factly, tucking the little bag back into her pocket and getting to her feet.

"Will it work?" Jett asked.

"Time will tell!" Gibbons answered. Cheerfully.

It was just before dusk. Gibbons had spent part of the day shooting the sun with a sextant (to determine the latitude and longitude of Alsop, she explained) in order to make sure they'd be back at the jail in plenty of time to watch Gibbons's subject revive.

This time, both of them reeked of cologne.

One of the things Gibbons had wanted was a list of the townspeople so their next of kin could be notified. Jett didn't feel right about picking over things belonging to dead people, but she'd found a big bottle of Florida Water among Dr. Butler's things, and, well . . . Meade Butler wasn't going to be needing it. She hadn't bothered to mention to Gibbons the two of them would probably be on that list themselves soon. Brother Shepherd might be done with Alsop, but he wasn't done with Texas.

That's what worries me. By the time anyone believes Br'er Shepherd can raise the dead, they're likely to be dead themselves.

She leaned back against the rough-hewn newel post and pulled out her watch. It was big and heavy and silver, like the one Father had owned. His was in some damnyankee's pocket now. She'd won hers at cards. She flicked the case open.

"Seven minutes to sundown."

The sky was still bright, but night came swiftly in the desert—once the sun made up its mind to set, down it went, and day became night before you could hit the ground with your hat.

Gibbons opened the door of the jailhouse. With a blue silk handkerchief tied over her nose and mouth, she looked like the world's most eccentric outlaw. She stepped inside just long enough to hang her lantern on its hook. In the light of the lamp, they could both see . . . exactly nothing happening inside the cell.

"Five minutes," Jett said.

"It might not be so . . . close . . . in there if we left the door open," Gibbons said in distaste. The rotting meat smell was strong enough to pierce through the scent of Florida Water, and the two mingled unpleasantly.

"And have every vulture in the Territories roosting on the roof," Jett said. "I don't know why they haven't showed up already."

"Because no matter what this smells like to us, it obviously doesn't smell like carrion to *Cathartes aura*," Gibbons said grandly. "The turkey vulture has a keen sense of smell and can locate prey up to a mile away, you know."

"Is there *anything*—" Jett began.

The corpse of Finlay Maxwell flung itself at the door of its prison.

It had moved so fast neither Jett nor Gibbons saw it get to its feet. The zombies they'd seen before moved with deliberation. Jett thought they couldn't move any faster.

She'd been wrong.

Its body hit the bars of the cell door hard enough that air was forced from its throat in an unearthly moan. The air in the jail had turned cold every time it rose—something Gibbons couldn't entirely explain, though she'd offered Jett half a dozen theories—but now the air pouring through the open doorway was as chill as the inside of an icehouse. Maxwell's mouth was open in a horrible silent scream, and Jett thought of every hideous story she'd ever heard about people who woke from illness only to find themselves in the darkness of a coffin, accidentally buried alive. How much more horrible would it be if life—if *awareness*—were called back into a body truly dead?

It drew back momentarily, but only to grip the bars in its hands and rattle the door in a frenzy.

"There was rust on the hinges," Gibbons whispered in a small voice.

For a moment Jett didn't understand. Then she did. Rusted hinges might give way.

"Get back," she said, drawing one of her pistols. "If it gets out, I'll shoot out the lamp." If she could spray the zombie with burning kerosene, its clothes would catch fire, and maybe that would slow it down. Jett didn't mention that even she might not be fast enough to get a shot off before it reached them.

"There's more kerosene in the saloon," Gibbons whispered, still in that dreadful airless voice.

Before Jett could say a word, Gibbons was off, running through the deepening shadows. Jett stood, so still she was barely aware of her own body, and watched the zombie tear and batter at the bars. It went from shaking the door to hammering the bars with its fists. Soon Jett couldn't hear the door rattling any longer, and she knew it was because the metal was lodged fast and starting to bend.

It was only a few steps to the stable. She could ride Nightingale bareback, come back for her saddle when it was safe to do so. She wished she was gutless enough to run. She knew she wouldn't.

"Here," Gibbons whispered in between gasps for breath. She had a wooden keg of kerosene in her arms.

"Pull the bung," Jett said. "Kick it through the door when I fire." Jett didn't know if Gibbons would be fast enough to do what she'd asked. If either of them would be. But she knew they weren't fast enough to get away from Maxwell.

Gibbons knelt on the boards of the sidewalk and began worrying at the stopper. The zombie had stopped beating at the bars of its prison and was now throwing its entire body at the bars. Jett imagined she could hear the protesting creak of the metal as it slowly gave way.

The popping sound as the bung finally came free was loud enough to make Jett jump. An instant later, she realized why: there was silence inside the jailhouse. The zombie had stopped moving, and now hung limply from the bars.

"Goodness!" Gibbons said, looking up. "That was close!"

"It's dead," Jett said in disbelief. "You killed it."

As Jett watched, the body sagged at the knees, slipped down the bars, and fell over. The night air was already starting to warm.

"I certainly hope so," Gibbons said fervently. She pulled the kerchief off and wiped her face with it, then sniffed the air. "It doesn't smell quite as bad now," she said analytically. With an expert whack, she set the stopper back into the keg.

"I guess one part of the legend isn't a legend," Jett said, drawing a shaky breath. "Whether it's 'scientific necromancy' or not."

"I guess it isn't," Gibbons said, sounding uncharacteristically subdued. She dug in her pockets until she found her little silver flask, and offered it to Jett wordlessly. Jett took a long swallow before handing it back. Gibbons drained it. "You did say when a zombie is released from the power binding it, its last act is to slay—or attempt to slay—whoever created it. I suppose you're going to say we should have just let it out."

"Not me!" Jett denied. "Even if we'd known that, all it'd do is tell Shepherd there's a posse after him."

"We're not much of a posse, I suppose," Gibbons said thoughtfully. "Still, we're here. And now I can start trying to find out how he creates the creatures."

"I'm surprised you aren't already in there with it," Jett said darkly.

Gibbons shuddered. "I think I'll wait for morning."

White Fox felt a shameful sense of relief at riding away from Alsop. It was not because he meant to flee the fight the spirits had led him to. The destruction of the zombies and the defeat of their creator would mean a justice he'd never thought to gain for his family, his people, his *tribe*. It was odd to think he was also to be the instrument of justice for his first family, but so it was. He'd marked the site of the wagon train's destruction on Gibbons's map without telling her what it meant or how he knew it, and it fit as perfectly into the pattern as another silken thread on a spiderweb.

No warrior rode into battle without preparation. He was willing to be patient until Gibbons had delivered the weapons for this combat. This journey might be a useless one, but at least it took him away from a place his thoughts populated with the ghosts of too many dead.

Flatfield was a full day's ride from Alsop, which was only to be expected: a ranch wasn't its land grant alone, but the "unclaimed" thousands of acres of open range around it, and the ranches themselves were widely scattered. He wondered what would change when a steel-rail road crossed the land. Or when Gibbons's Auto-Tachypode was as common a thing as a buckboard or a Conestoga.

It was just past noon when he knew something was wrong.

This was April, the end of the rainy season (such as it was) on the Staked Plains. The cattle drive that had disappeared a few weeks back had been one of the earliest ones; the drives would continue for the next two months, until the summer's heat became too fierce and the water holes and creeks dried up. He should have crossed paths with trailblazers, the cowhands who rode a day or more ahead of a drive to scout the way. Or with the chuckwagon (always driven as if wolves pursued it), that went ahead of the herd so the camp cook could have a meal ready and waiting for the tired cowhands at the end of the day. Or the *remuda*, the string of remounts every herd rider needed on the trail.

He saw none of those things, or even the tracks of their passage. But by midafternoon he saw the first corpses.

He'd followed the circling vultures to a waterhole heaped with the bloated bodies of cattle. More lay around it, their bodies black with flies and feeding birds. All the bodies he saw had been fed upon—by vultures and crows in the day, coyotes in the night—but they were still intact enough they could not have been dead for long.

There's a hundred head here at least, he estimated. *And this is roundup season. Mister Sutcliffe wouldn't have overlooked the absence of this many animals. He would have sent range riders in search of them. And when they found them ... they would never let a water source be fouled—or leave cattle dead of sickness unburned.*

Telling Deerfoot to stand, White Fox dismounted and walked slowly toward the corpses, flapping his hat to scare off the feeding birds. The vultures were too gorged to fly: they waddled away, shrieking imprecations at him. He searched until he found one of the bodies that was mostly intact and examined it quickly. He could not find any trace of a bullet wound.

And its neck had been broken.

It was the first such slaughter he found that day. It was not the last. By the time White Fox rode into Flatfield, he already suspected what he'd find there. He stopped at the gate to ring the iron bell, but no one came in answer. He rode on down to the outbuildings. Barns, corrals, bunkhouse . . . all empty.

He drew his pistol before entering the house itself. He'd circled it to come in through the back. That would be where any ambush was laid. But the kitchen was deserted, the pot of soup atop the stove congealed and half-evaporated, as if the household had been interrupted just before suppertime. He didn't find anyone in any of the common rooms, either. If not for Gibbons he wouldn't have known what signs to look for, nor found them as quickly. But as he went through the rooms a second time, searching them as carefully as he'd ever searched the ground for a trail, he saw more than he wished to.

The chimneys of the lamps are black with soot from a guttering flame. They have all burned dry. The logs in the fireplace are burnt to ash, and the ash has not been disturbed, yet every careful housewife saves ash for cleaning.

The keyboard on the spinet in the corner of the parlor was uncovered. No musician who treasured their instrument would leave its keys exposed to the dust of the plains.

In the library he saw two glasses half full of whiskey sitting on a table.

The bedrooms were prepared for bed, but no one had slept here.

When he returned to the pantry, he found the door to the root cellar open, and for a moment he dared to hope. But all that was there was a bible at the bottom of the ladder, open as if it had fallen. The cans and preserves, the bottles of whiskey and brandy that lined the shelves, stood untouched.

He searched for hours, until he realized he only

continued to search because he didn't want to admit Flatfield and all who'd lived here were another casualty of Shepherd's madness. The fact the house's furnishings lay undisturbed only meant its occupants had been lured—or *driven*—from it before they were killed.

But at last the red light of sunset warned him night was coming and he must seek shelter. He returned to the house one last time to collect some supplies: the still-full lamp he'd found in one of the bedrooms; salt and cornmeal from the untouched pantry; the humidor of cigars he'd seen in the study. The *wasichu* called what he meant to do "sorcery" and said it was wrong, but White Fox knew better. It was medicine for the spirit, just as herbs were medicine for the body. He didn't want to risk camping in the open—not with so many predators attracted by the slaughtered herd—and the house itself seemed too much like a place of ghosts.

He led Deerfoot into the stable and used the loop of braided leather she wore as a bridle to tether her to one of the center posts. He made certain she was settled, then closed the stable door and propped a full sack of feed against it. He couldn't bolt the door from within, but this would keep it from swinging open. When that was done, he took the meal and salt and walked around Deerfoot sunwise, drawing a wide circle of salt and cornmeal on the ground. Spirit medicine wasn't body medicine, but if the zombies returned, perhaps this would keep them from knowing he and Deerfoot were here. This was not Meshkwahkihaki medicine, but he dared to hope the medicine would answer his call, for in the long ago all the People had been one people.

Last of all he took apart several cigars to make four small piles of loose tobacco, one in each quarter of the circle. He lit one of the remaining cigars at the lamp flame, then used its coal to light the loose herb. The smoke was sweet, and the air was still. He watched the smoke stream upward for a moment before stubbing the cigar out, returning to the center of the circle, and dousing the lamp. The last light of day was visible through the cracks between the boards, but it fled swiftly. He sat quietly. The only sound was Deerfoot chewing the oats he had found for her. The only sight was the fading glow of burning tobacco.

With the leisure to think over what the day had brought him, White Fox realized he'd been counting more than he'd known on the possibility this journey would permit him to send word to the Tenth. Now— when it was too late—he realized he should have done so immediately upon their arrival in Alsop. Only he'd had nothing to report then, and by the time he did, the zombies had destroyed the telegraph office. His only alternative was a message rider, and he'd hoped to find one here. It wasn't that he'd expected help—Fort Riley was far away—but his report would have been a record of events that was beyond "Brother" Shepherd's reach.

There was nothing he could do about that now.

White Fox did not spend an easy night, but he spent a quiet one. When the dawn light shone through the gaps between the boards, he collected his belongings, swept the salt and meal away with a brief word of thanks, and rode for Alsop.

That morning Gibbons was so excited at the prospect of finally doing what she called "real research" she didn't even stop for breakfast before enlisting Jett to help her move the corpse from the jail to her makeshift laboratorium. It was too heavy to carry, so Jett rolled the body onto a blanket and the two of them dragged it up the street. In the daylight, the body looked even worse than it had in the cell. Its hands and face were battered and broken where it had tried to hammer its way from the cell, and its skin had a waxy grayish undertone, as if the body was slowly dissolving. On the other hand, it didn't smell quite as bad anymore, though that might have had as much to do with the half bottle of Florida Water Jett had poured over it as the removal of any curse.

"This—would be a lot—easier if we used—your horse!" Gibbons gasped as she stopped to rest.

"Nightingale's got more sense than both of us put together," Jett answered. "He wouldn't stop running till he hit the Rio Grande."

"Almost there," Gibbons said determinedly, grabbing her end of the blanket again.

It took them over an hour to cover the distance from the jail to the saloon, and when they got the body up the steps and onto the makeshift table White Fox had created from a door and two sawhorses, Jett collapsed into the nearest chair. *Couldn't have done that wearing a corset,* she thought. Now and then, her costume had real advantages.

"Now that you've got him, what are you going to do with him?" she asked warily, with the caution anyone would show who'd known Miss Honoria Gibbons of San Francisco more than a few hours.

"I'm going to take him apart and see how he ticks!" Gibbons answered happily.

Jett bolted to her feet as if she'd sat on a bee. "You—you *do* that," she said quickly. "I'll be—I'll be *around.*"

She made her escape before Gibbons could ask her to do anything else. Like *help.*

She'd seen a tin bathtub in the back of the barber shop. It took her far too many trips to the town pump to fill it with water, and it wasn't a hot bath, but she stripped to the skin and scrubbed herself until she'd scrubbed away the memory of having touched the cursed flesh that Gibbons was even now dismantling. By the time she emerged onto the street again, the Auto-Tachypode was back in front of the saloon. She'd heard the noise of it coming up the street, but by now that was a familiar sound. Jett could remember down to the day and hour the last time there'd been anything familiar in her life. It had been the night Court Oak burned.

I'm not going to think about that, she told herself firmly. *Not here, not now. Maybe not ever. I'll find Philip and . . . and maybe we'll go to California. Nobody cares who you used to be in California. I just have to find him first.*

To distract herself, she went down to the livery stable to check on Nightingale. He regarded her with disgust from the far end of the corral. He'd probably run out of the stable when Gibbons was moving her buggy.

"Don't look at me," Jett told him. "*I* didn't build it."

But she dragged a bale of hay out into the corral for him, then brought out a bucket of oats. The water trough here was dry, so then she had to go up to the town pump and carry more buckets of water until it was full. When she was done, she was as hot and sweaty as if she'd never had a bath at all. The water barrel at the back of the stable was closer—there were water barrels under every drain spout in town—but this late in the spring the water in them was stale and brackish. It would do for cleaning and bathing, but it wasn't something a body would drink if they had a choice.

She'd taken off her coat and her vest before she started carrying water. Now she dipped up a bucketful from the trough and poured it over her head. It was warmer than her bathwater had been, and made her linen shirt cling to every part of her, but there wasn't anyone here to see. When she set the bucket down, Nightingale walked up to her and began nudging her in the chest. He knew buckets meant baths, and he always thought it was hilarious to knock her flat in the dust when she was soaking wet.

She was laughing, threatening to lock him in the barn and sell the barn, when she heard Gibbons cry out and heard the sound of breaking glass.

She was wrong—I was wrong—the salt didn't kill it, it just made it get up in the daytime! Jett thought wildly as she ran toward the saloon. She'd reached the Auto-Tachypode when she smelled a foul odor. Not like zombie. Like burning hair and vinegar.

"Gibbons!" she shouted. There was no answer, and sucking in a lungful of that stink made her start to cough. She hauled her shirt out of her pants and dragged it off. Her neckerchief was in her coat, and her coat wasn't here. This would have to do. She held it over her face as she ran into the saloon.

The zombie was still where she'd left it, and now the bar was covered with jars and copper tubing. The contraption looked a little like a still at Court Oak she'd never been supposed to know anything about, and a lot like nothing she'd ever seen before.

And Gibbons was lying on the floor in front of it, unconscious.

"Dammit!" Jett's eyes were watering as if the room were filled with smoke. Even breathing through the wet muslin, her throat burned and she desperately wanted to cough. This was no time to stand around and ask what was going on. She ran across the floor to Gibbons, then wrapped a fist in Gibbons's collar and pulled. The twill fabric was sturdy. It held. And Gibbons didn't weigh quite as much as the late Finlay Maxwell had.

Jett hauled the unconscious Gibbons outside, but she didn't stop there—the air outside the saloon was nearly as foul as the air inside it. She felt sick and dizzy, but she dragged Gibbons along the street until dark spots danced in front of her eyes, then dropped her and clung to one of the newel posts, gasping for air. It didn't help much. The dizziness wasn't fading. Jett sat down on the edge of the sidewalk and leaned back against the rail, gasping for breath.

I learned how to pretend-swoon before I was fourteen, she thought, *years before I ever fainted for real, because Tante Mère said men liked delicate females. I don't think they'd like 'em near so much if they knew what it's really like.* She pressed the cold of her damp shirt against her face and neck for a moment, then struggled back into it. *Can't leave her lying out in the sun like that,* she thought tiredly, and went to pull Gibbons into the small shade of the sidewalk.

Gibbons began to stir even while Jett was moving her. She sat up weakly and began to cough.

"You just stay where you are," Jett said, but Gibbons had already dragged herself to her feet using the hitching rail, then staggered to the sidewalk steps to sit. Her hair had come partway out of its neat bun, and was a halo of gold-touched fire around her flushed face. Jett repressed an automatic twinge of envy. If she'd had Gibbons's looks, she would have had all the boys in Orleans Parish coming around.

In a time that was over. In a place that was gone. *I've thought more about home this week than I have in the past two years!* she thought angrily. *What's wrong with me?*

"What happened?" she demanded. "What were you doing in there?"

"Nothing!" Gibbons protested automatically. "Nothing that should have caused . . . what *did* happen?"

"Durned if I know," Jett answered. "I heard you

196

yelp and something broke. I came running. Whatever it was, it sure stinks."

"I was distilling some of the whiskey from the saloon," Gibbons said. She coughed again, experimentally, and then began taking her hair down to put it up again. "I'd brought the spirit lamps in from my wagon. They burn alcohol, not kerosene. They're a lot brighter, and I wanted plenty of light to autopsy Mister Maxwell. But I was running low on fuel for them."

"Whiskey's already alcohol," Jett pointed out.

"It isn't *pure* alcohol," Gibbons said. "That's why I was distilling it." She pulled herself to her feet, clinging to the post for support. "I need to find out what was in that whiskey."

"You just hold your horses," Jett said. " Let me get some air through there first. I'm not hauling you out of there twice."

She got to her feet, determined not to show a single sign of weakness Gibbons could use as an excuse to go with her, and walked down the street to the nearest alley. The buildings in Alsop hadn't all been built at the same time, and most of them didn't share a common wall. A fire could sweep through the wood buildings of an entire town in hours, and there was little way to stop its spread except by wetting down the wood of the adjoining buildings.

Jett hated fire.

She found the back door of the saloon and pulled it open, kicking a rock into place to serve as a doorstop. From the marks on the wood, the rock had served this purpose before. She could see straight through the building to the street. The saloon had double doors that could be closed behind the batwing doors in the unlikely event the saloon was ever closed for business. It was just as well Gibbons hadn't shut them. *Or tacked a blanket over that window I broke*, Jett thought. Those things had probably saved her life.

She got back to the street just in time to intercept Gibbons.

"Oh no you don't," she said firmly, taking Gibbons by the arm. "This dangfool *science* of yours can wait half an hour or so."

She hustled Gibbons over to the bench in front of the General Merchandise and pulled out her watch. When Gibbons started to get up again, Jett took off her Stetson and walloped her with it.

"For heaven's sake!" Gibbons said huffily.

"Yeah, you could have taken it up with the angels if I hadn't been here," Jett said. "I have no notion how you managed to live this long without a nursemaid, I swear."

"I am not a child, you know!" Gibbons said.

"Nope," Jett said agreeably. "Just an idiot."

Gibbons folded her arms across her chest and glared.

If one thing headed the list of things Gibbons truly abominated, it was the notion of being managed and minded and nursemaided. Those persons who appointed themselves to such a role usually did so as a first step to unleashing a long list of proscriptions, and Gibbons's entire life had been spent in a systematic overthrow of such things. Ladies did not wear Rational Dress. Ladies did not engage in intellectual pursuits. Ladies did not *invent* things. Ladies did not go anywhere without a suitable—meaning *male*—escort.

There were times Gibbons wondered whether her life would have been different if her mother had survived her birth. Jacob Saltinstall Gibbons had shattered convention—and earned the undying loathing of his Boston family—by marrying one of his servants. And not even his housekeeper, which the Gibbons family would not have approved of *either*, but at least he would have been marrying an upper servant, but one of his Irish housemaids. That marriage had been the true reason his family had banished Jacob Gibbons to Chicago, but Mary Gibbons—née Maire Caithleen

Donovan of County Cork, Ireland—had not lived to see her second wedding anniversary.

Perhaps Gibbons's mother had been as much an unconventional freethinker as her father was. Perhaps the three of them would have lived an ideal, if eccentric, life together. There was no way to know. Gibbons was merely thankful that her father—instead of returning to Boston to hand his child over to one of his female relatives to raise—had engaged a nurse and gone west.

Gibbons's childhood had been a happy one, spent doing essentially as she pleased, for though her father should have, by convention, hired a governess to succeed the nurse, he never had. Gibbons suspected it had simply slipped his mind. But if there'd been no governess standing over her to tell her what a "lady" ought to do and not do, there'd been plenty of other women eager to prove their worthiness to become the second Mrs. Gibbons by standing as moral preceptor to his daughter. Mister Gibbons had never noticed their overtures, and they'd only annoyed their target.

By rights, Jett's fussing should have irritated Gibbons as much as every other female's had. No matter how good Jett's masquerade was, Gibbons could see that was what it was: an act. Jett Gallatin might live as a man, but she was no more an emancipated modern woman than any simpering corset-wearing creature whose only ambition was to marry a man—*any* man!—and raise his children.

On the other hand . . .

Jett might be as ignorant as a troglodyte and utterly unemancipated, but she'd never once demanded Gibbons stop doing something on the grounds of her gender. It was true, Gibbons reflected, that Jett called her an idiot at least once a day and had no interest in learning anything Gibbons strove to teach her, but Gibbons suspected Jett treated *everyone* that way. In fact . . . in fact, if Gibbons had been a young man and Jett had found her—him—unconscious on the floor, Jett probably would have called him a fool and an idiot and walloped him with her hat. *I only wish she were more interested in the life of the mind!* Gibbons thought with a flash of irritation. *It would be nice to be able to talk with someone who was not constantly lecturing me on my unfeminine behavior.* Her father, of course, barely noticed she was a girl. But to say Jacob Gibbons was unworldly was to understate the case. And even dear Doctor Gordon had occasionally hinted gently that the freedom Gibbons enjoyed might not be . . . entirely suitable.

"Time's up," Jett said, closing her watch and getting to her feet. "Let's go see what tried to kill you *this* time."

Jett entered the saloon warily—*really, must she* prowl *everywhere?*—insisting Gibbons stay behind her. *As if some odd chemical reaction is something she can shoot!* But once Jett had satisfied herself there was nothing here that was going to pounce on her, she excused herself and left Gibbons alone in the saloon.

There was still a faint acrid odor hanging in the air. Since the only thing Gibbons had been doing had been distilling whiskey, the source must be the whiskey. But she'd performed the same distillation hundreds of times with no ill effects. So this whiskey must be different.

She just had to find out how.

She'd unpacked most of her equipment from the Auto-Tachypode already. She removed her microscope from its padded wooden case. It was only the work of minutes to fill a pair of her spirit lamps with the last of the pure (and safe) distillate and prepare a slide.

Nothing.

She took samples from the body of the zombie—hair, tissue, saliva, blood—and examined them beneath her lens.

Still nothing.

She returned to the whiskey and performed a flame reduction test. All that did was tell her there was *something* in it, for it released the same acrid scent as before, though in a much smaller quantity. Gibbons spared a moment's wistful longing for her laboratory in the basement of the Russian Hill townhouse—she would have liked to be able to administer this whiskey to one of her laboratory rats to see if it, too, would return from the dead. At least she had a lot of tainted whiskey, because the next step was to attempt to separate the contaminants from the whiskey for further analysis.

"I have it," she breathed in triumph. She'd nearly despaired as method after method had failed to yield the facts she sought. But she'd persevered. And gained victory.

"There's coffee," Jett said. "I made up some food, too. A couple of hours ago."

"I know how he's making the zombies," Gibbons said, turning around.

Jett was sitting at one of the two tables near the door. There was a deck of cards spread out on the table beside a coffee mug. On the other table was an enamel-ware coffeepot, a cookpot, a plate covered with a cloth, and a clean place setting. Jett had obviously returned to the saloon and been here for some time. The wonder wasn't that Gibbons hadn't noticed—she could be entirely single-minded in pursuit of a mystery—but that Jett's presence hadn't distracted her.

"It's probably cold by now," Jett added.

"Don't you care about what I've found?" Gibbons demanded, delight fading into her usual irritation with Jett's obtuseness.

"Sure I do. But in case you haven't noticed, the sun's about to set, so I don't guess anyone's riding out to Jerusalem's Wall right now. And you haven't eaten a thing since yesterday."

"I ate . . . breakfast?" Gibbons said doubtfully.

"Yesterday, maybe. I can put it back on the fire if—"

"No, this is fine," Gibbons said, abruptly aware of her growling stomach. She walked over to the table and sat down. Jett restacked the deck with a quick economical motion and joined her.

Gibbons filled her bowl with beans and bacon and poured herself a cup of coffee. She added a generous splash of milk, stirred, and sipped it. It was tepid (and boiled, since the arcanum of the percolator was apparently beyond Jett), but coffee was coffee. She uncovered the plate of tortillas, scooped some of the beans into one, and talked as she ate.

"I'm certain you have little interest in how I arrived at my conclusions, but I assure you they're correct. All the whiskey here has—I believe—been adulterated. It was those contaminants that turned Finlay Maxwell into a revenant—though I suspect they weren't what killed him."

"He fell over dead!" Jett protested. "We all saw him! Or heard him at least."

Gibbons shook her head. "I don't think so. When he left the jail—the morning you and White Fox went to Jerusalem's Wall—he came straight here and started drinking."

"Wouldn't've been anyone to stop him," Jett agreed, frowning.

"Exactly! And as a confirmed drunkard, his body was sufficiently adapted to the use of alcohol for him to remain conscious long enough to drink himself— literally—to death. It's possible to drink enough alcohol that one stops breathing, you know," she added, since Jett was still looking puzzled. "The effects are similar to a fatal overdose of laudanum."

"I guess I just don't know the right people," Jett commented dryly. "All I ever heard tell of was someone getting outside of enough whiskey to pass out."

"I admit it could be an expensive matter to drink yourself to death *quickly*," Gibbons agreed, "and a dipsomaniac rarely has unrestricted access to liquor, since they are usually impoverished as well. But that is beside the point! Imagine it, if you will. Maxwell, for the first time in his life, had all the liquor he could pour down his throat. So he did just that. Perhaps he drank as much from fear of what he had seen—perhaps because once he realized that no one could stop him, it was the first and only thing he wanted to do. Maxwell drank enough to poison himself to death—and rose from the dead because of what *else* was in those bottles. The first component I isolated was datura—you may know it as Jimsonweed—but while I am well aware illicit whiskey is sometimes adulterated with Jimsonweed to increase its effect—since datura can cause hallucinations and a number of other symptoms—it cannot cause an individual to rise from the dead. But then I also discovered the presence of *maculotoxin*!"

"'Defiling poison'?" Jett said, stumbling through the Latin credibly well, much to Gibbons's surprise.

"In layman's terms, puffer fish toxin," Gibbons said. "The puffer fish is a species of fish found only in tropical waters. In China and Japan they are considered a great delicacy, even though many parts of the fish are poisonous." She paused, brooding. "I do not think these two compounds can wholly account for . . . *zombification* . . . but I cannot discover what else may be present with the limited equipment I have."

Gibbons sighed as Jett directed a speaking glance toward the interior of the saloon, not even bothering with her anticipated gibe about "poisonous." It probably looked to her as if there was plenty of equipment here. Gibbons thought mournfully of her stock of reagents and catalysts, her rotary centrifuge, her *good* microscope. With the contents of her lab, she could have discovered every foreign element introduced into the whiskey.

"I guess we've got enough zombies that we don't need to make any more," Jett said at last. "Can we bury Mister Maxwell now?"

"I still need to find out why salt cured—or killed—him!" Gibbons protested. "Now that we know Brother Shepherd is drugging his targets with something that allows him to turn them into zombies once they die!"

"Look here," Jett said, her voice quiet and serious. "In case you haven't noticed, there isn't any ice within five hundred miles. That body is already going green. Another day in this heat and it's going to turn black and bust open. It's going to stink, it's going to attract vultures, and for all I know, it'll make us sick. I don't know what you're looking to find, but we need to get him into the ground."

Gibbons wanted to protest. But this wasn't civilization. In a city she would have been able to buy a dozen five-pound blocks of ice at high summer, let alone in April—enough ice to refrigerate a specimen until she was finished with it. Here on the frontier, an autopsy was a race against time—and she'd lost too much time already.

"I suppose you're right," she said reluctantly.

"There's a buckboard in the stables. You think your buggy can pull it as far as Reverend Southey's place?"

"I think so, yes," Gibbons said.

"Good," Jett said, nodding. "We've got just about enough daylight to get Mister Maxwell out there. I can put him in their stable for overnight. Tomorrow I'll dig him a hole while you figure out how Br'er Shepherd got his hoodoo juice into the whiskey."

Jett saddled Nightingale and used him to drag the buckboard from the livery stable to the saloon. The buckboard slewed maddeningly at the end of the rope, but taking it to the saloon was still easier than dragging the corpse the length of Alsop one more time. She hadn't been joking when she told Gibbons Nightingale wasn't a cart horse, but at least he was used to towing something tied to his saddle horn.

Since it had been made from a regular wagon the Auto-Tachypode had the usual iron staple bolted to the back of the carriage for hitching a drag team to. A wagon brake could stop the front wheels from turning when a wagon was descending a steep grade, but sometimes that wasn't enough to keep the wagon from either overrunning its hitch—or plunging over the side of whatever mountain it was trying to descend. It wasn't easy to rig the buckboard to that (Gibbons had to lower the steps so they could prop the buckboard's tongue on them), but it was possible. And between the two of them, they were able to drag the rotting corpse of Finlay Maxwell into the buckboard's bed.

For a moment Jett thought Gibbons had overstated her machine's capacity, but after a long moment when the Auto-Tachypode seemed to strain at the burden like a hitch of mules at plowing time, it began to roll forward, pulling the buckboard behind.

Jett rode on ahead to make sure there was space in the stable. The only thing in it was a battered old shay the parson—or his wife—had probably used for running errands. When Gibbons arrived, she turned the Auto-Tachypode to line both it and the buck-board up with the stable door, then backed the Auto-Tachypode until the buckboard was maneuvered neatly inside.

"You'll make a cutting horse out of that thing yet," Jett said. She waved Gibbons away as she came to cut the rope. A good piece of rope was a rare commodity out here. Jett wasn't a cowhand by any stretch—she knew she couldn't maintain her disguise if she didn't keep moving, just to start with—but she'd picked up their superstitious aversion to cutting a rope. A cut rope was bad luck. You burned it if you could, the same way you burned—or buried, or both—a rope that was worn out. She finally got it unknotted and coiled it up care-fully, then hung it over Nightingale's saddle horn.

Gibbons came back into the stable just as she

finished. "I found this in the church," she said, offering Jett a spade.

Jett took it. "Let's go see where we're going to plant him," she said.

White Fox rode up just as Jett was marking out the grave she'd have to dig tomorrow. She was about to ask him how his trip to Flatfield had gone when she saw his face.

She'd heard plenty of things about Indians long before she ever saw one. People called them "fierce, bloodthirsty, heathen savages," and that would have disturbed her more if she hadn't known Yankees called Southerners the same things. She'd heard plenty of talk about "murdering rebs" after Beast Butler and his gang of crooks took New Orleans—seen plenty of deeds from them, too. So she'd reckoned the Indians would be pretty much like folks anywhere: some might try to kill you, some might ignore you, and some would go out of their way to help you. She'd met all three kinds since she'd left home, but the one thing that was mostly the same about all of them was how they didn't wear what they were thinking on their faces for the world to see. (A preacher she'd traveled with once called it "savage inscrutability"; Jett just thought of it as good manners.) She knew White Fox was Meshkwahkihaki in all but body, so she'd never worried about not being able to tell what he was thinking.

The fact she could tell now scared her.

Gibbons was rattling on about all her discoveries—leaving out the part where she dang near killed herself—and talking about what she still needed to find out (Jett suspected Gibbons would be making the same speech on her deathbed). Jett just waited, watching White Fox's face.

"So what did Mister Sutcliffe tell you?" Gibbons finally asked. "Have there been any disappearances that he knows of? Were you able to send a message to Fort Riley?"

"No," White Fox said. "There was no one there to ask."

"They were all dead," Jett said. She tried not to show how much the news shook her.

White Fox nodded once. "So I believe. The house was deserted, as if its inhabitants had simply walked away. But there is more to tell."

Jett stuck the spade into the center of the shallow rectangle of earth she'd marked out. She pushed it down with her boot. The blade sank into the earth grudgingly, but it went. At least the clay wasn't baked too hard to dig. She left the spade where it stood.

"Tell it back in town," she said. "Sun's going down."

In the boardinghouse kitchen, Gibbons made biscuits to go with their meal as White Fox told the rest of his tale. The room was warm, both from the wood in the firebox below the oven and from the dozen lanterns they'd lit and placed on every available flat surface. Jett had stopped being afraid of the dark a long time ago—but that had been before she knew what it might contain.

"But why would Shepherd want to kill an entire herd of cattle?" Gibbons said. "They're worth money. And someone would be sure to see all those bodies."

"In another month—perhaps less—they will be nothing more than bleached bones scattered among the scrub," White Fox said bleakly.

"He had to kill them," Jett said thoughtfully. "Beeves'll wander halfway to the moon if you let 'em, and they'd be sure to get caught up in some roundup or other. The mavericks wouldn't be so much of a problem, but most folks in these parts respect a brand. They might ride over to the Running D to find out why Sutcliff hadn't cut his beeves out of their herd. And they wouldn't much like what they found."

"The transcontinental railroad—whatever route it takes—won't be finished for another two years," White Fox said. "Shepherd won't want to attract attention to his scouring of Texas before he's ready to claim ownership of the land."

"That makes sense," Gibbons said, nodding. She dumped her ball of dough onto the cutting board and began to roll it out. "And we have at least some idea of how the zombies are created, though we're obviously missing some of the steps. But how does the preparation get into the liquor?"

"Easiest thing in the world," Jett said. "Or do you think every saloon in the Territories gets cases of whiskey in glass bottles shipped by Overland Express?"

"I suppose not," Gibbons said thoughtfully. "Though it could come by train as far as Abilene."

"And in Abilene there's a freight yard, and every box and barrel comes with a bill of lading," Jett said. "All Br'er Shepherd needs is an accomplice somewhere along the way to lever open a few kegs and dose them. The kegs come off the stage in Alsop, get shipped in the same load as any empty bottle the barkeep might have ordered, he fills his empty bottles from the keg, and . . ." She shrugged. "Shepherd could get the surrounding ranches—and the teetotalers—the same way. Pickles come in barrels. So does vinegar."

"Or kerosene," White Fox said.

Both Jett and Gibbons froze, looking around the room at the lamps. Then Gibbons shrugged. "Too late to do anything about that—if his formula survives burning as well as distillation, we've all been exposed."

Jett sighed. "We know how he makes 'em. We know

what he's doing with them. And we know how to kill them. So what are we still waiting for?"

"Salt worked on Finlay Maxwell," Gibbons said, picking up a knife and beginning to slice the biscuit dough into squares. "But I don't know precisely why. Maxwell died of natural causes, so he isn't a typical case—maybe that's the only reason the salt worked. And that means I can't be sure of killing the rest of Brother Shepherd's zombies. I need *exact* details of how they're made."

"There's only one place that information can be found," White Fox said into the silence.

"Somebody has to go back to Jerusalem's Wall," Jett said.

"And preferably before Shepherd destroys another town," Gibbons added.

CHAPTER SEVEN

Jett slid down off Nightingale's back and sat down on a rock to remove her boots and the trousers she was wearing under her petticoats. She'd liberated a pair of overall trousers from the Merchandise, since it was better than riding halfway across Texas showing her bare legs to the world.

It felt strange after all this time to be wearing skirts and a bonnet, strange to be laced into the short canvas undershirt that was the frontier replacement for the boned corset. She'd just been lucky Mrs. Southey was near her height and build—they'd had to hunt all over town to find a pair of shoes that fit.

She got to her feet, staggering a little at the unfamiliar weight of petticoats, and walked over to Nightingale. Boots and trousers went into his saddlebag, shoes came out. Her Colts were in the other saddlebag. She felt more naked without their familiar weight than she'd expected to, but they'd look pretty odd with a calico frock. When she put the shoes on—the sturdy, ugly, lace-up kind you could walk for miles in—she suppressed a pang of unease. Tante Mère had always said wearing dead folks' shoes meant you'd be the next to be buried. Tante Mère had been right about a lot of things. Jett only hoped she hadn't been right about this.

Jett hadn't wanted to be the one to do this. But White Fox didn't move or act like a white, and Gibbons was . . . eccentric. It had to be her. It was too bad she'd already been to Jerusalem's Wall, but that had been as Jett. Few people seeing her dressed like this would make a connection between her and the black-clad outlaw who'd left so hastily. But she was hoping to get in and out before anyone saw her at all. She already knew Brother Shepherd didn't pay a lot of attention to the womenfolk in his holiness commune. Maybe that would work in her favor.

"You just wait right here," she told Nightingale. She'd ridden him to the stand of pines she'd stopped at before. It was the closest cover there was. "I'll be back in an hour or two." *I hope.*

Nightingale nodded his head enthusiastically. She'd whiled away a lot of time teaching him tricks, and now he showed them off whenever he wanted a treat.

"Sorry, fella," Jett said. "I'll find you something when we get back."

In answer, he nosed at her bonnet. It was tied on, but he managed to shove it cockeyed. She stepped out of his reach to re-tie the strings. At least—if it came down to bluffing—the length of her hair wouldn't be remarked upon. Most pioneer women cut their hair when insects made it a torment and alkali dust made it brittle as straw. And cutting hair was a sure way to break a fever.

You're stalling, she scolded herself. *Well begun is half-done.*

"I'll be back soon," she said again. "Wait for me."

She squared her shoulders and walked resolutely away.

Gibbons watched with barely suppressed misgiving as Jett rode away, clad in a dress and other articles of clothing that the former female inhabitants of Alsop were certainly never going to need again. She didn't like this, not one bit. If she had learned nothing else from her own adventures, it was the maxim *never divide the group.* On the occasions when she considered that she needed assistance, she hired it, and then made certain that no one went haring off on his own. Or, as one grizzled old, mostly drunk (yet still amazingly competent) gunslinger had said, "There are old shootists, and there are bold shootists, but there are no old bold shootists."

But that was another story . . . and in this case, Jett had been absolutely right. The only way to get a good look at that place was for a female to slip in and slip out. And the only one of the pair of them that could do this without giving herself away was Jett. Jett was used to playacting a part. Gibbons was . . . in this case, unfortunately . . . nearly incapable of prevarication. Let one of the Fellowship out there catch her unawares, and she would very probably speak before she thought and betray herself as no kind of believer.

That did not mean that she *liked* this.

Squaring her shoulders and turning her back on the disappearing speck, she headed for her makeshift laboratory.

It would be very nice if I managed to solve this conundrum, and we could go charging after Jett armed to the teeth with exactly what we need to put down an army of walking dead.

Pigs will probably learn to sing like larks first, but it would be nice.

It seemed to Jett she had to unlearn and relearn everything she'd ever known on that walk into Jerusalem's Wall. She strode instead of walked, flat-heeled shoes felt clumsy and strange, and her skirts whipped and tangled around her legs. The dress felt too narrow across the shoulders, though it hardly fit as closely as the demure glove-tight bodices she'd once worn without thought. The corset chafed. The bonnet cut off her vision on both sides. But when she found herself wondering if she'd *ever* be comfortable in female clothing again, it made her smile ruefully. *Reckon I could be dead by sundown, so there's no use fretting about it.*

Just as she'd hoped, the "dooryard" was deserted. It was why she'd left Alsop before dawn; she suspected everyone was somewhere else, at least until the dinner bell rang at noon. *I'll be gone by then*, she told herself hopefully.

She cut back behind one of the new bunkhouses—a dormitory, probably, considering how many people lived here—and followed White Fox's careful instructions until she reached the old bunkhouse. The one with no bunks and a door in the floor it shouldn't rightly have. The one that had to hold secrets, because who locked a door that didn't have anything behind it?

Her heart beat fast and her palms were wet as she walked up to its door. She'd stood in the middle of a street facing down a man who wanted her dead with more calm. But that had been different. Whoever died there wouldn't have gotten up and walked away.

She took one last glance around herself and lifted down the bar. It was new; the wood had darkened to brown but not yet faded to silver. Who put a bar on the outside of a door? What was Brother Shepherd keeping *in*?

She felt better once she had the door shut behind her. At least she was out of sight, even though with the windows boarded up it was just about pitch-dark in here. A little light came in through the chinks between the boards, but not enough to see by. She groped among her petticoats until she found the pouch she'd tied around her waist.

Wellborn young ladies had servants to escort them and carry their things, butlers to open their doors, family names respected enough that they could shop on account. Ladies who had none of those things carried reticules to hold their money, their keys, and—sometimes—their gun. And because they had no one to protect them, they carried their reticules tied to their petticoat strings, with a slit pocket in their skirts to reach them.

She hauled her skirt up enough to take the weight off the pouch's drawstrings, then groped around inside it until she found the candle and one of the Lucifer matches. Gibbons was the one who'd thought of them. When they were planning this, it had slipped Jett's mind that a shed with no windows would be pitch-dark even in the daytime.

She struck the match on the door and lit the candle. The bunkhouse smelled familiar. The smells of sweat, horse, tobacco, and wood-smoke were soaked deep into the wood, but they were all that was familiar. Just as White Fox had said, all the furniture was gone.

The doors in the floor looked like the entrance to a storm cellar. She'd seen one, once, when she and Philip had been sent east during yellowjack season. Its iron handles were bolted into the wood. A chain ran between them, secured in place with a lock. She walked over and knelt down in front of it, swearing softly under her breath at having to pull her skirts out of the way. She swore a little louder when she got a good look at it, and brought her candle close to make sure. White Fox was the only one who'd seen the lock, and that only very briefly. It wasn't the usual "smokehouse" type— easy enough to get past—but one of the newfangled "heart" locks, the kind the railroads used. Supposed to be burglar-proof.

He should have said something! she thought. The shape was distinctive, and so was the spring plate over the keyhole. But somehow she doubted an Army Scout spent much time trying to force padlocks. He probably thought the shape was just for decoration. *But I've got the key.*

I hope.

Gibbons had given her a selection of keys she'd found around the town. Maybe this was Jett's lucky day. She spilled a little wax and stuck the candle against the floor, then poured the contents of her reticule into her lap. Some of the keys wouldn't go into the lock at all. Others would fit the keyhole, but wouldn't turn. Jett sighed in exasperation once she'd tried the last one. *If I didn't have bad luck, I wouldn't have any luck at all.*

Gibbons had given—loaned—her something to use if the keys didn't work. She took a deep breath and unscrewed the little wooden case. Two heavy pieces of wire dropped out. *I guess we're going to see just how "unpickable" this lock really is.* She'd picked a few locks in her time, but ones where a hairpin would do the trick. Jewelry boxes and medicine chests—there'd been a hundred different locks at Court Oak.

The silver chest in the pantry, Mama and Tante Mère shrieking in anger and fear as the Union soldier threw it to the ground and scooped the utensils out of the wreckage. . . .

She spent five minutes of poking and twisting at the hidden interior of the padlock. Each time she got started, the lockplate sprang back to jar the picks from her hands. Finally she gave up. The folks who'd made this lock weren't bragging. The only way she was getting it open was with the key.

Where was it?

Not here. There's nothing here but dust, doors, and a lock and chain.

Shepherd must have it. If he carried it on him she was sunk, but the key for this lock wasn't small. He might keep it in his bedroom. Or his study. She was pretty sure he had a study where he could go to be alone, because she didn't think he wanted to spend all his time being holy for his faithful followers. And he wouldn't want to come out here to a hole in the ground every time he wanted to take a holiday from being the Fellowship's "Blessed Founder." If everyone else slept in the dormitories, there'd be plenty of room inside the house.

She tucked the lockpicks back into their tube, and the tube and the keys into her reticule, picked up the candle, and got to her feet. *I can still be on my way before dinnertime.* She wanted to believe that. But thinking it was too much like whistling past the graveyard.

Gibbons tried not to watch the clock as she paced up and down the wooden floor of her laboratorium. She only succeeded part of the time. When the last of her distillations brought her no closer to the answer she was looking for, she was forced to return to her mental resources.

The problem was, it was very difficult to concentrate when she kept picturing Jett getting into trouble. What if none of the keys fit the lock? What if Jett couldn't manage the lockpicks? Gibbons had learned the trade from an expert house-invader; picking a truly professional lock took more than a little expertise with a hairpin. What would she do then?

White Fox watched her pace. She noticed he stirred once or twice, as if to say something to her, then subsided again. He probably knew very well that nothing he could say would change her internal agitation, and having been trained in patience by Natives, he knew better than to flog *that* particular dead horse.

That's a lesson most white men could stand to learn, she thought, then added, with some wry irony, *including me.*

Front door or back? That was an easy one. Sister Agatha had come to the front door only because Jett had rung the bell, and she'd seen for herself the women weren't encouraged to stray from their drudgery. She eased the door open. The house was quieter than a church on Monday. She pushed her bonnet back off her hair as she called up a picture in her mind of all the rooms she'd been in the last time she was here, and turned left at the parlor instead of right.

She opened each door cautiously as she came to it. A couple of the rooms were bare to the walls; one of them had been the library, but the bookshelves were empty. A couple were still being used as bedrooms— the ones with boarded-over windows. All that was in those was a narrow iron bed and a couple of clothes pegs on the wall. By now, Jett knew, she would have been shaking like she had a fever if she hadn't spent month after month training herself out of it. A doctor might practice his profession with shaking hands. A gambler and gunslinger couldn't.

She realized she'd found what she was looking for the moment her feet touched carpet instead of tile. None of the floors so far had been carpeted, but most ranchos had carpet everywhere—Turkey carpets from back East for the wealthy, rag rugs or Navajo blankets for the regular folks. She didn't know which Lamar Chapman had had back when Jerusalem's Wall had been the Lazy J, but the runner under her feet was as lush and thick, patterned with the same intricate weaving of shapes and flowers as the one she'd once had in her bedroom. Back when she was a girl. She clapped her hand over her mouth to stifle her panicked giggling. She was a girl *now*.

Again.

There were two doors with carpet in front of them. She opened the first and slipped inside. Bedroom, and obviously Brother Shepherd's bedroom. It had a door that led through to the room next to it. She knew the bedroom was near the end of this wing. The room next door was probably his as well. Jett wondered how many of his "fellowship" had ever seen these rooms— and if they had, how they explained it to themselves. It had a thick Turkey carpet on the floor, and a cherry tester-bed plumped up high enough under its velvet cover she was willing to bet it contained a featherbed or two. There were night tables on both sides of the bed, carved with garlands and flowers to match the bedframe and set with gilded knobs, and there was a highboy bureau, too. The windows were hung with heavy velvet curtains—pushed back—and the washing table with its inset bowl and china pitcher matched the bed. The shaving set beside the bowl—mug and brush and straight razor—were ivory and silver gilt and fine porcelain. There was an oval mirror hung on the wall above it, too, the first mirror she'd seen any-where at Jerusalem's Wall. *Someone here* must *know about this*, Jett thought. *I'm going to bet Br'er Shepherd don't fetch his own wash-water of a morning.*

She searched the room quickly, but all she found was that Brother Shepherd had a taste for fine things—and probably as much clothing as the entire rest of the fellowship put together. Soft flannel night shirts, and woolen ones; fine linen shirts and a taste for good whiskey, because there was a bottle and a glass in the bottom drawer beside the big gilt-paper box of chocolates.

She didn't notice her fear giving way to anger until she had to stop herself from picking up the whiskey bottle and slamming it against the wall. She'd been afraid when the zombies had attacked Alsop. She'd been scared both times she'd come to Jerusalem's Wall. But now . . . ?

One Sunday after Mass, Philip had told her Catho-lics were raised on sin, and unfortunately for Philip, their brother Charlie heard him. Charlie went straight to Papa and ratted him out and Philip had to eat his meals standing up for a few days. Philip had said he was sorry, but he'd never said it wasn't true. Then the War came, and Jett had always tried to keep the Commandments in her heart even after she knew she'd broken pretty near all of them. It had been an actual heathen—the first Jew she'd ever met, and she'd thought they were all bible people and not real—who told her there was really only one Commandment for everybody. *Don't lie.* There was lying with words, and lying with deeds, and lying with thoughts, and out of all of them, Jett had decided that telling folks one thing and doing another was probably the worst. It was *hypocrisy*, and even the Greeks about a thousand years ago had a word for it (they were pagans, not heathens, so she guessed the difference was whether you were dead or not). Black heart and Sunday manners, Tante Mère had called it. Jett couldn't think of anything worse.

That was what Brother Shepherd was. Bad enough he was raising the dead and killing everyone for hundreds of miles around. She thought she could have maybe understood if he'd really thought he'd been Called to do it. But he preached about giving up worldly things and pretended he was too holy to even eat, and all along he slept in silk and velvet and gorged himself in secret. She would have walked out of his bedroom right this minute and called him out except for what Gibbons had said. If they didn't figure out how he was making zombies—and made sure nobody else could get their hands on that recipe—they'd just be leaving a stack of gunpowder kegs around and waiting for someone to walk by and light the fuse.

She opened the door that led to the next room. The moment she stepped through it she was sure the key was here, because it had to be here if it was anywhere. The room was at least twice the size of the bedroom, and twice as fancy, too. It had a couple of carpets on the floor, and more heavy velvet draperies at the windows pulled back to show off the curtains underneath, so she could see the windows were more of those French doors. There were paintings with big gilt frames on the whitewashed walls, and glass-fronted bookcases under them, and a desk almost as big as the bed in the other room, carved all over except for the top. On the wall behind the desk there were about half a dozen crosses, and every last one of them looked as if it belonged in a church. The sight of them made Jett a little queasy. She couldn't imagine anyone bad enough or crazy enough to loot a church, whether it was a real church or just a Protestant one.

The air smelled of dust and books, and there was a faint sweet scent beneath both. Incense. It made her more nervous than before, as if this room really was the holy place it worked so hard to resemble. She hesitated for a long moment, unable to step into that room. She told herself this was her best chance at the key, that if she *didn't* find it she'd light out of here and not stop until she was back in Alsop. Maybe Gibbons could think of something else.

Only Jett knew Gibbons couldn't, and that was what made her walk to the desk.

It had all the usual things on it—gilt writing set, humidor full up with good cigars, a couple of crystal paperweights, a lamp that was glass and brass instead of plain tin. There was a little silver box containing mysterious tarry black balls that smelled sick-sweet, and a bigger porcelain one that was full of incense.

The drawers were locked, and she was just reaching for Gibbons's lock picks again when she heard the knob on the hallway door rattle and saw it begin to turn.

Jett moved instantly. Bad enough to be caught in here. Worse to look as if she'd been trying to steal something. She got herself around to the front side of the desk and had her hands clasped in front of her by the time the door opened. It wasn't Brother Shepherd.

"What are you doing in here?" the woman asked sharply.

She was dressed in the same kind of shapeless faded calico dress Jett had seen on Sister Agatha. Her hair was gray, her apron was dingy—not dirty, but not white—and her skin had a gray tinge to it, as if her life was so hard even the wrinkles in her face weren't enough to tell about it.

"I'm sorry, I'm sorry!" *You've got about ten seconds to*

come up with a real good lie, a cold calm voice inside her said. "I heard— I heard tell there was a preacherman here, and I—I got me a bad need, ma'am!"

This wasn't her voice, not her words, but Jett recognized them anyway. Back in Orleans Parish, the Desbiennes had been a no-account passel of swamp trash who couldn't raise a crop up out of the ground if Jesus Lord had commanded it to come forth, and Mama had nursed their brats through fever and their women through childbed and rode out there at least once a month with a hamper of food and took Jett with her. Mama said it wasn't charity or compassion if it was easy, but Jett had hated to go.

"This is Brother Shepherd's private study," the woman said harshly.

Jett put her hands over her face. "Oh, miss, I didn't mean to go where I don't belong, truly, but I heard—I heard he's a powerful good man!"

The woman's face softened. "He is. Brother Shepherd speaks with God's holy angels daily. Come here, child."

Jett walked slowly across the carpet and stopped, head down. When the woman reached for her, she flinched automatically, but all the woman did was untie the bonnet-ribbons at Jett's throat.

"I am Sister Catherine," she said, handing Jett the sunbonnet. "What's your name?"

"J—Jayleen," Jett stammered. It wasn't a Bible name by any stretch, or even a proper name. It was the name of the eldest Desbiennes girl, and it was all she could think of. "Please, Miss Catherine! My brother's awful sick, and he's like to die if he don't get prayed over right quick!"

"Missus, Missus, come quick, the baby's come early and Mawmaw's like to die if you don't come right quick. . . ."

"You must not use those honorifics here, child, for we here of the Divine Resurrection have rejected the evils of the world," Sister Catherine said. "I am Sister Catherine. And I will call you Sister Jayleen." She put a hand on Jett's arm and drew her out into the hall, shutting the door firmly behind them. "You did wrong by sneaking in here this way. You should have come openly. Brother Shepherd would never turn away a soul in need."

"I was a-skeert, Ma— Miss— Sister, ma'am," Jett stammered. She thought of Phillip, laughing at her because she'd been caught in a lie by Tante Mère: *You have to believe it yourself, Pippa, before you can make anyone else believe it. They'll believe you if you believe you, that's the first rule.* It wasn't hard to let the tears come after that, or to scrub at her eyes until they were red. "My brother . . . he isn't really sick," she whispered.

Sister Catherine had been leading her back up the

hall. They'd almost reached the front parlor when she stopped.

"Does he drink?" Sister Catherine demanded. "There is no sanctuary here for drunkards and libertines."

"No," Jett whispered, her throat closing with unshed tears. "Oh, please, *please*, sister, he's done gone and got hisself shot and he, and we—we're rebs, ma'am. He never swore. They'll hand him over to the Army iff'n they ketch him."

Tyrant Johnson had issued a general amnesty to Confederates two years ago—pardoning them for the "crime" of fighting for their own country—but to claim that pardon, a Southerner had to swear an Oath of Allegiance to the Union. Without swearing that oath, you were a criminal in Yankee eyes, unable to vote, own property, operate a business . . .

But if you swore that oath, you were a traitor.

"The things of the world have no place here," Sister Catherine said, so calmly Jett wasn't sure she'd heard her. She started walking again. Jett followed. She forced herself not to look back at the study door. "Sister Jayleen" was interested in Brother Shepherd, not his possessions.

The kitchen of Jerusalem's Wall was familiar enough, even though Jett had never been in it: cookstove, pantry shelves, dry sink, wet sink, and a long marble counter down the middle. There wasn't much you could remove from a kitchen and still have a kitchen, after all. Jett saw there were two women were standing at the counter, rolling out tortillas. A couple of pots of something were simmering on the stove.

"This is Sister Jayleen," Sister Catherine announced. "She's come to join us."

One of the women looked up. It was Sister Agatha, and for a moment Jett held her breath, but Sister Agatha's gaze passed over her without recognition.

"Bet she hasn't come alone," the other woman said cynically.

"Sweetness and humility are the flowers we grow in Our Savior's garden of Righteousness, Sister Ruth," Sister Catherine said reprovingly. "If Sister Jayleen has had a true calling to come among us, our Blessed Founder will see it."

Sister Ruth returned to her work, her mouth folded in a thin line of disagreement.

Jett stood nervously at the edge of the kitchen as Sister Catherine went to the cupboard and took down two battered tin mugs. She picked up the kettle keeping warm on the back of the stove, but as she poured, Jett saw the liquid was thick and dark. *If drinking more of that Revealed Herb Tea is the worst that happens to me here, I'll count myself lucky*, she told herself.

Sister Catherine handed Jett one of the mugs and

motioned to Jett to follow her out of the kitchen. She led Jett to an alcove just off the dining room. Jett thought its purpose might once have been to hold cooling racks for cakes and pies, but its window had been bricked over, and now it was a gloomy place. There were benches on either side of the doorway. Jett sat as close to the wall as she could get. Sister Catherine sat beside her.

"Now," Sister Catherine said calmly, sipping her tea. "You must tell me all you know about our Blessed Founder, Sister Jayleen, and how you came to us."

"I guess I can't, ma'am—*Sister*," Jett said, bowing her head. The metal cup in her hands was uncomfortable to hold, but the pain was something to concentrate on. "I guess I heard about him a lot of places before I heard a name. We tried—Brother'n me—to join up with a wagon train up north of here. They wouldn't let us stay above a day or two. We didn't have any money." She took a deep breath, willing herself to *believe* so she could convince. "We headed on south, because he'd heard they didn't care if you'd sworn. And I heard there was a righteous man living here in the desert."

Sister Catherine nodded, as if she'd heard exactly what she'd expected to hear. "God has spoken to Brother Shepherd," she said. "You doubt and fear. Don't be ashamed. Once I did, too. Do you believe in the Resurrection?" she asked abruptly.

"I . . ." The question caught Jett off guard. What was the right answer? "I guess I'm as good a Christian as some, Sister Catherine."

"On the Day of Judgment, Jesus Christ our Lord will raise up both the living and the dead to weigh their souls and cast the wicked down into Darkness. But He will not come with a great fanfare, so that the wicked may lie and pretend to righteousness. No! He will come so softly and quietly that many—even among those of us here—do not realize He is already here."

"Oh, Sister Catherine," Jett said. She'd wondered why Brother Shepherd let Sister Catherine enter his private rooms just as she pleased, and now she thought she knew why. Brother Shepherd was bad crazy in the smart way. Sister Catherine was just crazy.

Jett suspected she knew why. "I am sorry for your loss, Sister Catherine," she said softly.

Jett was all too familiar with bereavement and the terrible toll the death of a loved one took on those left behind. Louisiana had been one of the Seven, the first seven states to secede. It had gone out in January of 1861. New Orleans—and Orleans Parish—had fallen to the Yankees fifteen months later. Yankee occupation had meant they got the bad news quickly. The casualty lists: husbands, fathers, sons who had gone off to fight and would never come home again. Many of the bereaved had turned to planchette writing, desperate for a last word from those who'd gone on ahead. Others had just gone quietly mad, insisting a husband, a son, a father was alive—coming home soon, already here, never left.

"You're a good girl, Jayleen," Sister Catherine said, patting Jett's knee. "But I have no need to grieve! Brother Shepherd has promised my David is to come back to me very soon. Would you like to see his picture?"

She didn't wait for Jett's answer before bringing out a locket she wore beneath her dress. She opened it and held it for Jett to see. There was a daguerreotype picture of a man on one side and of a young boy on the other.

"That's my David. My angel baby. Henry and I always hoped for children, but for years we were not blessed. I'd given up hope when the Lord took mercy on me. But he punished me for my doubt as well. From childhood David was frail and ill—but a good boy!—and the doctors told us he had an incurable consumption. This time I didn't despair, and again my prayers were answered, for I saw a newspaper article saying it was merely the heavy wet air that troubled him so, and the desert would make him well again. Henry was against it, but I prevailed upon him at last. What mother wouldn't fight ten lions for her child? And once we had begun our journey, I discovered Henry meant us to press on to California, but I knew we must not. Like you, I'd heard rumors that Christ our Lord had returned to Earth. Oh, I did not know who He was, then! In fact, He does not yet know his true nature, for God does not send burdens we are too frail to bear, and it will be a hard task for Him to sit in judgment upon the nations. But we must not speak of such things yet. All that matters is that David has been made well again."

"What about Henry?" Jett blurted out, unable to stop herself.

Sister Catherine's momentary animation faded. "Some are called to the Divine Throne before their time," she said softly. "Henry was not willing to embrace his salvation—but I do not grieve for him! I shall see him again when Brother Shepherd—as we must still call Him!—erects his Jerusalem of Fire for the righteous to inhabit."

Jett felt as if she was drowning in the flood of Sister Catherine's confession, but one thing stood out. "You say David is coming back to you?"

"Oh, yes," Sister Catherine said brightly. "He died two days ago—but our Blessed Founder has promised to raise him up on the third day. He promised me David would live forever, you see. He promised."

Jett couldn't decide whether she wanted to scream, slap Sister Catherine silly, or just run for her life. What she was afraid she'd do was start laughing, the terrified hysterical laughter that came when even tears weren't enough. "Does—does he do that often?" she asked, wincing at the inanity of her own words.

"Oh yes," Sister Catherine said. "Everyone who dies here—and there are many!—goes with Brother Shepherd to his house of prayer. Not the outer one you will see soon, but the inner one, where the angels come. There he calls them back into life once more. But not like my David. My David will be special!"

"That must be—must be a hard thing to accept," Jett said, gripping her mug so hard her fingers ached.

"God does not send burdens we are too frail to bear," Sister Catherine reminded her. "Those the blessed resurrected have left behind often hope for some word of reassurance, but the reborn only speak the tongue of Heaven as it was spoken by Father Adam and Mother Eve before their Fall from Grace. Brother Shepherd conveys their messages of hope and reassurance to their surviving loved ones for them. Perhaps you will see for yourself."

"I'd like that," Jett said, hating herself. "My brother's a soldier."

"What did you say his name was, again?" Sister

Catherine asked. When she'd been talking about her husband and son her voice had been soft and dreamy. Now it turned sharp and accusing again.

"Johnny," Jett said wildly. *Johnny Reb*. "Sister Catherine, my brother's bad hurt. That's why I didn't bring him. I think he might be a-skeert of thinking about . . . well, about passing on, and maybe . . . If I could just *see* this special prayer house, maybe I could tell him it would be all right. Only I don't want anyone to know I—I maybe had doubts," she added in a rush. "Could I see it and, and not let anyone know?" She didn't think Brother Shepherd would show it to her. Not without making her one of his "Blessed Resurrected" first.

Sister Catherine sat silently for so long Jett thought she might have gone off into a trance. "Many people have asked what you're asking," Sister Catherine finally said, her voice so calm and reasonable that Jett had to bite her lip to keep from showing how frightened she was. "Brother Shepherd has always told us anyone who wishes may visit there. But he also warns us the angels are often present within it, and anyone who isn't pure of heart will be struck down instantly at the sight of one."

I just bet he has, Jett thought grimly. "I think I already saw it," she said, her voice shaking. "It had a door in the middle of the floor, all chained. I have to see it, Sister Catherine. Johnny—" She couldn't finish the sentence.

The lie choked her. 'Johnny' was a lie, but *Philip* wasn't. And Philip *did* need her.

Sister Catherine got to her feet. "When Brother Shepherd ministers to your brother, He will take away all fear, I promise you. And I know you are anxious for that. Let us see if we may discover when He will return. When He goes to pray, sometimes He remains lost in adoration for days, communing with the angels and the Blessed Resurrected. If the Keys to Heaven are in their place, He is merely upon some errand, and will return soon. He always takes the keys with Him when He goes to pray—I think they are a sign to us of the times we should not disturb Him. Let us go and see."

"Thank you." Jett got hastily to her feet, setting down her untouched cup. Maybe she should have said more, maybe she should have told Sister Catherine she was good and pure and stainless and all those words they flung around here at Jerusalem's Wall a mite too freely, but Jett thought if she said another word, she'd just blurt out the whole truth. Sister Catherine wouldn't want to hear it. Brother Shepherd had said he'd raise Sister Catherine's boy from the dead.

Sister Catherine didn't want to hear he couldn't.

Sister Catherine led Jett to the front door, and indicated a ring of ornate brass keys hanging on a nail beside it.

"Here are the Keys to Heaven," she said, pointing. "Even though Brother Shepherd has said any may freely enter His Holy Tabernacle, it would be wrong of me to encourage you to use them." Despite her words, she took them down and handed them to Jett. There were almost a dozen of them, and Jett knew there was only one lock. She guessed maybe some of them opened things down in the cellar.

"I guess I'll just . . . you . . . you want to come along?" Jett asked hoarsely.

Sister Catherine shook her head, smiling gently. "I have no need to peer into mysteries not meant for me. I'll see my son again before tomorrow's sunrise. That's all I care about."

I forgot my bonnet, Jett realized as she stepped outside. It didn't matter. Riding back to Alsop bareheaded wouldn't kill her.

She was two steps across the compound before she realized she should have asked to take a lantern with her, and three more when it occurred to her she was holding a large ring of keys in plain sight. She wrapped a fold of her skirts around them and hoped no one would see her (though if anyone but Sister Catherine saw her, she was in trouble just to start with). This had been supposed to be a *secret* reconnaissance. She'd been supposed to get in to the secret bunkhouse without anyone seeing her, grab anything written down, sneak back to Nightingale, and ride hell-for-leather back to Alsop. And that plan had gone south the moment Sister Catherine found her.

Well, I've got matches and a candle. I guess I could set the whole place to blazes and hope that settles things.

And get out of Jerusalem's Wall before anyone smelled smoke.

It was a relief to reach the bunkhouse again, even though she'd have to go back to the house afterward to return the keys. If she didn't, Brother Shepherd would know somebody had been in his "inner prayer house." Jett was pretty sure that wouldn't end well.

Just as before, she closed the door behind her, then pulled out the candle stub and lit it. She stuck it to the floor beside the locked doors once again. Her heart was beating fast as she tried the first key.

The first key wouldn't even go into the lock. The second one wouldn't either. By the time she got to the third key, Jett had a horrible suspicion. She quickly fanned out all the keys on the ring and measured them against each other, then tried two more to be sure.

None of the keys on the ring Sister Catherine gave her would fit this lock.

It's a trap. Oh holy mother, it's a trap. These aren't keys—to Heaven or anywhere else. They're bait!

Anyone unhappy with Jerusalem's Wall would want to get into the "inner prayer room"—whether to loot it or to find proof Brother Shepherd was a fraud. His tarradiddle about people who entered his inner prayer house "without a pure heart" being struck dead was just a useful excuse for them vanishing.

Jett knelt in place for almost a minute, panting as if she'd been running. Her only hope was to get the keys back into the house before anyone else saw they'd been gone and tell Catherine she'd . . . reconsidered.

You have to. You run off now, and Sister Catherine's going to tell everybody in that ranch house you were struck dead by an angel. And there's one person at least who won't believe it.

She had to assume someone here could track her back to Alsop. All Shepherd would have to do was burn the town to flush them out—or kill them. By the time Jett got there to warn Gibbons and White Fox, there wouldn't be enough time to cover their tracks, let alone get far enough away they couldn't be spotted.

You have to take those keys back to the house and tell Sister Catherine you lost your nerve. She'll believe that.

She pushed herself to her feet. Only when she was halfway to the door did she realize she'd left the candle burning. It was hard to go back and snuff it out. It was even harder to open the bunkhouse door, and Jett nearly forgot to bolt it again.

Jett glanced toward the sky as she stepped out into the sun. Her stomach knotted. It was almost noon.

Hurry! she told herself.

Head down, keys clutched in her fist, she crossed the compound as quickly as she dared.

"Hold up, girl!" a man called out. Jett stopped. She had to. Any female who belonged here would. She shoved the keys into a fold of her skirts and turned, then drew a quick sharp breath.

It was Brother Raymond. He was red-faced and sweating and kept pulling his hat off to fan himself and putting it back on as he hurried toward her. "Where do you think you're going?" he demanded.

"Ahhh . . . the kitchen!" Jett said desperately. It was plain to see that Brother Raymond didn't connect the female he was bullying with Jett Galatin, gunslinger. That was a piece of luck. Unfortunately, her ability to tell a convincing story seemed to have vanished.

Brother Raymond's eyes narrowed suspiciously. "Kitchen's that way," he said, jerking a thumb toward the house. "All there is where you were coming from is— What are you hiding there?"

He grabbed at her arm. Jett jerked free, but the

movement had brought the keys into sight. Brother Raymond grabbed them, then grabbed her wrist. "Spying, were you?" he demanded.

"Let me go!" Jett gasped, trying to twist free.

But Brother Raymond was already shouting for help.

CHAPTER EIGHT

The draperies had been closed before Jett was brought to Brother Shepherd's study (again). The only light came from the lamp on the desk. She sat on a chair facing the desk. Her wrists were handcuffed behind her back. The cuffs were chained to one of the chair rungs with a second chain, and it was padlocked. The key to the padlock was lying in the center of the desktop. Even if she could get out of the cuffs, the chain went around her waist, too, so she'd still be chained to the chair unless she could get the key and get at the padlock. (It was a good heavy oak chair, too. She probably couldn't smash it.)

She couldn't even try, because she wasn't alone.

"What's your name, girl? Your *real* name. Don't be afraid."

Brother Shepherd's hands were folded on the desktop. He was smiling, doing his best to look kindly, but Jett could see the wolf under the fleece.

"I reckon I'd be less afraid if I wasn't chained up like a lockbox," Jett answered sharply.

"What did you come here to steal?" he asked, as if he hadn't heard her. "We're a small and humble congregation of good Christian men and women. We have nothing of value."

Jett couldn't keep herself from glancing around the library in disbelief. Just one of the gold crosses on the wall behind him was the price of a blood horse.

Brother Shepherd's smile faded, as if she'd mocked him aloud. His expression sharpened. "Sister Catherine said this was where she found you. Was any of the story you told her true?"

"I don't know—" Jett began. She broke off as Brother Shepherd got to his feet and strode quickly around the desk. He took her chin in his hand and forced it upward, peering at her intently. She struggled to shake him off, but his grip was too strong.

"You've been here before," he said, releasing her. "You were dressed as a boy."

She hoped the galvanizing shock of fear that hit

her didn't show in her face. She struggled to keep it hidden.

He looked shocked at the thought—and impressed, too, which was the last thing she wanted. "I don't—" she said, trying to buy some time.

"Oh, don't bother lying," Brother Shepherd said, waving her words away. "It was you. You called yourself Jett Gallatin. You told Sister Agatha you were looking for your brother. But you weren't. You'd come to spy—or to steal. Do you even *have* a brother, I wonder?"

"You go to blazes!" Jett snapped, letting anger take away her fear. "T'ain't none of your business!"

"And where's your horse? A magnificent animal, I do admit. He must be somewhere nearby. I'll send some of my faithful followers to look for him. After all, you aren't going to be needing him any longer."

"You think I'm going to *join* you?" Jett blurted in disbelief. She wasn't worried for Nightingale—Brother Shepherd's "faithful followers" were going to return with broken limbs and smashed skulls if they tried laying a finger on the stallion. But—

Brother Shepherd smiled unpleasantly. "Of course I do. The army of the blessed resurrected is always eager to welcome a new member." His smile widened as a shudder passed over her. "But I see you take my meaning. You'd already been to Alsop when you came here.

Don't bother to lie. You saw the power I can command."
He leaned back on the edge of his desk and looked smug.

"Wouldn't call it much of a power, Mister Shepherd.
I saw everything you could throw at Alsop two nights
running and got off scot-free," she taunted. Right now,
words were her only weapons. If she could make him
mad enough, maybe he'd get careless. Or leave. Something she could use to escape before he sent her soul
to Hell and raised up her body as a walking corpse.

"So that's your game! You want my discovery!" He
pushed himself to his feet and began to pace back and
forth in front of the draperies. "Do you think you can
use it yourself? Whatever your plan, you've already
failed!"

"Well then, I don't reckon you've got anything to
worry about," she said tranquilly. She'd been afraid
when Brother Raymond caught her, but now the calm
Jett felt before every gunfight had descended on her,
the same calm she felt each time she stared down someone's gun-barrel at her own death.

"And yet—and yet—Yet it is for the conquerors to
show mercy to the fallen." He stopped pacing and
folded his arms across his chest. "Before you die, I'll
show you what you came to steal."

He walked back to the desk and pulled out a small
gold key he wore on a long chain around his neck. He
used it to unlock the desk and brought out an Army

Colt. She thought he might unlock her chains next, but instead he set the pistol on the desk beside the key and walked over to the draperies. He pushed them open, and then the curtains behind them, and unlatched and opened the French doors. The hot wind spilling into the room made the lamp flame dance and gutter.

Shepherd came back to the desk and picked up the pistol. He thrust it through his waistband, then picked up the key and walked behind her. Jett held absolutely still as he fumbled at her restraints. She heard the soft thump as the padlock dropped to the carpet. The slithery feeling of the chain around her waist coming free made her shudder.

"Stand up, Miss Gallatin," Shepherd said. "I'm going to give you your heart's desire."

"Only if you shoot yourself with that thing," she snapped as she got to her feet.

Shepherd struck her between her shoulder blades hard enough to make her stagger and fall facedown across the desk. Just as she gathered herself to knock the burning lamp to the carpet—the kerosene-soaked wool would go up like a torch—Shepherd grabbed the chain of her handcuffs and used it to haul her to her feet.

"Now, now, my dear girl, there's no need to act the termagant with me. I'm only the groomsman, come to conduct you to your bridal couch," Shepherd said. He pulled upward on the chain until her arms were bent painfully behind her back. She started to struggle until she felt the cold metal of his pistol against her neck.

Shepherd pushed her toward the open doors. She'd thought of screaming and trying to get away as she was marched through the house: all Shepherd could have done was tell his followers to ignore her. Or shoot her. But they were going around the outside of the building.

The air was baking hot and utterly still. Heat radiated from the adobe wall, and the shards of broken roof-tiles—the usual substitute for gravel or for crushed shells—crunched under their boots. They reached the front of the house and began the long walk across the compound. There were a few windows on this side. Anybody riding up to the front wouldn't see anything amiss—at least in the main house. But somehow Jett didn't get the feeling the Fellowship spent much time looking out the windows.

I know I wanted to find out what was in that basement, but being frog-marched there at gunpoint by a crazy Yankee wasn't what I had in mind.

She could probably outrun Shepherd even with her hands manacled behind her back, and he'd have to let go of her sooner or later. But nobody could outrun a bullet. He wouldn't even need to be a good shot to hit her before she got ten steps. She hoped she'd get her chance when they reached the bunkhouse—it only took one hand to get the bar off the door, but to free a hand he'd either have to put away his gun or let go of her. But to her disappointment, the door was already unbarred and ajar.

Shepherd hustled her inside. He closed the door behind him, and Jett saw there was a lantern lit and waiting beside the cellar doors.

"Walk to the back wall and get down on your knees facing it," Shepherd said, releasing his grip on the handcuff chain. Jett hesitated until she heard the click of the Colt's hammer being pulled back. "I don't care whether you enter glory with a hole in you or just as God made you. While I'd enjoy showing you my work, I don't insist on it."

Jett moved quickly to the rear wall. It was hard to get down on her knees with her hands behind her back, but Shepherd wasn't taking any chances that she'd rush him while he was unlocking the doors. *He thinks I'm some typical nervous female. Maybe I can use that. How? Think!* She leaned her forehead against the wall and listened to the sounds coming from behind her. The chain locking the cellar doors rattled through the handles and the doors thumped open. She caught the scent of damp earth—and beneath it, the stink of dead flesh.

"Get up. Jett, Jayleen, whatever your name is," Shepherd said.

"I can't move with my hands behind me like this," she said. She'd heard him cock his pistol before. Had he eased the hammer back down? Or would the next thing she knew be the impact of a bullet in her back?

She heard him cock the Colt again.

"I can't!" she repeated desperately.

She heard footsteps—Shepherd coming toward her—then he grabbed her wrists and yanked them upward. But his intention wasn't to haul her to her feet. She felt both hands on her wrists as he fumbled with the lock of the handcuffs.

He's put the gun away—or he's left it by the doors.

"Now—" Shepherd began.

The cuffs fell away from her wrists. Jett sprang to her feet, shoving Shepherd off balance. She turned as he staggered, and punched him in the jaw as hard as she could.

He wasn't expecting that. Girls slapped, they didn't punch. But she'd had five brothers, and one of them had taught her everything he knew. As Shepherd fell backward, she saw he had his gun stuffed into his waistband again. She lunged for it but she wasn't quick enough. Shepherd scrambled back out of the way and yanked the gun free. Jett was on hands and knees, her skirts tangled around her legs. She had an instant to register what was about to happen and try to ride the blow as he reversed the pistol and hit her with the butt as hard as he could.

Light flared behind her eyes as she was knocked sprawling. Pain—nausea—dizziness—this wasn't the first time she'd been hit, and she screamed inside her head that she had to get up, get moving. . . . She didn't get very far before she felt a boot on her stomach holding her down. She forced her eyes open. Shepherd was standing over her, pointing his gun at her. As she watched, he wiped a trickle of blood away from his mouth with the back of his free hand. When he saw her looking at him, he stepped back out of reach.

"Get the cuffs," he said. "Slowly."

She sat up and drew a slow breath at the new surge of nausea it brought, then got carefully to her feet.

"You're just like all the rest of them," Shepherd said conversationally. "The liars, the deceivers, the flatterers. You're no different."

"You're going to kill me!" Jett flashed angrily. "What the Sam Hill did you expect?"

"I thought you'd have more interest in learning about my work," Shepherd said. He actually sounded hurt. "I've discovered secrets lost to Mankind for thousands of years."

Yeah, and if Gibbons was here I'm sure she'd be chomping at the bit to go visit your secret zombie-making factory,

Jett grumbled silently. "Why, yes indeed and thank you kindly, sir," she said cuttingly. "Bless your heart! It would be a pleasure I'd never hoped for, sir, if you were to do me the honor of showing me your work." Jett pulled her skirts wide and swept Shepherd a deep curtsey, her back very straight. She rose to her feet again and trudged over to where the handcuffs were. She had to walk past the open cellar. The stench wafting up made her heart beat faster in panic. Her head hurt vilely and she was probably going to be dead by sunset. *But he doesn't know about Gibbons and White Fox! And even if he does, even if he kills both of them too, Gibbons's papa knows where she is. He'll come looking.*

She picked up the cuffs and held them out to him. "Do you care for the pleasure, sir?" she asked evenly.

"Put them on and close them," Shepherd said, ignoring her defiance.

He didn't spell out front or back, so she chose front. The ratchets clicked as she closed them in place. She left them loose enough that she might be able to squeeze out of them. If she was left alone for long enough.

"Now pick up the lamp."

She walked to the lamp and picked it up carefully. She could smash it to the ground—or just chuck it into the cellar. She could even throw it at him. If she dropped to the floor fast enough, Shepherd's first shot might miss in the sudden darkness.

But Jett wasn't sure how fast she could move just now. And Shepherd had six bullets. Enough to hit her if he was lucky. More than enough to summon help. She was still hesitating when he spoke again.

"Now go down the steps. Slowly."

When she held the lantern over the cellar opening, she could see an adobe brick staircase. She'd thought this "inner prayer house" couldn't be much larger than the bunkhouse, but the stairs went down farther than she could see by the lamplight. *Whatever's down there, he won't want to shoot it up if he can help it, and I might be able to find a weapon,* she thought. It was more of a chance than she had standing right here. Jett didn't doubt he had her marked for death. But Shepherd was like a stump preacher with an empty hat. He'd want her to listen to him first. Even better, she was betting he'd need to put in an appearance at the ranchhouse long before he was done talking—so he'd lock her up, and he'd leave her alone, and that would be her chance. Shepherd would be confident because she was behind doors he'd chained shut. And Jett was just as confident she could pry them open if she had to.

Carefully, she took the first step. It wasn't difficult to move as slowly as Shepherd wanted, the hard part was getting down the steps without falling. She didn't have a hand free to hold her skirts out of the way, and her boot caught in her hem with every step. A dozen steps down she froze at the sound of a loud booming sound behind her. Shepherd had closed the cellar doors. She turned quickly to look back to see if he'd just locked her in, but he was standing a few steps above her. He gestured meaningfully with the Colt. She turned away, steadied herself, and went on.

By the time she could see the bottom of the steps, she realized she'd far underestimated the size of the cellar. The ceiling must be twenty feet high, and she couldn't see the walls. She reached the bottom, took a few steps forward, and stopped.

"Here we are, all nice and cozy," Shepherd said. He took back the lamp. "Don't go anywhere."

Jett did as she was told. She knew there wasn't any point in trying to escape while he was here. He'd hear her if she ran up the steps, and she didn't think she could get the doors open before he started shooting. Suddenly she realized what she was seeing. Jett drew a sharp breath. The lamp Shepherd was carrying wasn't shining off walls or ceiling, and its flame had dwindled with distance. Whatever this place was, it was enormous. Some natural cave he'd found? That was both good and bad. It meant more places for her to hide once she got free—if she couldn't get all the way out. But if she got lost, she would have signed her own death warrant.

Suddenly the lamp went out. The darkness surrounding her was absolute and choking, and she drew a long steadying breath, fighting the dizzying pain in her head. It was day. If there *were* any zombies down here, they wouldn't be able to move. Suddenly a tiny blue flame flickered into life, and Jett bit her lip sharply. "Corpse candles," they called them back home. You could see them at night in any graveyard—if you were crazy enough to go into a graveyard at night—eerie blue flames dancing over the graves.

Oh Blessed Virgin help me—he's brought me to a tomb, and if I can't see I'll never get out!

The first blue light was swiftly joined by a dozen more, then one of them flared white. In its glow she could see Shepherd holding a lamp that burned with a bright blue-white flame. *Spirit lamps*, she thought in relief, exhaling a shaky breath. *Just like the ones Gibbons has.*

By the time Shepherd returned, her momentary panic was gone, and she could gaze at him blandly. He seemed a little disappointed she wasn't more impressed.

"Come with me," Shepherd said genially. "These will be the last sights you ever see—but they're worth dying for, I assure you!"

"You ever bring anyone down here who agreed

with you on that?" Jett asked with feigned interest. She didn't think Shepherd would shoot her now. Only folks scared of what you might do shot you just for slanging them, not someone sitting in the catbird seat and holding all the aces. That kind would talk your ear off until you wished they *would* shoot you and give you some peace.

"Mock me if you must. The world has mocked all great visionaries. Alexander—DaVinci—Galileo!"

"They live in Texas?" Jett asked, just to be annoying, but she didn't think Shepherd was paying much attention.

He grabbed the chain between her wrists and towed her behind him. They were moving toward the other little flames, but she couldn't get her bearings. Her feet skidded on tile for a few steps, then she tripped and nearly fell over the edge of a carpet as she hurried to keep up. If he accidentally pulled the cuffs off by dragging her behind him, he'd be sure to put them back on good and tight. She'd never get free then.

Suddenly he turned and shoved her. She staggered, tripped over something she couldn't see, and fell backward. Light flared behind her eyes, even as she realized she'd fallen onto something soft. *A chair!* She heard it creak, smelled buckram and horsehair and the ticklish dusty smell of goose feathers. It was low and soft, and she wouldn't be able to get out of it quickly.

Shepherd turned up the other lamps until they all burned white. There were eight of them around the edge of a wagon wheel; their combined light was too bright to look at. She looked away and heard a homely, familiar sound: the squeak of a pulley. When she looked back, he'd finished raising the chandelier. The room was bright enough to read in now.

This place looks like Ali Baba's Cave! Jett thought in amazement.

She could only get a measure of the room's size by fixing her gaze high on the far wall. The room was at least forty feet across and longer than it was wide. She was pretty sure you could drop all of Alsop in here and have room left to dance. It was difficult to be sure because the room itself was so cluttered. She saw stacks of gilt-framed mirrors and paintings, rolled-up carpets, marble-topped dressers and tables, one, two, *four* silver tea services, and a stack of wooden chests that obviously held sets of silver. A pile of pelts, fox and beaver, stacked so high they'd slipped and spilled over onto a stack of buffalo robes. And that was just what she could see. There was more, piled and stacked halfway to the ceiling. If Shepherd had gone through every townhouse and plantation house in all of Orleans County, he might have been able to fill this room as it was filled now. The thought made her dizzy. How long had he been looting towns and ranches with the help of his zombie army?

But if this room was where Shepherd kept his loot, there were two things that didn't fit.

One was the two doorways she could see leading out of it, cyclopean archways built to the same brobdingnagian scale as everything she'd seen so far. If Shepherd had more than one treasure vault like this one, Jett couldn't imagine what he needed with Texas. He could just *buy* himself a railroad.

The other was the enormous something covered by a white cloth. He hadn't covered any of the furniture. What was so special he needed to hide it under a dust cover?

Shepherd walked nonchalantly over to a japanned secretary desk and lowered the door. On the desk inside were two painted wooden boxes. He opened one and popped several sugarplums into his mouth, then opened the other as he chewed and withdrew a cigar. He clipped off the ends and walked to the table where he'd left the other lamp, still chewing. *Manners of a pig hog!* Jett thought scornfully, but she watched him carefully. The pistol was back in his waistband, but she couldn't get out of the chair quick enough to get it.

Shepherd removed the glass chimney and bent over the flame. He puffed his cigar alight and then turned to look at her.

"Normally I'd ask before smoking in the presence

of a lady," he said with an ironic bow. "But you, Miss Gallatin, are no lady."

"And you're no gentleman," she snapped.

"Gentlemen are useless idlers, growing fat off the toil of those of us whom they deem to be their inferiors," he said grandly. "They lack vision. Give one of them the least iota of power, and they will use it to oppress their betters."

"Like you, I suppose," Jett said.

"Like me." He took a few steps closer and blew a jet of smoke into her face. If he expected her to cough or flinch away, she disappointed him. "You've already seen proof of my ability to raise the dead—and put them to good use. All this," he added, gesturing grandly at their, surroundings "was accomplished by my resurrected *allamatons!* It's a word of my own creation. From the Greek. It means 'other acting.'"

"Funny thing, but back home we just call them 'zombies,'" Jett drawled.

"My creation owes nothing to the heathen superstitions of Africa," Shepherd said. "No, my *allamatons* owe their being to Goetia, queen of the natural sciences! They are raised and given purpose by the application of 'Musica Universalis'—not sorcery, but *science!*—a mathematical concept first discovered in ancient Egypt! *Aiguptos* the Eternal, that dark kingdom of sorcery and alchemy!"

I thought you said this was science—not sorcery? Jett knew better than to say that aloud. If there was one thing she'd learned in her brief acquaintance with one Honoria Gibbons of San Francisco, it was that folks who went on about "Science this" and "Science that" got really miffed when you pointed out the holes in their arguments.

Jett realized she'd been right about Shepherd being starved for an audience. He'd been so careful to keep her out of sight as he brought her here she was pretty sure nobody else at Jerusalem's Wall was in on his schemes—and that meant he had nobody to brag to. She just hoped that meant he wouldn't give her up—meaning *kill her* and turn her into a walking corpse—until he'd given his tonsils a good airing, because that meant he probably wouldn't be satisfied with just one gabfest. She folded her hands in her lap and sat very straight and gazed at him as if he were the most fascinating thing going. He ate it up, of course. He wasn't that different from the boys back home, all of them thinking anything they had to say was just what a girl wanted to hear. She really was listening, though. For one thing, Gibbons would want to know every word Shepherd said. For another, he might eventually say something useful.

It took him almost an hour to run down, and by then Jett had pretty much his whole life story—and she could read between the lines of it, too. His actual born name was George Wilson Shepherd, and he'd been born in 1822 on a farm near Chillicothe, Ohio, the middle of eight children. As a boy, he'd wanted to study law (he'd wanted to study anything that would get him out of doing an honest day's work, Jett figured). Unfortunately his poor (but humble) family's fortunes were wiped out by a flood. The Shepherd farm was bought up by the bank, and young Mister Shepherd's daddy drank himself to death. His mama tried to keep the household together on her own for a few months, then packed up his younger sisters and threw herself on her own sister's mercy, and that of her sister's husband. He would have been happy to count himself in on the deal, but none of his surviving kin could see any reason an able-bodied young man couldn't support himself, and they weren't keen about loaning him any money either, so George Shepherd became a schoolteacher (a career that lasted longer than Jett expected). But he still wasn't minded to turn his hand to a job of work—he lost one position after another for spending more time on what he called his "researches into Natural Philosophy" than he did on the work he was paid to do.

From the way he skated over the details, Jett guessed there was a little more to it than that, but it wasn't as important as the bee Mister Shepherd got in his bonnet about coming up with an "elixir" he could use to make his fortune. *That* got him run out of town on a rail over what he called "ignorant superstition and arrant persecution" (and what Jett suspected ordinary folks might call "poisoning"). But by then, he was hot on the trail of what would become his "Elixir of Allamatonry."

"But the Elixir is only a part of the whole, magnificent achievement though it is!" he said, striding back and forth in front of her as if he were giving a public lecture (or was a pigeon on a sidewalk). "It is not enough to create the *allamaton*! One must then *control* it! I nearly despaired, Miss Gallatin! But the life of the mind which was my comfort and refuge came to my aid! For you see, the ancient pagans believed that audible sound had the power to heal or to kill. From that bare hint, my genius refined upon their primitive superstitions in ways they never dreamed of. You see—in fact, as you will soon see for yourself"—he emended with an obscene chuckle—"once a body has been prepared with my Elixir of Allamatonry and undergone the purging alchemy of extinction, I can instruct it with my "Musica Universalis" to act at my command!" He paused expectantly.

"You poison folks and then caterwaul at 'em until they do what you want?" Jett asked doubtfully. She supposed what she'd heard the night he'd brought the zombies back to Alsop must be that "Musica Universalis" he was going on about.

"More! Far more! I will show you!"

He strode to the muslin-shrouded object and pulled away the sheet that covered it. It was the biggest pipe organ Jett had seen outside of a church. Its brass pipes gleamed in the lamplight. Brother Shepherd walked around to its side. Jett couldn't see what he did, but whatever it was made a glugging sound like water being poured out of a stone jug, followed by a low constant drone. The pipes rang faintly, as if a wind was blowing through them.

"Behold the power of Musica Universalis, Miss Gallatin!" Shepherd shouted, seating himself on the organist's bench.

He brought both hands down on the lower keyboard.

The blast of sound was the loudest thing Jett had ever heard short of cannon-fire. The floor beneath her feet vibrated, and she desperately wanted to put her hands over her ears. *They've got to be able to hear that all the way to Alsop—let alone back at the ranch house!* she thought. *What does the Fellowship think he's doing out here?*

The sound brought her headache back full force. But that was only the beginning. Chord followed chord—none of them anywhere near the same key—before the blasts of noise began to resolve themselves into . . . something. Certainly not any kind of melody. The jangling jarring discords certainly made *her* want to rise up—if only to do in Shepherd's instrument. Soon the organ notes were being accompanied by a thin glassy ringing, as every piece of glass and china in the 'inner prayer house' vibrated madly. There was a crash as something she couldn't see fell to the floor. Shepherd didn't seem to notice. Or maybe he just didn't care. As he played faster and faster—and louder, if that was even possible—Jett leaned forward cautiously. Maybe he'd be so caught up in raising the dead that he wouldn't notice if she moved.

The sudden silence was as deafening as the sound had been.

"You see, don't you? The music moves you—don't deny it." Brother Shepherd sprang from the organist's bench and strode over to her.

"If anything could raise the dead, it'd be that," Jett answered. She hadn't meant it as a joke, but Shepherd seemed to take it that way. He laughed, then put a hand under her elbow.

"But come! You have not seen the full extent of my genius!" he said, picking up the lamp on the nearby table.

Jett followed docilely, still waiting for him to lock her

up somewhere private for an hour or two. She found herself wondering if Mister George Wilson Shepherd of Ohio had forgotten he'd brought her here at gunpoint and intended to kill her once he was done showing off. She didn't think she could be that lucky. If she was Gibbons, she bet she could have talked him into it (on the other hand, if Gibbons was here she might just improve his zombie-making methods).

Brother Shepherd led her past the pipe organ and through the archway. It didn't lead to another room, but instead opened onto a corridor. The clay walls were damp, and the scent of decay grew stronger with every step she took. Shepherd didn't seem to notice.

"Up until now I've been creating my *allamatons* slowly, so the disappearances won't attract too much attention. A farm here, a settlement there—I admit Sheriff Mitchell forced my hand. But no matter! Very soon I'll have enough *allamatons* not merely to scour the rebel state of Texas clean of traitors, but to wipe out the godless savages as well. The Comanche, the Apache, the Pawnee, and the Ute will be no more."

"I reckon you aren't the first feller who's said that about the Apache," Jett said. "Don't you think somebody's going to notice?" she added quickly, since Brother Shepherd was giving her a sulky look.

"Let them!" he said happily. "Every fallen enemy will increase the strength of my unstoppable army! The wealth I've amassed has nothing to do with Earthly enrichment, just as my Fellowship does not exist merely to gratify some base longing for adoration!"

He glanced at her expectantly, but Jett didn't know what to say. She was too busy trying to keep from gagging at the stench. And she wasn't sure what she *could* say to someone who'd just said he was going to wipe out thousands of people with an army of walking corpses.

"Behold!" Brother Shepherd said, bringing them to a stop. He released her arm and raised his lantern high above his head and took a few more steps forward.

For a merciful instant Jett didn't understand what she was seeing. When she did, she raised her bound hands and pressed them over her mouth. If she hadn't, she would have screamed.

The bodies in the doorway sagged or leaned or lay heaped and tumbled like the tenants of an open grave. The ones behind them and to either side were pressed so tightly together they stood upright. She couldn't see the back of the room, or its edges, but every square foot of the space was packed with zombies waiting for the sun to set.

"Come closer," Shepherd urged, as if he were proudly showing off his prize roses.

"Mister, you can shoot me right here before I do any such thing," Jett said hoarsely.

He lowered his lamp, looking disappointed. The shifting illumination gave the dead faces a hideous appearance of life and movement. Jett took an involuntary step backward.

"You think my plan won't work," Shepherd said quietly. For the first time since he'd brought her down here, Jett thought he sounded almost sane. "You believe everyone will share your repugnance, and so I won't have willing followers to stand guard over my great army during the hours of daylight. Ah, but you're wrong, Miss Gallatin. You're wrong. And I will show you why."

He walked back to where she stood and ushered her ahead of him. At this exact moment, Jett didn't care where they went, as long as it was away from that room.

CHAPTER NINE

That morning, while the predawn shadows were still cold and blue, Gibbons and White Fox had watched as Jett rode out of sight, then they returned to the make-shift laboratory she'd created in the Alsop saloon. Hours passed as he watched her pace back and forth muttering to herself. From time to time she would stop and leaf through some notes—notes she had surely memorized by now—or go to stare at the makeshift map on the wall. As inscrutable as her work might be, Gibbons's frequent detours to the street to gaze at the position of the sun—and then at the watch pinned to the front of her jacket—were utterly transparent.

Jett was late.

"Jett Gallatin is a very resourceful individual. I am certain this delay in her return has a wholly innocent cause," White Fox offered at last, voicing a certainty he was far from feeling. Many of the Anglos who came west seemed to feel neither law nor custom bound them any longer. The Army functioned as much as policeman as a military instrument, and in his time with the Army White Fox had seen things he once would not have scrupled to name madness. He knew (perhaps better than Gibbons or even Jett) what men and women were capable of when they felt they were beyond the reach of punishment.

Gibbons grumbled something under her breath and resumed her pacing. From time to time she'd settle into her chair to consult her notes and the tiny spell book belonging to Trooper Lincoln, but such stillness would only last for a few minutes before she was on her feet once more. Finally, as the afternoon light slanted across the floor, White Fox could bear Gibbons's pacing and semiaudible mutters no longer.

"My friend Doctor Singer was a wise and educated man," he said. Gibbons gave no indication that she had heard him, but White Fox was reasonably convinced she was able to think and listen at the same time. "The two things are not necessarily the same," he added dryly, slanting a sideways glance at Gibbons. She continued to ignore him.

"One day, when I was still among the Meshkwahki-haki, there came a day I happened to be with him when he was urgently summoned—so he was told—to a deathbed," White Fox continued. "He asked me to accompany him, and I did. The lady had been traveling when she was taken ill, and when we arrived at the stagecoach stop, he found several other females present at her bedside. They had removed her outer garments, but despite the fact she was unconscious, and obviously in deep distress, none of them was doing anything. 'It's that patent corset she is wearing,' one lady cried out to Dr. Singer as he moved to examine her. 'We can't get it off her—'"

"Exactly why I refuse to wear the miserable things!" Gibbons interjected crossly. White Fox reflected that she was surprisingly charming when she was annoyed. Her cheeks flushed a becoming pink and her eyes sparkled. She might have said more, but White Fox prevented her by resuming his tale.

"Doctor Singer snatched his scalpel from his black bag. 'Clearly you ladies never heard of Alexander the Great!' he growled, and in an instant he sliced through the knotted laces. The lady's breathing eased at once." White Fox smiled faintly. "Doctor Singer was persuaded of her full recovery when she snatched up her parasol and—"

He broke off at the sudden sound of hoofbeats.

Nightingale. From the sound, Jett was returning with urgent news. Perhaps his anecdote would not be needed after all. He hurried to the street to greet her, but the moment he saw the empty saddle, his heart sank. Nightingale had returned alone.

The stallion shied violently when he reached White Fox and danced to a halt a few yards away. He was covered in foam, and his mouth was bleeding where the bit had cut him. White Fox had seen Jett ride often enough to know she could never have done this damage. Someone else had obviously grabbed the stallion by the rein.

"Something has gone wrong," White Fox said as Gibbons joined him.

"Yes," Gibbons snapped. "That much is clear even to me. I wish you could talk," she said to Nightingale.

The stallion skittered even further out of reach, ears flat back, then extended his neck hopefully.

"I'm not chasing you all over the landscape," Gibbons said crossly. Nightingale minced toward her and finally nudged her shoulder. Gibbons reached up to stroke his muzzle. "Where is she?" Gibbons asked the stallion.

"Captured," White Fox said needlessly. "Perhaps she is already dead," he added in reluctant tones. He hated to think it, but he remembered Jett's tale of her escape from Alsop. He'd later seen with his own eyes what Nightingale had braved to rescue her, and so he knew Nightingale wouldn't have abandoned Jett. Not if she'd been anywhere in sight when he was attacked.

"No!" Gibbons exclaimed. Nightingale flung his head up at her vehemence. "Not you," she said, patting his neck. White Fox saw her set her jaw in determination. "We'll see about that," she said grimly.

Under Shepherd's supervision, Jett retraced her steps back to the main room, down its length, and through the second doorway. She'd expected a second corridor, but it opened at once into another room at least the size of the one she'd just left. There wasn't enough light to see clearly, but between the light from the other room and the lamp Shepherd carried, Jett could see the shadowy outline of a long marble-topped table. The shroud-covered body on it gave the table the look of a mortuary slab.

Shepherd ushered her further into the room. When she was standing where he wanted her, he set the lamp down on the end of the table and walked away to light more lamps.

This was a chance at escape.

She turned and ran for the doorway. But before she could reach it, the sound of a shot echoed loudly through the room. The bullet struck the wall ahead of her and sprayed her face with dust. Jett recoiled and staggered sideways, falling against the wall beside the doorway.

"The next one goes into *you*, Miss Gallatin!" Shepherd called cheerfully. "Do not try me!"

She turned around slowly. He brandished the Colt.

"Now come here," Shepherd said.

He motioned her forward with the gun barrel until she was standing within reach, then dragged her into the shadows. Before she could get a good look around, he yanked her hands up over her head and shoved her back against the wall. She tried to lower her arms, but he'd hooked the handcuff chain over something. As she struggled, Shepherd stuffed the Colt back into his waistband and reached toward her neck. For an instant Jett thought he was about to strangle her, but what he did was worse. He closed an iron collar around her throat. When she tried to pull away from the wall again, she couldn't.

"I'm sure this is more comfortable for both of us," Shepherd said, smirking unpleasantly.

"Happy to swap places with you," Jett said tightly. *You damned fool! You should have run when he walked you out of the house! You let him waltz you down here like a calf to the branding, and now he's got you roped and tied!*

Shepherd ignored her remark and walked away.

No matter how hard she struggled, Jett couldn't pull free of the collar. She hadn't heard a padlock click, and she didn't hear one rattle as she struggled. It was probably held shut by a simple latch. She'd left the cuffs loose when she put them on, and whatever they were hooked over was something she could pull against. *So if I can get my hands free, maybe I can get loose again.*

At least Shepherd was ignoring her right now. As he walked around the room lighting lamps, the shadows receded until Jett could see clearly. There was a barred door—like a jailhouse door—off to her right. It was set flush to the wall, and all she could see behind it was shadows. She didn't want to think about what Shepherd might be keeping in that cell.

As she worked doggedly at pulling her hands free, she studied the room. It was as large as she'd guessed. Shepherd only had five bullets left, and she didn't think he was carrying more. If she could make him empty his gun, it would come down to a brawl. She was pretty sure she could win it. If she had her hands free.

The opposite wall held shelves filled with jars and boxes. It had a worktable in front of it. *Why, I bet that table could seat thirty for supper and not leave them to bump elbows,* she thought in disbelief. It was covered with a litter of bottles and tubing and jars and looked like the fancified cousin of the mess Gibbons had made of the Alsop saloon.

"But as I was saying—before you so rudely interrupted me," Shepherd said, replacing the last chimney on the last lamp, "if you place your hopes in my failure to enlist willing followers in my crusade, you underestimate my genius. I've always known I must be able to count upon my acolytes' unthinking devotion. Which means I must indicate that I can both punish and reward, as did the Biblical Patriarchs of old."

He walked back to the mortuary slab and yanked the sheet from the body. It was a child. A boy. He was thin and frail, and dressed for burial in his Sunday suit.

"That's Sister Catherine's boy, Davey," Jett said hoarsely.

She'd stopped struggling with the cuffs the moment Shepherd turned his attention to her again, but she knew now she could get them off if she had a little peace and privacy. If he meant to leave her like this, he was in for a surprise when he came back.

"How insightful of you, Miss Gallatin," Shepherd said. "You guess my methods already. Dear loyal Sister Catherine. She never realized I had no intention of curing her boy—as if anyone could cure consumption. And yet, I will *reward* her by raising him up into eternal sinless life—"

"She'll never believe that!" Jett said. "He's dead! Anyone can see it!"

"Oh, I beg to differ. He will smell of the flowers of Paradise instead of the stink of the grave, and seeing that, what grief-crazed mother would prefer to believe her beloved son was dead? A pity that he's been chosen for a great Heavenly task and so is called away—but a great honor, as well. But rest assured: I shall give her his words of love and devotion myself."

"There isn't any word vile enough for what you are," Jett said. Of course Sister Catherine would believe everything Shepherd told her. She'd seen David die.

"Visionaries are scorned by the common herd," Shepherd said airily, tossing the shroud casually over the body again. "But just as I reward my faithful, you—I am very much afraid—are going to become an example of my wrath."

Shepherd walked to his workbench, hunted around for a moment, then picked up a tiny syringe. He removed the stopper from a bottle filled with dark liquid and filled the syringe. Jett began to struggle with the handcuffs again, not caring now if Shepherd saw her. *I don't know what's in that, but I'm damned if I'm opening my mouth so he can dose me!* One of her hands slipped halfway through its cuff, then stuck fast. *Just a few more seconds,* she prayed silently. *That's all I need—*

"A *hypodermic syringe* can be used to introduce a concentrated dose of my Elixir directly into the body,"

Shepherd announced. "It's far more efficient that way. As you're about to discover."

Jett didn't know what a "hypodermic syringe" was, but it didn't sound good.

As Shepherd walked toward her, she saw there was a needle on the syringe's end, and she redoubled her efforts to escape. Suddenly her right hand slipped free. The chain clattered over whatever her cuffs were hung on, then caught fast. She kicked out at him and tried to hit him, hauling against the remaining cuff with all her strength. He evaded her blows easily and grabbed her arm. Jett screamed in panic and outrage as Shepherd stuck the needle into her flesh just above her elbow. Her mouth went dry and tasted of metal. A burning pain spread through her arm, and she broke out in a cold sweat. When Shepherd released her arm it flopped to her side. She couldn't raise it—not to smack that smug smirk off his face, not to wipe the sweat from her eyes. The floor seemed to shift and slide beneath her feet. Her knees buckled, and she began to gasp for air. Now the only thing holding her upright was the collar around her throat. Her whole weight was hanging from it, and it was choking her . . .

From somewhere that seemed very far away, she heard Shepherd's voice.

"The beauty of my Elixir is that it can be administered either before or after death. But 'before' is so much more entertaining."

Nightingale finally permitted White Fox to lead him down to the livery stable. Gibbons returned to the saloon to pace, her mind working furiously. She refused to believe Jett was dead. Certainly Brother Shepherd was no stranger to murder, but how would he react to someone simply trying to break into his secret lair? *He will decide she is a common thief,* Gibbons told herself determinedly. *Jett is in trouble, probably captured, but I must believe Brother Shepherd means to question her. And that means she is still alive.*

Would Jett tell him anything? Betray what she knew, admit she wasn't working alone?

Not likely, Gibbons decided. She knew something of Jett's history by now. Jett considered herself the citizen of a conquered nation. If the destruction of her home couldn't break her, one lunatic preacher never would. *Or at least*—Gibbons amended to herself—*not in less than a day.*

White Fox returned from settling Nightingale in the stables. He looked utterly grim. "I should have gone with her," he said.

"Then I would be faced with the need to rescue

both of you," Gibbons answered sharply. "At least this way we're free to plan." She frowned. "But without the information she went to find, I am not certain just how we're going to rescue her." She knew she didn't need to go into detail. They'd both seen the "zombie army" Brother Shepherd could command. Even if she pushed the Auto-Tachypode to its top speed, Jerusalem's Wall was hours away. And reaching Jerusalem's Wall was only the first step. They'd have to find Jett and free her. If they succeeded, Shepherd would know his secret was out—and that would be bad enough. It would be worse if they were delayed at Jerusalem's Wall until after sundown.

White Fox regarded her silently for a moment. "As I was saying before Nightingale arrived, Doctor Singer—"

Gibbons stopped to glare at him. "I assume there is some obscure and inscrutable reason to tell me this story *now*, Mister Fox," she said wrathfully. "But I cannot imagine what it could be. So why don't you just tell me what you want me to know?"

"The gentleman who summoned Doctor Singer to attend his wife assumed she was ill, yet the truth was far simpler. In just that way, you wish to know how these "zombies" are created, because you believe knowing that will tell you how to lay them to rest. But I think you might well be hunting the wrong hare. You already know how to kill them. Salt."

"I know it put down *one* of them, Mister Fox," Gibbons replied, her irritation growing. "But Mister Finlay wasn't one of the ordinary run of zombies—if one can even imagine such a thing! I can't assume the same method will do for all of them, because—"

"But you *do* know that, Gibbons," White Fox persisted. "You have not just the answer, but its proof. Remember what Jett told us about the meal she was served?"

He didn't say anything more. Her eyes narrowed and she dredged the fragment of information out of her memory. Suddenly her eyes widened in realization. "There was *no salt* in it, not in any of it."

White Fox nodded. "That must be deliberate. If Brother Shepherd has, as you think, engineered a scientific method of creating walking dead, the absence of salt—"

"Tells us he *knows* salt will put them down!" she almost shouted. "By heaven, I would bet that there is not one grain of salt anywhere on that property! Tarnation! I *have* been hunting the wrong hare! I need to determine a way to get salt into a great number of the creatures at once—and as quickly as possible!"

She went to her makeshift desk and began feverishly sketching and scribbling. There was no time for fear. She had work to do.

Hours later, her sketches had become a weapon.

Gibbons could only thank Providence (and her own determination to be prepared for anything) for the fact that she carried a length of fire hose in her supplies. Normally she filled the Auto-Tachypode's boiler with buckets. But water sources weren't always conveniently situated. She kept the hose stored under the wagon to save space, but now she'd need to have it instantly ready for use. She rummaged out another hose-clamp. In her first test, the hose had immediately torn free of the pipe end when it was pressurized, though White Fox had clearly gotten the valve wrenched down as tightly as it would go.

"The only way we are going to fly to Jett's rescue is if we can get this thing working properly! Otherwise we will surely fall beside her, which is not, I think, what she would wish! Hand me that screwdriver, please, and come lean on this wrench!" Gibbons said. "You are much stronger than I am."

Gibbons stepped back. White Fox moved quickly to obey. He hadn't made a single protest all this time, though Gibbons knew he doubted Jett was still alive. It might be that this rescue attempt was a forlorn hope— and possibly foolhardy was well. There were only two of them. And if Nightingale had come tearing back here without Jett . . .

Then Jett was almost certainly already dead. Or worse, one of the zombies by now. The sensible thing to do would be to point the Auto-Tachypode north and not stop until they reached the walls of Fort San Antonio. They could say Brother Shepherd was building a militia, that he planned to take over this part of Texas, that he had an arsenal and was going to make himself into a little tin-crown king. That would get the Army to come on the double, and Gibbons could make sure she was there, and handy with answers, when they discovered just what sort of force Brother Shepherd had under his command. The best thing, the most intelligent thing, the most logical course of action was to carry a warning to others.

"Bother logic!" Gibbons snarled aloud as she screwed down the final fitting on her device. "Help me get this into the back of the Auto-Tachypode!" she commanded. "We're going after Jett."

The first thing Jett realized was how cold she felt. For a moment she thought Nightingale must have thrown her, because she was lying against something hard and every muscle ached. Then memory returned. Shepherd. The zombies. The "inner prayer house." She floundered upright, gritting her teeth at the surge of nausea and pain. But at least her hands were free.

She had a muddled memory of Shepherd removing the collar and the remaining handcuff bracelet, then walking her over into the cell. Was he gone? He'd left the lamps lit. She crawled over to the cell door and used the bars to drag herself to her feet. She tried the door, but of course it was locked. Still getting her bearings, she held her breath, listening intently for any sign she wasn't alone. Nothing. Still holding on to the bars for support, she turned around to look at the interior of her prison.

David's body was lying on the floor at the back of the cell.

The sight of him galvanized her to full alertness. *"He died two days ago—but our Blessed Founder has promised to raise him up on the third day."* Sister Catherine's words echoed through her mind.

Today was the third day.

David was going to rise as a zombie *tonight*.

It had been around noon when Shepherd brought her down here. What time was it now? How close was it to sunset? What did Shepherd have to do to raise up a zombie besides dose somebody with that swamp water of his? He'd injected *her* with it—

If that poison's going to kill me, I'm going to make sure he goes first, Jett vowed grimly. She had to get out of here. How? The walls and the back were solid rock, and the bars went all the way up into more rock.

The keys! Gibbons gave me half the keys in Alsop!

Had the jailhouse key been one of them? Had

Shepherd taken her reticule? She patted herself down quickly. No. She still had it. She dredged up her skirts and wrenched the neck of the bag open to pull out a fistful of keys. She sorted quickly through them to find the likeliest-looking one. She might be able to pick a lock, but she couldn't pick one blind and working backward.

Was this the jailhouse key? It looked like it. She groped around the lock plate to make sure it had a regular keyhole, then clutched the key in her fingers and reached through the bars until she was at the best angle she could manage. She closed her eyes so she could concentrate. Her fingertips ached with the strain, but if she dropped the key she might be dropping her only means of escape.

There. It was in the keyhole.

She tried to twist it, but it wouldn't turn. She had to get a better grip, and to do that, she had to let go of it. The moment she did, the key fell from the lock and bounced away.

She could see it. It was caught in the raised fringe at the edge of the carpet. Was it out of reach? She got quickly down on her knees, then stretched out full-length, straining to reach as far as she could through the bars. Her fingertips just brushed the teeth of the key. She scrabbled frantically and brought it under her fingers.

The air turned suddenly cold.

Jett recoiled, clutching the key in her hand. Everything down here smelled of putrefaction—to the point she'd almost gotten used to the smell—but suddenly the stench was stronger. She dragged herself to her feet again, glancing anxiously over her shoulder. The corpse in her cell was still immobile.

Once more she fitted the key into the lock. It fit, but nothing she could do would make it turn. With a muffled curse, she threw it through the bars. The air was cold enough now to make her shiver. She breathed through her nose, trying to ignore the stink of corruption, because when she breathed through her mouth, she could *taste* it. Over and over she held her breath to listen. She was almost sure she could hear something. A sound like a wind blowing through dry autumn leaves, or a hundred voices all whispering at once. She bit her lip so hard she tasted blood and chose another key. If she wanted to escape, she didn't dare hurry.

She fit the second key into the lock, gripped it tightly, and twisted.

The key turned.

Suddenly she heard a distant thud, loud enough to drown out the whispering Jett wasn't sure she heard. Another. Then: footsteps. Shepherd had opened the cellar doors. She'd been unconscious too long. He was coming back.

An instant more and she was easing the cell door

open. The room spun dizzily as she stepped through it. She was weaker than she'd realized. But if Shepherd was back, the cellar doors were unlocked. She looked around frantically for a weapon, any weapon. At last she picked up one of the lamps. It wasn't much, but it would have to do. She moved toward the doorway to hide.

But she'd miscalculated the time it would take Shepherd to get here. He came through the doorway when she was still in plain sight. She threw the lamp at him and ran toward another one. He batted the first lamp reflexively away. It struck the floor, where the alcohol inside it spilled from the reservoir. And suddenly the carpet was in flames.

"Get her!" Shepherd shouted.

He hadn't come alone this time.

She grabbed another lamp and whirled around. The man behind her lunged for it—and for Jett—but he missed. The lamp arced through the air, struck the edge of the table, and smashed. A second man seized her around the waist, swinging her around. Jett kicked and fought, forcing him to lift her off the floor, then flung her head back as hard as she could. There was a crunch. *Broken nose*, she thought with a flash of glee. She managed to land a lucky kick that sent his partner sprawling into the middle of the flames. He howled in fear, beating out the fire with his hands.

Shepherd threw a pitcher of water over him before stepping up to Jett and punching her in the stomach. Hard. As she choked and gagged, he hit her across the face. It was an open-handed blow, but it was on the same side he'd hit her with the gun-butt earlier. For an instant, the world went white.

It took both of his bullyboys to hold her down on the marble slab as Shepherd wrenched her arms behind her back and cuffed her again. This time he closed the cuffs so tight she knew she would soon be unable to feel her hands.

The others yanked her upright, one holding onto each arm, and turned her to face Shepherd. She fought and struggled, but she couldn't get loose.

"It's time for you to join the purified army of the Blessed Resurrected, Miss Gallatin," Shepherd said.

"No!" she shouted desperately. "Listen to me! Shepherd isn't a holy man! There aren't any Blessed Resurrected! He doesn't bring the dead back to life—he animates corpses! He's a thief and a madman!" For a moment she dared to hope her words had some effect.

"He pays well," one of the men said.

Shepherd chuckled. "Brother Nathan was one of my first followers. He is a pure spirit, truly blessed with the wisdom of the Lord. As is Brother Saul."

"I'll see the lot of you burn in Hell!" Jett cried.

The man Shepherd had called Brother Saul laughed. "Save us a seat, darlin'."

Shepherd gagged her with a handkerchief. She tried to spit it out, but he tied it so tightly it dragged her mouth open into a parody of a smile. Now she couldn't speak.

But she could still scream.

They carried her up the stairs into the bunkhouse. The bunkhouse was bakingly hot, but after the chill of the underground rooms, the heat was a relief. Shepherd opened the outer door without stopping to close the cellar doors. As her captors dragged her outside, she saw it was just dusk. Shepherd's whole "congregation" was standing in patient rows outside the door of the ranch house, as if they were soldiers on parade. Bizarrely, the organ she'd seen in the chapel had been brought out and placed to their right. A dozen tall wrought-iron candelabrum, their fat tallow candles flaring and guttering in the night air, provided light. Their presence gave the scene a weirdly exotic look.

But Jett spared only a passing glance for the grotesque set-dressing. The thing that riveted her attention was in the center of the compound. A post had been placed there, sunk deep into the ground. It was taller than she was, the raw wood still oozing where the twigs and bark had been hastily trimmed away. As Brother Nathan and Brother Saul dragged her toward it, Sister Catherine stepped forward carrying a length of rope. Brother Nathan took the rope, and Brother Saul forced Jett back against the post. She smelled the sharp scent of pine gum. Brother Nathan lashed Jett quickly and efficiently to the post, then stepped back.

Sister Catherine came forward. Jett tried to speak, to warn her—*It's a lie, everything Shepherd told you is all a lie, your boy Davey's dead and he isn't coming back*— but she couldn't form intelligible words through the gag. She shouted as loud as she could and whipped her head from side to side.

"Don't worry, Sister Jayleen," Sister Catherine whispered, leaning close. "Brother Shepherd is a kind and merciful shepherd. You'll see that soon."

Jett stared at her in horror, her heart sinking at Sister Catherine's words. Sister Catherine leaned closer and kissed her on the cheek, then turned away to resume her place among the congregation.

"My dear brothers and sisters in the Fellowship of the Blessed Resurrection," Shepherd said. He walked forward to stand between Jett and his congregation. "I have told you many times that to build the Jerusalem of Fire is no easy task. Its path is a hard path—a stony path—a path walked in renunciation! The weight of such privation lames the foot and twists the back! Yet the body broken for everlasting Glory is raised up in health and strength at the walls of the Jerusalem of Fire!"

As Shepherd began to preach, Nathan and Saul moved to stand on either side of the organ.

"Have I told you it is a hard road? I tell you yet again—your eyes will be washed in salt tears a thousand times before you see its end! And at its wayside stand many—the liars, the idlers, the thieves, the drunkards, the unchaste—eager to offer you comfort and ease! Many times have I spurned them! But you must have faith only in God, and from men ask proof! *Here* is my proof—the woman sent to seduce me from the path of righteousness!"

Shepherd gestured sweepingly toward Jett as a murmur ran through his congregation. He moved closer to them and spoke in confiding tones, but Jett could still hear him perfectly well.

"You might say to me, Brother Shepherd, you are a humble and a God-fearing man. You might say to me, Brother Shepherd, God has given into your hands the power of the patriarchs of old. Surely—*surely!*—it is your right to strike down this red-mouthed harlot who has set herself against the ordained will of God! And I would say to you, it is not I, but God Almighty, the Throne of Wrath, the builder of the Jerusalem of Fire who will punish or pardon. I have already forgiven this woman, and I will do so again before you all."

He turned back to face Jett. "Corrupt vessel of sin and evil, I hold you blameless for your vileness and error! And yet—" He turned to face the congregation once more. "And *yet,* surely it is God's right to punish—if He will punish—or pardon—if He will pardon! And so I have prayed to Him to send His holy angels to mete out his judgment!"

He strode to the organ and seated himself on its bench. As he did, Brother Nathan stepped behind it and began to pump the bellows. From the first terrible chords Shepherd wrung from the instrument, Jett realized what was about to happen. The Fellowship began to chant in time to the music, turning it into a grating wail of despair. Jett couldn't get free, but there was nothing to keep the knotted ropes holding her from sliding around the stake. With a great effort she could turn herself until she was facing the bunkhouse. If she was going to die, she wanted to see it coming.

The wind turned suddenly, bitingly cold.

A moment later, the first of the zombies staggered from the open door of the bunkhouse. Somehow it was worse not being able to see them clearly, but from the movement of the shadowy shapes in the flickering candlelight, Jett could tell that more and more zombies were coming. The first ones had walked a few steps away from the door and stopped. As more emerged, they jostled the ones in front of them forward a step at a time. There didn't seem to be any rhyme or reason to which ones stayed at the back, which ones moved to the edges of the mob, which ones pressed forward.

There'd been—Jett thought—sixty zombies (at most) in Alsop the night the town was killed, and not many more the following night. There were three times that number here, and somehow she couldn't keep herself from thinking there must be more down there in the dark: rotted corpses that had fallen to pieces, fragments too decayed to walk but still (horribly) animated, twitching bits of decaying flesh pulling themselves toward the stairs any way they could. Shepherd played on, but none of his congregation was chanting any longer. And still the zombies stood motionless. There was light enough for Jett to see the zombies clearly. The ones at the front almost looked as if they were still alive. Some of them.

What are they waiting for? Jett raged, even though she knew. They were waiting for Shepherd's order. However it would be given. "Come if you're coming!" The gag reduced her scream to unintelligible grunts. She didn't understand why Shepherd hadn't set them on yet. Suddenly a horrible suspicion struck her. *He knows! He's known all along I wasn't alone!* Maybe he'd seen Deerfoot's tracks. Maybe he'd sent Nathan or Saul to Alsop to spy. Maybe he'd gone himself.

Suddenly Jett realized the rhythm Shepherd set had stumbled, as if someone was banging a drum just out of time. The chanting faltered, and in that moment Jett realized what she was hearing.

Not a drum.

An *engine*.

Her friends were coming for her.

The Auto-Tachypode was moving with unimaginable speed—as fast as a steam locomotive. She could tell by the steadily louder sound of its engine. At the gallop a good horse could cover a mile every two minutes, but it couldn't run flat out for hours. A horse was flesh and blood, not unliving fire and steel.

A horse would have more sense than to gallop into the middle of an army of zombies.

Jett didn't think Shepherd knew what the sound of the Auto-Tachypode meant—he might not even be able to hear it over the renewed frenzy of his playing. And Gibbons had no idea what was waiting for her at Jerusalem's Wall—even if she had, she wouldn't believe there was anything her brains and her damnyankee *science* couldn't face down. And White Fox . . . well, he was as loyal a *compadre* as Jett could ever hope to ride the trail with. He wouldn't let Gibbons come alone, no matter what Gibbons was riding into. There was no way for Jett to warn her friends—or tell them to flee. Even if she hadn't been gagged, Jett knew she couldn't ever be heard over the sound of Shepherd's playing and the noise Gibbons's hellish conveyance made.

Suddenly Jett could see light moving over the ground. The Auto-Tachypode was almost on top of her. She heard scattered screams behind her—almost loud enough to drown out the sound of the engine—and lancing through them, the shriek of the organ.

Shepherd struck a final howling discord from his keyboards. The music stopped.

The zombies began to shuffle forward.

The Auto-Tachypode jerked to a halt beside Jett. The burning lanterns hanging on each corner of the wagon gave it a spectral appearance, as if it were a Death Coach. Despite herself, Jett flinched. The Death Coach only came when someone was going to die. *It isn't a Death Coach!* Jett snarled silently. *It's Gibbons's dangfool contraption!*

Before it stopped bouncing against the brake, Gibbons and White Fox jumped down from the bench. Gibbons hadn't vented the boiler, and the clatter of the engine was deafening. But even so, Jett could hear Shepherd start to play again.

"Don't worry!" Gibbons shouted in Jett's direction. But Gibbons looked terrified, and Jett had never seen her show fear. Jett had assumed this was a rescue mission—even if it was a doomed one—but instead of coming toward Jett, Gibbons ran to the back of the wagon. She opened the door and leaped inside.

Run! Jett begged silently. *You have to run!*

White Fox got to the back door just in time to receive a narrow coil of canvas. He was wearing heavy leather gauntlets. One end of the coil had a gleaming brass nozzle attached. The other was still inside the wagon. He ran toward the zombies with the nozzle in his hands, unrolling the canvas behind, just as the Auto-Tachypode let out an ear-splitting shriek. Suddenly the canvas writhed and began to thrash as if it were alive. Now it was a long tube—like a hose, only not made of leather—and its entire length steamed gently. Even from where she was, Jett could feel its heat.

The first of the zombies was barely a dozen feet away now. White Fox stood pointing the brass nozzle at the zombies as if the hose were a weapon. Jett could see how hard he had to struggle to hold it steady. But still he waited.

Suddenly—though Jett hadn't seen any signal—he released a coupling behind the nozzle. Water so hot it was half steam jetted out to strike the first ranks of the zombie army. In an instant, White Fox was hidden by billowing clouds of steam.

Steam that smelled of salt.

As the hot salt jet touched each zombie, it broke

from its halting shuffle into a lurching run—but not to retreat. They moved forward with grim purpose. The congregation began to scream again—not just a few of them this time—and Jett spared a moment to hope the sounds meant they were too scared to fight back. The organ had fallen silent once more, but suddenly Jett heard a sound that vibrated through the air like the lowest note of an organ a hundred times larger.

The zombies were wailing.

Steam turned the clear arid desert night into an eldritch landscape obscured by mist—but even now, Jett could see White Fox standing his ground.

The first of the zombies reached him. Its clothes were wet and steaming, as if its body was afire. It ignored White Fox as if he didn't exist. Others followed, and all of them ignored him. Jett tensed in fear as they reached her, but they passed her too. Now White Fox raised the nozzle of his hose so the spray of water showered over the remaining zombies as if it were rain.

The creatures continued to ignore him.

Every one of them was heading for Brother Shepherd.

The hose went limp. The wagon's reservoirs were dry. As the last of the water sputtered from the nozzle in a falling arc, White Fox dropped it to the ground. In the instant it took Jett to realize the temperature was rising, every zombie in the compound fell to the ground. Limp. Lifeless.

At last.

There was utter silence for a moment, then Jett heard a loud mechanical rattle and looked away from the corpses in time to see a trap door open in the side of the Auto-Tachypode.

"I very strongly suggest that no one do anything rash!" Gibbons called, leaning out of the back of the wagon.

White Fox walked toward Jett, a Bowie knife in his hand. He slipped the blade under the rope and began to cut her free. Suddenly she felt absurdly self-conscious. Her masculine disguise was armor as much as weapon, and at the moment she had neither one. The ropes fell free and she stepped away from the stake.

"I hope you brought my clothes," she snapped at him to disguise her unease. She tried to bring her hands around in front of her, only belatedly remembering the handcuffs still on her wrists. She couldn't feel her hands at all.

White Fox smiled at her. "I've brought something more immediately useful," he said, sheathing the knife again. "You're fortunate Gibbons carries handcuff keys at all times."

"Likely because anybody who meets her wants to throw her in jail," Jett muttered.

White Fox stepped behind her to unlock the cuffs. The moment she could, Jett wrapped her arms around herself, then inspected her hands, flexing the fingers critically. They were discolored and swollen, and there were deep bruises on her wrists.

But she was alive, which was more than she'd expected an hour ago. She turned around to look behind her. Her eyes widened.

Everyone, Union and Confederate both, had seen Mister Mathew B. Brady's photographs of battlefields. Jett had never expected to see anything similar in person—but such was the sight before her. The ground was scattered with bodies. There was a mound of them where Shepherd and his organ had been—she had no doubt what was left of Shepherd was at the bottom of that pile—but not all his creations had managed to reach him before he died. Some were sprawled flat as if they'd been running. Others lay in tangled heaps. Some had fallen to their knees and been braced upright by the bodies behind them.

Tante Mère was right. A zombie's last act is to take vengeance upon its creator.

Most of The Fellowship of the Blessed Resurrected had fled in terror. She didn't see either Brother Nathan or Brother Saul, which didn't surprise her. But to Jett's amazement, about two dozen of Shepherd's congregation had stood their ground. They huddled together in the open doorway of the ranch house. Some sobbed openly, men and women both. Some prayed loudly.

"Now you listen to me!" Gibbons strode from the back of her wagon, her coach gun prudently cradled in her arms. "I don't know what this Brother Shepherd told you, and I don't care! He wasn't a saint or a prophet! He was a thief and a murderer! If he told you he could raise the dead—he lied! These bodies are dead flesh— zombies—walking corpses, nothing more!"

Gibbons walked toward them. Jett followed her. Jett wasn't armed, but she didn't have to be. The fact she was standing here was her weapon. Mister George Wilson Shepherd had tied her to a stake and called down God's judgment on her—and she was still alive and Shepherd wasn't. She stood beside Gibbons on one side, White Fox on the other.

"If these bodies had really been alive, do you think a little dose of hyper-salinated steam could have killed them?" Gibbons demanded. "That's all this was: salt water. And it didn't kill them! It just broke your Brother Shepherd's hold over a bunch of carcasses."

As Gibbons spoke, a few more members of the Fellowship came out of hiding to join their fellows. Suddenly a woman broke away and ran toward the three of them. Jett tensed, and Gibbons swung her gun around, but this wasn't an attack.

"Oh forgive me! Sister Jayleen, forgive me for doubting you!" Sister Catherine said. She fell to her knees and clutched at Jett's hands. Despite herself, Jett recoiled.

"I take it you know each other?" Gibbons asked.

"This is—" Jett began.

"I told him everything!" Sister Catherine said, her words nearly unintelligible through her tears. "Brother Shepherd said if anyone worked against him, God would punish them by denying their families angelic resurrection!"

(Zombies) Jett mouthed at Gibbons, who was frowning at her quizzically.

"Least said, soonest mended, my good woman," Gibbons said crisply. "All water under the bridge! Now, if you'll—"

"I had to tell him, don't you see?" Sister Catherine went on as if she hadn't heard. "It was for my boy! My boy, my—"

Suddenly Sister Catherine faltered to a stop, realizing that if Shepherd was a fraud . . .

Her son was truly dead.

As she broke into hysterical howls of grief, Jett stared at Gibbons and White Fox in horror.

There was still one zombie unaccounted for.

Chapter Ten

Considering that they still had Shepherd's acolytes to deal with, Gibbons was just as glad to discover Shepherd had apparently confiscated all firearms brought to Jerusalem's Wall as a matter of course. A panicky mob was bad enough. An *armed* panicky mob was worse. More than a third of the Fellowship were unaccounted for. They would probably come back at sunrise, since the ranch was the closest source of food and shelter. Most of the rest them had decided to gather in the ranch house chapel to pray (whether to be struck dead or forgiven, it was hard to say).

The more Jett told her about "Brother Shepherd," the angrier Gibbons got. Not only had he been a bully and a killer, he'd let pride and greed corrode what seemed to have been a first-class scientific mind. For a while she'd wondered if the zombies might be proof that magic actually existed, but now Gibbons wasn't as sure. Sound had a measurable effect on a living body, after all. At a high-enough volume, it could even kill. Who was to say whether Shepherd had resurrected dead bodies—or simply drugged people into a deep coma and then used sound to control them? It was even possible the zombies had been truly dead, and the corpses host to some form of insect or parasite or bacterium not yet known to science. She wouldn't be able to hazard a guess until she could examine his laboratory in depth. She could begin tomorrow.

But there was one matter that couldn't be allowed to wait, and with all her heart, Gibbons hoped Jett was wrong. *She is not a trained observer—though I grant she is a good one—and the disciplines of Science are as yet a closed book to her.*

But it is best to make sure.

White Fox chose to remain above to ensure the safety of the Auto-Tachypode—a necessary precaution among a group of people who'd had every certainty destroyed in a few brief hours. Now, accompanied by Jett, Sister Catherine, and—to Gibbons's faint surprise— half a dozen of the braver souls of the Fellowship, Gibbons descended into what Brother Shepherd had called his "inner prayer house." According to Jett, Brother Shepherd's "*allamatons*" had built it. Gibbons wasn't sure she credited that, but it was an amazing piece of engineering all the same—a space vaster than the foyer of the San Francisco Opera House, carved by hand out of Texas limestone. The rooms were still brilliantly lit by lamps showing the blue-white smokeless flame of pure alcohol, and for a moment Gibbons wished they weren't, for the first room Jett led them to was filled with what Gibbons could only categorize as "loot."

Behind her, she could hear the unhappy murmurs of Shepherd's former dupes—though perhaps fortunately, they were all still too stunned to work up much in the way of shock or indignation. It was additional proof of Shepherd's dishonesty and their own credulity, but to Gibbons it was more. It was her first real evidence of how long he had been left to build his empire of death and plunder beneath everyone's noses. Even if he'd done nothing more than follow the wagon trails to scavenge those items abandoned by travelers (and it did not matter how precious an heirloom had been loaded into the back of a Conestoga at Independence, Missouri, it became merely dangerous makeweight a few hundred miles west), it would have taken him years to acquire the contents of this room.

And she knew he'd done more than that. Far more. But what? And for how long?

Jett led them to a doorway at the far end of the chamber. She hung back, allowing the others to enter before her. The room wasn't as brightly lit as the other one. Gibbons smelled scorched wool as she crossed the threshold, and beneath it the unmistakable sharp-sick stench of zombie. *I did hope she'd been wrong*, Gibbons thought sorrowfully.

"He's alive!" Sister Catherine cried. "My boy is alive!"

In the cell at the end of the room, a boy perhaps twelve years old was pacing back and forth. When he saw them, he thrust both arms through the bars, his mouth open in a silent howl. Sister Catherine ran to him before Gibbons could even think of stopping her.

"You were wrong, you were wrong, oh, praise the Lord, he's alive, *alive!*" Sister Catherine laughed and sobbed as she fumbled at the door. The dead child flailed blindly through the bars. "He sees me! He knows me! He's alive!"

If there is anything left of David in there... Gibbons shuddered.

Jett walked up to Gibbons and wordlessly offered her something. A key. Gibbons shook her head quickly and walked to Sister Catherine. She put a hand on Sister Catherine's shoulder.

"No," she said. "He isn't. I'm sorry."

"But you see, don't you?" Sister Catherine said desperately, turning to address her words to all of them.

"He is. The others are dead, but they— They were dead flesh, like you said. Not my boy! Not my Davey!"

Gibbons reached into her pocket and pulled out her small silver flask. "No," she repeated unhappily. "If he drinks this, you'll see." She held out the flask to Sister Catherine.

"What is it?" Sister Catherine demanded sharply, her eyes narrowing in suspicion.

"Nothing but salt water," Gibbons answered softly. "Just plain salt water."

"You have to tell him to drink it," Jett said. "He'll do it if you ask. You're his mother."

"Of course I am!" Sister Catherine said laughing a little, as if Jett had made a joke. She took the little flask from Gibbons and unscrewed the top. She took a sip of its contents to test it, then turned back to the cell.

"You're alive, Davey," she said, holding the flask through the bars. "I know you are. All you have to do is prove it to them by drinking this, and then—and then we can be together! We can be happy! I told you I'd find a doctor for you. I told you I wouldn't let you suffer. Just drink this. That's all you have to do."

Was there a kind of dull desperation in those eyes? Gibbons thought there was. The thing fastened its blind gaze on the flask.

Does it know? How can it know? Impossible of course,

and yet . . . Gibbons thought she saw a spark of . . . something . . . in that dead gaze.

Hope?

His mother was still talking—promising her son what they'd do, where they'd go—when the child-zombie clumsily pawed the silver flask from her hands, as if the flask held the water of life. It held it awkwardly between its palms and tipped it up to pour the contents into its mouth.

It fell backward, dropping the flask. Dead.

Sister Catherine began to scream, clutching the bars and shaking the cell door. Jett shoved her sideways and thrust the key into the lock. Sister Catherine yanked the door open and rushed inside. She fell to her knees and gathered the lifeless body into her arms. "Wake up, Davey," she said, rocking him. "It's time to wake up. You're cured. You're healed. He promised me. He promised. Wake up. Prove to them how wrong they are. Oh please, please, please wake up . . ."

Gibbons felt her eyes sting and her throat close a little. The poor child . . . and his poor mother. She blinked the tears away with determination. Crying would do nothing to change what had happened, and David had been doomed in any case. Shepherd had made a promise he'd known he could not keep.

No one could cure consumption.

Yet.

And so he'd lied, and given the boy's mother false hope. That was worse than letting the child die—

She made a mental note to add medical research to the scope of her investigations. In a proper world—a *scientific* world—there would be no Davids, no Sister Catherines, no desperate parents watching their children die of a hundred diseases.

"If that bastard wasn't already dead, I'd kill him myself," Gibbons snarled, so low only Jett could hear.

"I'd help you," Jett said grimly. Then, to Gibbons's faint surprise, she crossed herself and began to speak, her lips moving as she whispered almost soundlessly. "*Inclina, Domine, aurem tuam ad preces nostras—*"

Gibbons translated the words automatically. *Incline Thy ear, O Lord, to the prayers with which we suppliantly entreat Thy mercy . . .*

It was a prayer for the dead.

It was the end of April, and even at midmorning the temperature was ovenlike. The steady wind provided no relief from the heat, and Gibbons thought longingly of San Francisco's cool breezes. Thanks to her Auto-Tachypode, she would be home again within the week. Despite her eagerness to return to familiar surroundings, it was with a certain amount of regret that Gibbons made her last preparations for departure.

"Think they'll be all right?" Jett asked, walking from the ranch house to stand beside Nightingale. The black stallion was saddled and ready to go. Deerfoot stood beside him.

"As 'all right' as possible," Gibbons said. She picked up the spool of fuse cord and used a scrap of twine to tie the spool to the rear door of the Auto-Tachypode. The fuse ran across the compound and through the open doorway of the bunkhouse that led to the underground cavern. The best thing to do, they'd all decided, was to destroy all trace of Brother Shepherd's work, and give the rest of the dead as decent a burial as possible under the circumstances. Among the things they'd discovered while searching Jerusalem's Wall was more than a dozen kegs of gunpowder. Early this morning, Gibbons had run a length of fuse cord down to the makeshift powder magazine she'd constructed—with White Fox's help—in the underground complex.

"They can use Alsop as a starting point to resume their lives, or even become its new citizens," she continued. "Even if—technically—they are accessories to murder."

"What story could we tell that anyone would believe?" White Fox finished as he, too, exited the house. He stepped to Deerfoot's side and vaulted onto her back in a single fluid motion.

Jett snorted. "I'm pretty sure making them tote

corpses for a week was punishment enough," she said. She tucked the toe of her boot into the stirrup and swung onto Nightingale's back.

The survivors of Jerusalem's Wall had chosen to bury all their own dead in the cemetery in Alsop. The number of "blessed resurrected" who had been friends or kin of the former members of the Fellowship had been shockingly large, and if they'd attempted to bury all of Shepherd's "allamatons" as well it would have taken months to dig enough graves. At Gibbons's suggestion, they'd placed the rest of the bodies in the dormitory building closest to the old bunkhouse. At least a couple of sacks of quicklime scattered over them had made the presence of the bodies bearable while the final investigation of Jerusalem's Wall took place.

While Jett and White Fox resettled Brother Shepherd's former congregation in Alsop, Gibbons searched Shepherd's "resurrection chamber" for information. She'd been troubled to discover Shepherd had been in regular correspondence with someone who'd encouraged his theories on "Musica Universalis" and helped him to expand them. Unfortunately, he'd copied those letters into his personal journal and burned the originals, so the name and location of his correspondent remained a mystery. And to her disappointment, she'd found little about Shepherd's actual method of creating and controlling his *"allamatons."*

Perhaps once I return to my own laboratory and examine my sample of the "zombie cocktail" I will be able to discover the formula, she thought hopefully. *I do not wish to borrow trouble, but until I have discovered the identity of Shepherd's correspondent, I cannot be certain this . . . plague of zombies . . . has been ended once and for all. But at least it is ended* here—*and now I can tell Papa the disappearances have nothing to do with his "phantom airships"!*

"And yet, Brother Shepherd's followers truly weren't aware of Brother Shepherd's crimes," White Fox said to Jett. "You did a good deed, Gibbons, to distribute his ill-gotten gains among them."

Gibbons felt her cheeks warm at his praise. She looked quickly away. "It wasn't as if any of us could—or wished to!—carry it off with us. And I abhor waste," she added uncomfortably.

"You couldn't fit so much as a silver teaspoon of it into your buggy anyway," Jett pointed out. "Not with all those books and papers."

"Vital to my ongoing investigation," Gibbons said crisply, her composure restored. The Auto-Tachypode was indeed crammed full to bursting with the documents she'd salvaged from the "resurrection chamber." She'd even lashed a trunk of papers to the roof.

"Investigate all you want," Jett said. "Just don't make any more of those things."

"No," Gibbons said, shuddering despite the warmth of the day.

There was a moment of silence. The three of them looked at each other. "There's just one thing left to do," Gibbons said.

She was confident that this detonation would obliterate all trace of the madness and horror that had taken place at Jerusalem's Wall. While Jett and White Fox had been sure the gunpowder would be suffcient, Gibbons knew that neither of them was as well versed as she in the properties of explosive substances. Fortunately, Shepherd's laboratory had contained extensive stocks of sulfuric acid, glycerin, and white fuming nitric acid. It had been a simple matter for one of her education and training to use those chemicals to make *pyroglycerine*—or as it was now more commonly known in scientific circles, nitroglycerin. The volatile compound was not well known in the States as yet, though Mister Ascanio Sobrero had first synthezised it at the University of Turin in 1847. It was far more potent than gunpowder, and she had made quite a large amount of it. Once the gunpowder exploded, it would set off the jars of nitroglycerine . . . and bury the last evidence of Wilson Shepherd's madness.

As Jett and White Fox waited at a safe distance, Gibbons mounted the driver's bench of the Auto-Tachypode. Once she had, the other two rode to a safe distance. *Here goes nothing*, Gibbons thought, taking a deep breath. But to her pleased delight, her machine started smoothly and (more or less) quietly. It really was both reliable and efficient. She released the brake and pushed the tiller forward.

"Gibbons's device could be useful, once it is fully perfected. Such a conveyance will be able to reach places too distant or thinly settled for the railroads to go," White Fox mused as he watched the Auto-Tachypode approach. They were still too close to the compound to weather the explosion safely, but neither of them truly trusted the Auto-Tachypode not to quit at a very inconvenient moment. Their horses twitched their ears at the sound of its engine, but made no other sign they'd noticed it.

Jett laughed. "I'll keep Nightingale. Horses don't explode. Or run out of steam in the middle of nowhere. And they can get you where you're going even if you're sound asleep."

"I suppose you're right," he said. "It isn't really very practical." White Fox studied Jett covertly from the corner of his eye. The young desperado on Nightingale's back wouldn't be taken for a girl on even the closest inspection. "What are your plans?" he asked at last. Gibbons had a home to return to, and even he had a home of sorts.

"Head on up the trail," Jett said, shrugging. "I sure as shootin' don't want to be anywhere around Alsop once word gets out—whatever word that might be," Jett said. "This neck of the woods is going to be up to its ears in law after that."

And "law," White Fox knew, meant only one thing to Jett—the Union. The Northern oppressors who had put down the rebellion of the Southern states, and whose policies of "Reconstruction" weighed so heavily upon them.

"Perhaps," White Fox agreed neutrally. "Though I suspect Brother Shepherd's former congregation will be grateful simply to forget the entire matter."

"Just as well," Jett said thoughtfully. "This is 1867. Folks would have a powerful lot of trouble believing in a zombie army."

"I hope you're right," White Fox said. Shepherd had believed. And so had his unknown correspondent.

As the Auto-Tachypode rolled toward them, the last of the fuse uncoiled from the spool attached to the back of the wagon and fell to the ground. Gibbons drew level with them and set the brake on her machine, then jumped down and ran back to the coiling end of the fuse.

"We're going to be here a while," Jett predicted, tilting her hat back. "Too much wind out here to strike a light."

"I believe you underestimate Gibbons's resourcefulness," White Fox said mildly.

They watched as Gibbons pulled a tin about the size of a deck of cards from her pocket. The match she struck not only caught fire instantly, it didn't blow out. She touched it to the end of the cord. There was a flare of light, and the end of the cord caught fire. In the sunlight, the tiny spark that sped down its length was nearly invisible. Gibbons turned and ran back to them, one hand holding her sunbonnet in place. Unencumbered by skirts or corset, she ran as fast as a young deer.

"What the devil did you light that with?" Jett demanded.

"They're called 'safety matches,'" Gibbons said breathlessly, as she clambered onto the driver's bench. "They were invented by Mister Gustaf Erik Pasch of Sweden, and they are far superior to both the common Lucifer match and the so-called noiseless, or white phosphorous, match invented by—"

In a loud ratcheting of gears, the Auto-Tachypode moved grandly forward.

Gibbons continued lecturing as she drove, but Jett knew by now there wasn't a subject under the sun that Gibbons didn't know upside down and backwards. Come sundown she'd probably still be talking about the cousins and sisters and brothers of whatever new-fangled match she'd used. Jett was more interested in what it had *done*. As the Auto-Tachypode's speed increased, Nightingale and Deerfoot moved from a walk to a canter. Seconds passed. Jett counted silently under her breath. *It should reach the powder magazine just about—*

Suddenly there was a roar as fire and stone fountained into the sky. Even in the saddle, Jett could feel the ground shake. The force of the explosion took her completely by surprise. Nightingale reared, laid his ears flat back, and bolted.

If it hadn't been for the possibility Gibbons's go-devil would refuse to move—requiring her or White Fox to drag Gibbons (undoubtedly protesting) to safety—Jett would have left the stallion somewhere further from the explosion. But now she didn't think *Mexico* would have been far enough, and that would probably have been where he stopped running if she weren't in the saddle.

"Easy, easy, easy," she murmured until he finally slowed. *She said she'd found some gunpowder*, Jett thought weakly. *And you dang fool, you took her at her word!*

She looked around. Deerfoot and White Fox were a few hundred yards behind her—he'd managed to get his mare to angle away from Nightingale, for if the two horses had been running neck and neck, they would have egged each other on. Behind her, she could see a huge billowing cloud of dust. Of course Gibbons was turning the Auto-Tachypode around to head right back toward it.

Jett stuck her fingers in her mouth and whistled shrilly, then yanked her hat off to wave it in Gibbons's direction. When she was sure White Fox had seen, she pulled the bandana around her neck up over her nose and mouth and turned Nightingale back the way he'd come. He tossed his head reproachfully.

"I know," Jett said. "Bet they heard that all the way to Atlanta. Come on. I need to keep that dangfool Yankee from killing herself—her and her dangfool *science*."

Nightingale went as much sideways as forward as Jett coaxed him back the way they'd come. The dust was already starting to clear—or at least, to be blown somewhere else by the steady desert wind. Jett could see tiny limestone pebbles scattered over the ground. They looked like out-of-season hail. She could see only the vague outline of the Auto-Tachypode now. It had headed directly into the dust cloud.

"Wait up!" Jett shouted uselessly, over the racket of the engine. She spurred Nightingale to the gallop, still shouting. She overtook Gibbons and forced Nightingale across the wagon's path. Gibbons braked to a halt in a squeal of machinery. Jett saw with vague astonishment that she was wearing a sort of leather domino mask with what looked like spyglass lenses set in it. The engine noise dropped from an ear-splitting roar to a quieter idle, making it possible to converse—even though it required shouting.

"Where do you think you're going?" Jett bellowed.

"All I was doing was—" Gibbons broke off suddenly. Jett looked around quickly for the threat.

The wagon—and Nightingale—were barely a dozen yards from the edge of a gigantic crater.

"What the Sam Hill did you *do*?" Jett demanded.

"I didn't think the gunpowder we found would be enough!" Gibbons shouted. "I made some nitroglycerine to increase the force of the explosion! Hardly much at all! Nitroglycerine is much more powerful than gunpowder—it's the advance of Science!"

" 'Science', my—"

A movement behind Gibbons drew Jett's attention. White Fox and Deerfoot appeared through the billowing dust, moving toward the Auto-Tachypode at a cautious walk. White Fox's hat and coat were white with dust; Jett looked down at her own clothes and snarled. She looked like somebody had hit her with a bag of flour.

"She used science!" Jett shouted to White Fox in exasperation.

White Fox nodded silently, signifying he'd heard. The three of them sat in silence for some time, just watching. As the dust cloud rolled majestically northward, herded by the wind, the scope of the destruction became visible. Jett knew what the ground looked like where a cannonball had hit. This was the same crater magnified a thousandfold. More. The bottom of the crater was mounded with broken stone, and despite her immediate irritation at nearly having been blown to Glory, Jett was privately relieved at the size of the explosion. She could hear the clicking and sliding of the stones in the crater as they settled. There was no longer any sign of any of the buildings that had once been Jerusalem's Wall—or of the catacombs beneath it, and their contents.

"Nobody's ever going to be able to figure out what that sidewinder was doing here now!" Gibbons said in satisfaction. Her words were an uncanny echo of Jett's thoughts.

"'Sidewinder'!" Jett shot back, repressing a grin. "Listen to you! If you aren't careful, you're going to go native on us."

"No chance of that," Gibbons said feelingly. "I like clean sheets, hot food, and a roof over my head."

"Except when you are tracking a mystery," White Fox teased.

Gibbons favored him with a radiant smile of agreement. "Sure I can't persuade either of you to come back to San Francisco with me?" she asked, sounding hopeful.

White Fox shook his head. (With a certain amount of reluctance, Jett thought.) "I must return to Fort Riley," he said. "I've been absent from my duties for too long. And I owe Caleb Lincoln the answer he sent me to find, sad news though it will be." He glanced toward Jett. "You are more than welcome to come with me."

Jett was already shaking her head. "Got no use for Yankee soldiers, beg pardon," she said. "Figure I'll head on up the trail and see what's there." She hesitated, then touched the brim of her hat to Gibbons in salute. "I reckon this is 'good-bye' for sure, then. For all of us." Despite her constant complaints, Jett knew she'd miss the spunky Yankee firebrand. And White Fox, well . . . no use crying for the moon. Besides, her brother was out here. Somewhere.

"Maybe it's good-bye and maybe it isn't," Gibbons said. "I have a feeling we might just meet again. All three of us."

"Don't tell me *you* believe in woman's intuition?" Jett asked mockingly.

"Call it a scientific theory," Gibbons answered lightly, and White Fox smiled.

"Then I won't say 'good-bye,'" Jett said. "I'll say *vaya con Dios* instead."

"Go with God, Jett Gallatin," White Fox answered.

Jett turned Nightingale and spurred him to a trot. She was almost too far away to hear when the ear-splitting sound of the Auto-Tachypode's engine reached her ears. *I wonder if she's right . . .*

"Come on, partner! We're burning daylight!" she shouted, and Nightingale moved from a trot to a gallop. The sound of his hoofbeats drowned out all other sounds.